THE SURGEON'S SIN

ATONEMENT

DEAN C. LOHSE, MD

Copyright © 2020 by Dean C. Lohse, MD

All rights reserved.

No part of this book may be reproduced in any form or by any electronic or mechanical means, including information storage and retrieval systems, without written permission from the author, except for the use of brief quotations in a book review.

ISBN: 978-1-7352559-0-3, print

ISBN: 978-1-7352559-1-0, e-book

This is a work of fiction. Any similarities to people or events are coincidental.

Cover art design by John Wollinka at DesignCorps.

❋ Created with Vellum

For the doctors and nurses in the ORs, the ICUs, and the ERs who take on the tough cases every day.

CHAPTER ONE

An easy mistake to make. Easy, not forgivable.

"No," Dr. Peter Jenson said. "I am not okay. *We* are not okay. Her tumor is on the right side of her brain, and we are drilling holes in the left side of her skull."

"I'm sorry, Doc," Carl, the scrub tech, said. "We didn't know. The schedule said left."

Nancy, the circulating nurse, confirmed. "The schedule said left." She tapped the printout hanging on the door. "In the time-out we all agreed to the left side. The procedure line on the consent form . . ." She swiped on the computer tablet until a copy appeared. ". . . says 'temporal lobe tumor.' We didn't read the X-ray reports, but that's not our job. We just brought the images up on the monitor."

"You set the room up wrong," Jenson said. "Look at the MRI. Here's the tumor. Here's the right-side marker. We've made the wrong incision."

Nancy stood from her stool and put her hands on her hips. "We set the room up like it said on the OR schedule. You booked the case and filled out a consent without a specific side.

We had a time-out, Doctor. If there was a mistake on the OR schedule, you had a chance to fix it."

Archie Davis, the anesthesiologist, looked up from his place on the other side of the drapes. "Nancy's right, Pete. *We* didn't make the wrong incision. You did."

The room went silent again, except for the monitors. Peter's gut tightened and heat rushed to his face. His hands started to shake, the embarrassing visible sign of his distress. He checked himself to keep from screaming. He wanted the mistake to be Carl's fault, Nancy's fault, Archie's fault.

Or Joe Bell's fault.

Bell, the chief of surgery, had motivation and opportunity. Bell had delayed Peter's case for an "emergency" that was really seniority privilege, snatching away an earlier surgery start time. Bell even might have engineered the delay. After all, they had argued bitterly about it, and afterward he'd seen Bell leaning over the scheduling secretary, touching her and pointing at something. He could have been getting her to mess with Peter's OR schedule.

If Bell hadn't delayed his case, Peter would not have rushed. He would have caught the error before it was too late. If he hadn't been in a hurry, if the schedule or permit had been more clear, if he'd used the navigation equipment . . . if, if, if. But the scalp lay open before him with holes drilled in the wrong side of the skull. His incision, his responsibility.

The consequences would belong to him, too. To him and one other. He deserved the consequences, but she, Megan Kaiser, the anesthetized woman beneath the drapes, did not.

Guilt tempered his rage and brought him back from his panicked paralysis. He broke the silence, erecting a wall between his feelings and his actions.

"Fine," he said, "but *we* still have the same problem we did when we walked into this room. The patient still has a brain tumor. We have done her a disservice by a wrong-side incision, but we will do her another disservice if we don't get her tumor out."

Nancy and Carl both stiffened at his use of the term *we,* but Carl reorganized his instruments. Nancy notified the control desk of the delay and filled out the reports required when things went wrong.

Peter held out his hand and asked for sutures, needle holders and forceps. His right hand shook visibly.

"You all right, Doc?" Carl stared down at his hand. "Take a break? Sit down, maybe."

"I won't be all right if you don't hand me the suture right now. Let's get this thing fixed."

"Sure, Doc."

Peter began closing the long scalp incision. Action tranquilized his stress. With each stitch, his hand tremor lessened, and his breathing steadied. Recriminations would come later. This was how he approached problems—by working harder, faster, longer. But he still felt this one in his gut.

The room remained quiet. He reviewed what excuses he could make for such an egregious error and came up with nothing. Everyone else in the room was no doubt distancing themselves from the mistake, and from him.

With the first incision closed, Peter removed the drapes and repositioned the body and head. He shaved the right side of her head, leaving a ridiculous haircut and regretting the reassurances he had given her about her post-op appearance.

A new skin prep and drape, another incision, another operation. This one was textbook pretty, with neat incision lines, precision bone cuts and dural openings, and a nice, clean resection of the right temporal lobe that gave the widest safe margin of resection.

The tumor was sent to pathology. Peter could have gotten a

preliminary report, but he knew without the report that it was likely malignant. Today's troubles had been enough. Tomorrow would be soon enough to receive the official report.

He wrapped her head in a turban dressing that covered both incisions. At least she looked as if everything had gone according to plan. Technically speaking, Megan's surgery was successful. The tumor was resected. Biopsies would lead to a definitive diagnosis and the best treatment plan. But "technically successful" was little comfort.

Archie extubated Megan and supervised her transfer to the anesthesia recovery room. "These things have a way of working out," he said on his way out.

Peter nodded, hiding his total disagreement in silence. He stripped off his bloodied gloves and surgery gown, deposited them in a biohazard container, and washed the glove powder and sweat from his hands. The many hours of surgery were over, but recrimination and blame lay ahead. Good news travels slowly in hospitals, but bad news spreads faster than the limits of physical science. By now everyone—including the janitors just coming to work and food service workers isolated deep in the kitchen—knew he had made a mistake in the operating room. The risk manager would be waiting in the recovery room. Bell would be gloating.

Everyone knew except Megan Kaiser.

And Ellen, his wife. Peter now allowed himself to look up at the OR clock. Six p.m.— too late to meet her, too late to call. Too late for his marriage.

Megan en route to the recovery room, he sat alone on one of the steel stools in the OR, surveying the carnage: discarded drapes stuffed into biohazard containers, bloody towels on the floor, and urine collection bottles in the corner. The coppery scent of blood and acrid smell of burned flesh still hung in the air.

He put his elbows on his knees, his head in his hands.
He said softly to no one, "Oh, Jesus."

CHAPTER TWO

Peter replayed the day, trying to find the fork that had put him on the wrong road, hoping to find his way back. Before the surgery, he had slipped off his wedding ring in the locker room and examined it, feeling its weight in his hand and his heart. He had closed his fist around it and released it into his trouser pocket. He had been slipping that ring off for nearly twenty years, but he wondered how much longer he would have the privilege of slipping it back on.

Next, he took off his watch, a gift from Ellen, and slid it into the same pocket. The watch had come with a handwritten note: *Time is not money; time is love. Measure it . . . and spend it wisely.* He remembered that as he put on his scrubs and told himself that he had no choice. Megan Kaiser's brain tumor had to come out, and it had to come out today. Waiting, even overnight, entailed a risk that she could fall into a coma or die. But if he operated now, he would miss the psychiatry appointment at 4:30. Ellen had cut time out of her business as an interior designer and planned the appointment around his schedule. She was worried about their son Daniel. Peter was less worried about Daniel, but certain she was ready to walk away from their marriage. They, all three, had to be there, no matter what, and he had agreed. He had promised.

And his plan had been good. If Megan's case had started at 7:30, as it should have, it would have finished by noon, a four-plus hour buffer before the 4:30 appointment. But his case had been bumped by Joe Bell. Bell's "emergency" operation was a lumbar disk surgery that he wanted to do first so as not to disturb his afternoon office hours. Bell was the chief; he did what he wanted.

Initially, Peter didn't worry about it. He'd still make the appointment. But Bell was too old to be good and too young to know it. The case should have taken two hours. It took four. Add the turnover time for the room, and Peter was running late before he'd even begun. And he'd made the mistake of letting Bell know how slow and incompetent he thought he was. When he had turned away from Bell, he saw the shocked expression on Archie Davis's usually stoic face. Perhaps he had gone too far.

Although he had been angry, he regretted his words. Bell would be just as slow the next time, and now he had made an enemy. No good would come of this; Bell would get even. Peter had done what he always did before an operation, only this time it was a bit harder. He drew a deep breath and exhaled, shutting out the vision of Bell's red face. Then he shut out the vision of Ellen's disappointed face. Then Daniel's. Then he breathed again and visualized the MRI images of Megan's tumor, focusing on the first of the thousand perfect steps that made up a good operation.

Peter took comfort in seeing his usual OR team: Carl, the scrub tech, and Nancy, the circulating nurse. Everything would go faster and smoother with experienced help. He had looked at the clock. One-fifteen. A four-hour operation. A four-thirty appointment.

The neuro-navigation system used images from the MRI

and CT scans to correlate with three-dimensional information gathered in the operating room, much like the GPS systems used in phones and cars. With the device, he could pinpoint critical locations within the head to sub-millimeter accuracy in real time. He used it with nearly every tumor case. But it added time, fifteen minutes, maybe a half hour, and Peter still had hope. He could finish this four-hour operation in three and get to the appointment before it was over. He could apologize profusely to Ellen and Daniel, and move on.

"Shut it down," he said.

Nancy narrowed her eyes and stood still. "Really? You're sure?"

This was the moment that could have changed everything, the fork in the road. It would have been nearly impossible to begin a wrong-sided operation while using that equipment.

But the tumor was only a glioma; the old-fashioned way would be good enough.

"You're the doctor," Nancy said. She shut down the equipment.

Peter approached Megan, anesthetized on the OR table. When she first sought help, she had been a person, a single, young waitress with a headache. After her MRI scan, she became a patient, a thirty-two-year-old white female with a right temporal lobe brain tumor. Now, asleep, her humanity slipped even further away, allowing him the psychological distance he would need to perform the violence that was surgery.

The scalp was prepped and draped as Peter scrubbed his hands and donned his gown and gloves. He held out his hand for the scalpel.

"Time out," called Nancy.

The "time out" was a rule that mandated the entire surgical team to stop whatever they were doing and confirm the patient identification and surgery plan.

"Come on. Get it over with," Peter said.

Nancy stared him down and called out, "The patient is Megan Kaiser. The consent form is 'craniotomy for tumor.' The schedule states 'left temporal craniotomy for tumor.' Vancomycin was given as the pre-op antibiotic at twelve noon. Are we all agreed?"

"Agreed," Archie said.

"Yeah, yeah," said Peter. "Let's go." He tapped his foot and shook his outstretched hand, waiting for the scalpel. This time Carl handed it to him.

That had been his last chance to get back on the right road. The hour following that moment could cost him his career and his marriage. And Megan Kaiser? What could he say except that he had betrayed her trust. She would die believing he could have saved her and didn't.

Peter lifted his head from his hands as Archie came into the room and went straight to his anesthesia cart. As Archie started filling several small syringes, Peter forced himself to his feet and walked over.

"She's all right?" he asked.

Archie startled. "Didn't see you there. Ah, yes, she's fine. I just came back for some drugs." His hands were shaking. He had filled the syringes from vials labeled *fentanyl*, a short-acting narcotic.

An alarm bell rang in Peter's head. Six vials would be enough for a whole operation. Megan shouldn't need them. "I don't want her getting any more IV narcotics," he said. "You know that. Not until she wakes up."

"Sure, sure." Archie looked around and slipped the syringes into his pocket. "Just wanted to have it ready."

"Six syringes?"

Archie moved to the door. "I'd better be getting back."

Peter grabbed his arm. "Is there a problem here, Archie? Something I should know about?"

Archie met his gaze, and Peter saw panic.

"I'm fine, Pete. Fine."

Peter continued to hold him. "You don't look fine."

"You can't say anything, Pete. Please. You gotta understand."

"Understand what, Archie? What you're doing with six syringes full of narcotics in your pocket? Drugs that you've got no business giving to my patient?"

"It gets to me. Cases like this. Days like this. The stress." He tried to shake his arm out of Peter's grip. "When I was a resident, it was such an easy way to get a little rest, a little relief."

"Are you out of your mind, Archie? How long before you can't cover it up?" Peter released him and stepped back. "How long before you hurt someone?"

"You're right, you're right. I swear I was just thinking about it. But don't say anything. I'll handle it."

Peter searched Archie's face. Sweat beaded on his forehead, and his hands clutched Peter's arm. No one had ever appeared so sincere.

"Please," he implored.

Addicts always lie, and Archie was probably lying. But no one was perfect, and today they had been imperfect together, a weird kind of brotherhood. When the world heard about what he had done, Archie's narcotic theft would seem like a small asterisk next to a big headline. Furthermore, if Peter reported him, he would seem to be simply drawing attention away from himself. And all Archie had to do was deny wrongdoing; who could say the drugs were not intended for a patient?

"This time, Archie, this one time, I look the other way. But you've got to get help. If I see the least hint of a problem, I'm calling it. You understand? This is the last time."

Archie hugged him. "You're the best, Pete."

Peter remained stiff to the embrace. "The least hint, Archie. A constricted pupil, a yawn in the middle of a case. A tremor when you start an IV."

"You won't be disappointed." Archie released him and turned to go to the Post Anesthesia Care Unit.

"The syringes, Archie. Empty them while I'm watching."

"Yeah, sure, Pete. I was just going to do that. Really. I owe you, man."

Peter watched him empty the syringes. Then he walked with him to the recovery room, disturbed by his friend's weakness, wondering if he had made the right decision. On another day, a day when he had done a perfect operation, would he have been so merciful?

Debbie Schafer, the hospital's risk manager, waited in the recovery room, sitting at the dictation desk in the open ward. She wore a lab coat with empty pockets over a white silk blouse, a dark wool skirt to just below her knees, sheer nylons, and shiny black, low-heel pumps. Recovery room nurses in maroon scrubs and athletic shoes scurried around her.

"Dr. Jenson," she said before he had a chance to sit, "a Code Fifteen violation has been reported."

Peter waved her off. "You need to give me some time to dictate the note and write the orders."

"Yes, but it's a *Code Fifteen*," she said, breathless, quivering.

Peter sat at the desk next to her, held up a hand like a traffic cop, and started working.

She nattered on, uncomfortably close to his right ear, as he wrote the post-op orders. "Dr. Bell is on his way right now, you know."

Peter grimaced and wrote instructions for the nurses in the recovery room and the critical care unit on how to monitor Megan's safety over the next few hours: IV fluids, food—what and when—and how high the head of the bed should be elevated.

"And the family," Schafer went on. "I should be there with you for the post-op conference."

Peter continued writing instructions for medicines to prevent seizures and reduce brain swelling, pain, nausea, and fever. Most importantly, he wrote about how to recognize the signs of things going wrong and the steps to take while he was being notified.

"We need to file a report with the Department of Health. Right away," added Schafer. "Well, not right away, but sometime in the next two weeks. If we don't—"

Peter held up his hand again. He wrote a brief note in the chart about the operation, and then picked up the landline to dictate the operative report. When he finished, he turned to Schafer. "There's no family."

"What?"

"No family, Debbie. No conference."

Schafer looked disappointed.

"But I do need to make some calls," he said.

"Well, sure. Maybe I could . . ." She stopped, appearing disappointed. "I'll just wait for Dr. Bell." She folded her arms across her clipboard and hugged it to her chest.

He clenched his teeth and dialed the next-of-kin number on Megan's chart.

"Waffle House," a gruff male voice answered.

Waffle House?

"This is Dr. Jenson from St. Luke's Hospital. I was asked to call this number about a Megan Kaiser."

"Oh yeah, Doctor. This is Bert, the cook. Thanks for calling. We been worrying all day. Well, I mean, we're the three-to-eleven crew, but the day shift, they been worrying, too." He exhaled into the receiver. "I'm sorry, Doc. I'm not making much sense, but we been just sick about Megan. How's she doing?"

What to say next? Families only heard one thing in the initial post-op conference: "okay" or "not okay." Was there a way to say that the operation had gone poorly, yet she was okay . . . but only for now, since tomorrow they would find out the tumor was malignant?

"Doc, are you there?" Bert asked.

He had hesitated too long. Delayed replies transmitted bad news.

"She's fine," he said.

"Oh, thanks, Doc. She's kinda family here."

"She's in the recovery room now waking up from the surgery. She'll spend the night in the ICU, but we hope to have her in a regular bed tomorrow, where she can have visitors more easily."

"We'll have some people over to see her in the morning. Maybe bring over some cheese grits. We make real good cheese grits. That'd be okay, right, Doc?"

Some people get chocolate; some people get cheese grits. But Peter puzzled over how to deal with a dying woman's "kinda family." Although listed as the next-of-kin, they had no legal standing. For now, though . . . "I'm sure that would be fine," he said.

As he hung up, he glanced at Schafer who sat at the dictation desk hugging her clipboard, sighing, and tapping her foot. Perhaps his reluctance to talk with her made it easier to face his next call, the required one to the referring doctor—Luke.

If Luke picked up, should he start by talking about Megan Kaiser? Or should he start with *I'm sorry*? He wondered if *sorry* had an expiration date.

The phone signaled a ring; the call had gone through, breaking ten years of uneasy silence. He hoped for voicemail.

"Dr. Ryan here."

"Luke? This is Peter Jenson."

Silence—it had accumulated its own weight and inertia, unwilling at first to be moved by a few words over a phone.

Then Luke spoke, curt and sharp. "What do you want, Jenson?"

"I'm calling about Megan Kaiser."

"Let me guess. You're about to tell me she doesn't have insurance, and you're sending her to the University Hospital."

"No, that's not it. And about that thing when we were residents—"

"That thing? Is that what you call it?" His voice rose in both tone and pitch.

"I'm sorry."

Another silence, longer this time. Yes, there seemed to be an expiration date.

"You called about Megan Kaiser," Ryan finally said, perhaps a shade more calm.

Peter exhaled, relieved to return to the present. "She had her operation today."

"And?"

"She's in recovery, tumor's out, path's pending."

"The scan looked like a glioblastoma."

He should have known Luke would anticipate the diagnosis. "That's what it looked like in surgery, too."

"Seems like all I ever get out of you is bad news, Jenson."

"I'm sorry." It sounded like an echo, but Luke didn't seem to notice.

"She's a good woman."

"She seems nice."

"Nice? You've got no idea."

"One more thing," Peter said. "There was a complication

with her surgery. Shouldn't affect the outcome, but something you need to know about."

"What?"

"There was confusion about the OR schedule, and her initial scalp incision was on the wrong side."

Another pause fell before Ryan replied, his tone and pitch back up to danger levels. "Same old Jenson. In a big hurry, and she's just an uninsured waitress with a malignant tumor. You didn't even care enough to get the side right."

"I do care," Peter said. Yes, he felt like he had cared. "I'm going to make this thing all right."

"You care that you look bad. You always think you can say *sorry* and fix it. Some things you can't fix."

Luke kept ranting about Megan's operation. "How hard could it be . . ."

But Peter tuned out. This was a lecture he had already given himself. His mind went back to twelve years ago, when he had been a fourth-year resident and Luke had just started his neurosurgery residency. Luke was a hard-working and trustworthy junior resident, a friend, until his son Ethan had a nosebleed, and the world changed. After a trip to the ER, Ethan left the hospital with a pack of gauze in his nose, a platelet transfusion and a diagnosis of leukemia.

For the next two years Luke's wife, Jane, bore the brunt of Ethan's care, but some nights, she collapsed, and Luke took over. His work suffered. Everyone's did, because the other residents, including Peter, had to cover for him. He breathed a guilty sigh of relief when Ethan died. A few days after the funeral he placed Luke on the regular night call rotation, justifying the move as a chance for Luke to distract himself from his grief. All the residents were relieved. What no one had anticipated was Jane's inconsiderate suicide two weeks later.

Inconsiderate should have been the wrong word. But that's

how Peter had felt about it. And he was pretty sure the other residents felt the same way. The call schedule was brutal, the nights sleepless, the days stressful. Why couldn't Jane have just taken the Prozac, seen the shrink, and let Luke work through his grief on the job?

Only later did Peter learn what it was like to have a son and what it would be like to lose him. For years now, he had felt guilty, even partly responsible for Jane's death. Of course Luke hadn't forgotten or forgiven. He expected no more. But he prayed that Luke was wrong about Megan.

". . . and so what exactly do you think you can do to 'make this all right?'" Luke asked.

Peter didn't know, not beyond a vague hope. So he pressed on, hoping to end this call quickly and let their relationship lapse again into an uncomfortable silence.

"Do you know if she has a next-of-kin?"

"She's been out of contact with her family for years. Doesn't know if they're alive and doesn't really care. Not after what they did to her."

"How about a surrogate?" Peter asked.

"Me. I have durable power-of-attorney for health care."

Peter could not have been more disappointed. Now, at least until Megan Kaiser was dead, he would have to be on speaking terms with Luke. Painful speaking terms. He took a moment to regain his voice. Then he said, "I'll call you tomorrow with the path report."

He hung up and swiveled his chair to face Schafer. Behind her, Bell strode through the double doors, smug and confident.

Bell stopped, surveyed the room, and frowned. "Executive conference room," he said. "Now."

Schafer sprang up and, with Bell, looked back to Peter.

"See you there in five minutes." He had to stop at Megan's bedside first.

Peter had forgotten Megan was beautiful. Perhaps he hadn't noticed. A patient is a case, beautiful or not. But now as she rested peacefully, still unaware of the invasion of disease in the most precious part of her, he noticed.

He took her hand and called her name. Slowly, her eyes opened—blue, dark like sapphires. Had he noticed that before? She blinked, clearing her vision, and finally focused on him. Her rapid return to consciousness encouraged him to believe she would recover quickly.

"You're here," she said, searching his face for clues.

He nodded. "I'm here."

"Then everything must have gone well." She smiled and closed her eyes.

He wanted to tell her everything, bathe in the cleansing that was confession, promise atonement, and beg for forgiveness. But she wouldn't understand. Not tonight, anyway. Maybe never.

"We'll talk in the morning." Explanations would have to wait, at least until the anesthesia didn't cloud her thoughts. He squeezed her hand and headed for his meeting with Bell.

In the executive conference room, Bell and Schafer occupied two of the twenty upholstered chairs around the giant mahogany table. Their heads together, Schafer took notes on a yellow legal pad. They both looked up as Peter entered and sat opposite.

"Code Fifteen, Jenson. We're obligated to report this," Bell said.

Peter gritted his teeth and nodded.

Schafer asked a series of questions apparently drawn from a corporate checklist. Bell tried to look paternal. Finally Schafer asked, "The OR schedule in the computer listed Kaiser's surgery as left-sided. Did you book it that way, Dr. Jenson?"

Peter saw Bell's eyes flick down and the shadow of a smile cross his face. Did he know something?

"No," he said. "I'm certain that I didn't. Did you ask Amanda?"

She flipped a few pages back on her pad. "The schedule clerk? She believes you did."

Bell continued to smile.

Schafer continued. "The consent form says 'craniotomy for tumor.' Here is a copy." She flipped her computer tablet over to show him. "Did you electronically sign this?"

Peter tried without success to imagine making the double error of a mistaken surgical booking and a mistaken consent form. "I'm quite sure I filled it out and signed it for a right-sided tumor."

Schafer looked doubtful. "Then how do you explain this?"

"Could the consent be altered in the computer?" Peter asked.

"I don't believe so," she replied.

"How about the schedule? Could that be altered in the computer?"

"Sure. Schedules have to be flexible."

Beside her, Bell looked Peter in the eye and smiled.

"Then maybe the same person altering the schedule could alter the permit," Peter said.

Schafer looked doubtful. "Why would anybody do such a thing?"

"Just ask Information Technology if it's possible."

She made a note. "Were there any extenuating circumstances?"

Peter ignored her. "Anything to add, Dr. Bell?"

Schafer puffed up. "We are trying to get the facts here, Doctor Jenson. Dr. Bell's opinion of the events is not relevant."

Bell continued to smile.

"You wanted to get to me," Peter said to him.

Bell spread his hands. "Dr. Jenson. I understand you're

upset, as well you should be. But I certainly have no idea what you are talking about."

Peter shook his head. Even if Bell had set the trap, he had stepped into it. He turned to Schafer. "No extenuating circumstances other than the team had a late start and was in a hurry to get the tumor out. You could make a note that the mistake was discovered before irreversible damage was done, and the tumor was removed as planned."

"She'll be cured then?" Schafer asked hopefully.

Peter frowned. "She'll get her best chance."

"Likely she's going to die from a malignant brain tumor after an operation that you botched," Bell said. "Everyone's going to think you killed her."

"You know that's not true."

"What I know is that perception is reality, Doctor. And because of the perception of this case, the Board of Medicine is going to eat you alive. You'll be lucky to still have a practice."

Peter looked from Bell's smug expression to Schafer's prim notes and knew he had nothing more to say. He touched his naked ring finger and longed to go home.

CHAPTER THREE

He entered a deserted kitchen. The nightlight above the stove illuminated stainless steel appliances and granite countertops devoid of any evidence of meal preparation. A pizza box on the center island smelled of pepperoni, garlic, and stale crust. The dim glow of a television, the only light, came from the family room.

"Ellen?" he called.

No answer.

"Ellen?" he called again, this time crossing the kitchen to the family room, where the Weather Channel was cheerfully predicting unseasonable storms and flooding. He heard ice cubes tinkle before he saw her. She lounged in the oversized leather chair, crossed legs resting on a footstool. Her dark hair outlined her face, her expression hidden in shadow, her silver earrings catching reflections from the thin light from the TV. In one hand, she held a glass of scotch. In the other, a prescription bottle.

"Ellen," he said again, turning on a lamp.

"Ah, the great and glorious Oz." She raised her glass in a mock toast.

"What are you doing?"

She held up the scotch and the prescription bottle. "I am deciding."

"Deciding . . . what?"

"Deciding whether or not to be a twentieth century cliché—the doctor's alcoholic wife." She tinkled the ice cubes. "Or," she said, rattling the pill bottle, "a twenty-first century cliché—the bipolar professional."

"Oh, for God's sake, Ellen." He picked up the remote to shut off the TV. "This is embarrassing."

"Embarrassing? This? This is nothing like showing up for the last-ditch, save-your-marriage, rescue-your-son psychiatry appointment without your husband."

He silenced the Weather Channel's chirpy predictions of meteorological doom. "I'm sorry, okay? I can explain."

"The way I see it," she said, "is if I think I'm sad, I should drink. An age-old Irish tradition." She took a small sip and grimaced.

"I had a tough case today. Something happened."

She turned to him with false innocence. "Oh, I'm sure." She eyed the prescription bottle. "Maybe I'm crazy. Maybe I expect too much of life. Of our child. Of you. Of us. After all, the psychiatrist gave me these. Antidepressants." She shook the bottle. "Maybe I should take them and be happy with the pitiful existence we've created."

"Ellen. Can't you listen to me for just a minute?"

She almost smiled. "I have another prescription for Daniel. Isn't that great? A nine-year-old on antidepressants."

"Ellen, I'm trying to tell you something important."

She put down the scotch and the pills, and stood, her face tilted up, inches from his. "You had your chance to tell me something important—at four-thirty."

"It couldn't be helped. It was an emergency."

She came close enough that he smelled her perfume and her scotch. Her eyes blazed. "Of course. It always is. But when is it Daniel's turn? When is it *my* turn?"

He reached out to hold her shoulders, to make her listen. She jerked and spun away.

"Don't touch me," she hissed. "Never again."

Peter froze. So did his heart. So many words rushed into his mind that none would come to his lips.

She walked away, her heels clicking on the hardwood, but when she reached the stairs, she turned. "It's over. Get out." She said it clearly and coldly, as if dismissing the cleaning service. Then she climbed the stairs, Peter's heart following behind until her long legs finally disappeared. The bedroom door slammed shut, and the lock clicked.

Anger replaced his shock. She knew what he was before she married him—not a neurosurgeon yet, but dedicated. Patients first, always. Then family.

An inner voice asked him if there was a difference between "patients first" and "himself first," but he silenced it. They had always played by the "patients first" rule. He had the duty to be the doctor; she had the duty to wait. And Daniel could wait, too. He certainly waited less than the forever that Peter had waited for his own father.

Peter uttered an expletive, jammed his hands into his pockets, and kicked the footstool. She had no right to change the rules now.

This is my house and my son, as much as it is hers.

He ran up the stairs and pounded on the bedroom door.

"Go away." Was she crying?

He pounded on the door again. "You're not the only one having a bad day."

"If you hit that door one more time, I'm calling 911."

At least she hadn't thought of using the handgun he kept in

his bedside table. He stepped back and turned sideways. He lifted his leg to kick the door just as his phone rang. He relaxed his leg, steadied himself, and breathed. Hands still trembling, he pulled the phone from his pocket and looked at the screen. Message from the answering service. Call the ICU about patient Kaiser.

Another expletive.

He stepped back from the door and made the call.

"She's had a grand mal seizure," the nurse said. "We gave her four milligrams of lorazepam and the seizure stopped. But now she's out of it."

"Out-of-it comatose? Or out-of-it post-ictal?"

"She's breathing on her own and her O_2 saturations are ninety-nine percent, but she's not talking. I don't know."

He looked at Ellen's locked door, the flame of anger cooled by the urgency of duty. "I'll be there in fifteen minutes. Get a stat phenytoin level and a CT scan. Keep a vial of lorazepam with the transport in case she has another seizure."

He hammered the door again. "I'm leaving, Ellen. But I'm not the only one who messed us up." He put his ear to the door. She *was* crying.

He turned away, hoping Daniel had not heard the screams. When he knocked on his son's closed door, electronic sounds were his only answer. He pushed his way in.

A video screen flashed images, the only light in the room. Daniel slouched on his bed facing the screen, controller in hand and earphones on, Peter thankfully noted. Daniel graced him with a brief glance before turning back to the game.

Vapors of remorse tempered Peter's impulse to go straight for the power button. His own father would have thrown the machine out the window. He stepped between Daniel and the screen. Daniel paused the game and looked up, still sullen, still wearing the earphones.

Peter motioned toward the screen. "*Grand Theft Auto?*"

"What?"

Peter tapped his ear, and Daniel pulled the earphones down. Peter repeated the question.

"*San Andreas*," Daniel answered.

"Good," he said, having no clue what San Andreas meant, "because your mother and I think you're too young for *Grand Theft Auto*."

Daniel rolled his eyes.

Peter thought about the missed appointment, about apologizing. "You've got homework?"

Daniel shrugged. "What do you care?"

Peter felt his face flush. "I care, okay? I care a lot."

"Good to know, Dad." He replaced his earphones.

Peter felt the anger rise. He turned and slapped the power button on the game machine. The room went dark. He stood in the silence, his anger turning inward. Edging toward the faint light from under the door, he reached the switch. When the ceiling light flicked on, the flash caught a moment of pain on Daniel's face before the rebellious expression returned.

"I've got to go," Peter said.

Daniel glared.

"But I'll be back. We'll talk tomorrow."

Daniel shook his head.

Peter closed the door behind him and heard the video game resume. It sounded like *Grand Theft Auto*.

Fifteen minutes later he stood silently next to Megan's nurse, Emily, as the CT images appeared on the monitor. No signs of hemorrhage, no tumor, and less brain swelling. All good things. Post-op changes only. But on both sides of the skull.

He stared at the bone cut on the left and silently berated himself for his stupidity.

"Doctor Jenson?" the nurse asked. "The scan?"

He refocused on the moment. "The scan is okay. Her phenytoin level?"

"Lab just called. Seven-point-three."

"Get her back to the ICU and give her another five hundred milligrams fosphenytoin. She should be okay."

Emily handed him a computer tablet. "Got to write it down, Doctor."

He cursed under his breath. He had trained at a time when a doctor could simply speak an order and a nurse would follow it. The era of the electronic medical record—the EMR—irritated him. Now that he suspected the system had been manipulated, he was even more distrustful.

After he tapped the instructions and handed the tablet back, he went into the CT chamber and did a quick neurologic assessment of the still sedated Megan.

"This a special patient, Doctor?" Emily asked. "I could have called you with the report."

"Hearing is not the same as seeing. I needed to be here."

"Sure," she said, wheeling the transport stretcher out of the scan room. "You're the doctor. I'll call if she has any more seizures."

Peter would always deny that one patient was more important than another. But Megan did seem special. Perhaps because of unfinished business: he owed her an apology and an attempt to set things right and, for the moment, he could do neither. Or perhaps because being here at her bedside tonight was easier than being at home.

He hoped against his knowledge and experience that the pathology report would surprise him, and the tumor would turn out to be benign. She might find forgiveness easier if her life had just been saved. But if he was right, the tumor was going to end her life within the next few months, and grace would be hard to come by. How could he make amends to a dying woman?

He sighed and walked away to face the more immediate concerns of getting through the night. He found a hospital blanket and headed for the couch in the surgeon's lounge, where he pulled the thin cover over himself. He closed his eyes. Images from the day fought against the exhaustion that begged for sleep. He flipped to his other side, then back. Finally, exhaustion won. His muscles relaxed, and his thoughts faded. Ellen *was* crying, though. She cared enough to cry.

CHAPTER FOUR

As he stood at the foot of Megan's bed, Peter felt grainy and vulnerable. A saggy lab coat covered his fresh scrubs, the only fresh thing about him. He picked up a tablet containing Megan's EMR, tapped to the page with the most recent vital signs, and held it like a shield.

"There's something you should know about your surgery," he said to her.

Dark circles lined her eyes, her striking blue pupils nearly hidden by her swollen lids. She was a small woman, making only a few lumps in the blankets of the hospital bed. On her tray table sat a Styrofoam container of cheese grits.

"There's a lot I need to know," she said.

"Yes. But—"

"Like why Nurse Schafer was here asking if you'd been in yet. She said she was from risk management."

So that damn busybody couldn't wait. "What did she tell you?"

"Nothing. That's what scares me. What risk is it that she's supposed to help me manage?"

Schafer was an idiot. Showing up to say nothing was not

discretion. Megan was now terrified. The message he had to deliver would be that much harder.

"I hate to say it, but she's not worried that you *have* a risk," he said. "She's worried you *are* a risk."

"I'm not following, Doctor."

Now was the moment for him to do the right thing, to confess. But his mouth went dry; his tongue felt stuck to the roof of his mouth. To confess was to give another person power over you. It was weakness, vulnerability.

He jammed his hands in the pockets of his coat and swallowed furiously, trying to regain his voice. The second of hesitation seemed like an hour.

Finally he said, "Here's the thing: I made a mistake, a big mistake, during your surgery."

Her head lifted, and her swollen eye slits widened slightly.

"Your tumor in your right temporal lobe was removed as planned. But before I got that far . . ." His mouth still dry, he made himself go on. "Before I got that far, I made an incision on the left side of your scalp down to the bone. A clerical error on the schedule led us all in the wrong direction, and I didn't pick up on it until after the incision was made."

Megan stared at him, puzzled at first, but her shock quickly turned to anger. "How could that happen?"

Peter looked down. He set the EMR tablet on the tray table, shoving his hands into his coat pocket. "I'm sorry. I had a lot on my mind. Mostly you, but a lot. I fixed it the best I could."

"But I mean, like, right and left. How hard can that be?" She shook her head.

"We'll try to make it up to you."

She gingerly touched her bandaged head. "What about my hair?"

It was the only concern she had voiced before the surgery. "We'll change the bandage later and you can see," he said.

She glowered back at him.

Peter looked down, silence filling the space before his next words. He still had to tell her about the tumor, but he had to be careful. She would have to face a difficult truth, and he wanted her to be prepared. "The surgery itself went well," he said. "Your tumor is out as far as I can tell, and you are not in danger for the present."

"For the present? What else aren't you telling me?"

"I'm not telling you what I don't know. The future—your prognosis—depends on the results of the biopsy more than the success of the surgery. I don't know those results yet." He was not exactly lying. The final biopsy report was not ready yet.

She frowned. "So when will you know?"

"Probably by this afternoon. I can come back."

"I'm not going anywhere," she said, still glowering.

He left her room. He needed a shower, clean clothes, and a quiet place. He needed to tell his side of the story to the only person he trusted, the only person who always had his back, the only person who loved him. He needed to go home.

Maybe Ellen had cooled down this morning. He was sorry; he could explain. He dialed her number, but the call went straight to voicemail. He hung up before leaving a message, unable to come up with something that sounded both contrite and confident.

The phone immediately signaled a text from Ellen: *Locks and alarm codes changed. Your stuff in plastic bag on front step. Don't try to come in.*

He barely restrained himself from throwing the phone, venting his frustration by kicking the nearest baseboard. For the first time in his life he doubted his ability to suck it up and go on. Then he took a deep breath, blew it out, told himself to not be a wimp. Surgeons have complications; couples get separated.

Get the bag, get a hotel room, and get back to work. Patients need you.

At one o'clock, he returned to the hospital and headed to the pathology department to find Bill Roberts. Dr. Roberts' knowledge of neuropathology was exceeded only by his magnificent pessimism.

"Nice day, Jenson," he said.

"It's fifty degrees and raining, Bill."

Roberts smiled. "Yeah. What can I do for you?"

Roberts *would* love this miserable weather. Looking at malignant tumors and dead bodies must have lead to such desolate joys.

"Kaiser. Brain tumor from yesterday afternoon. You got anything yet?"

Roberts nodded, allowing his smile to fade. "It's over here. Take a look." He gestured to a chair next to a microscope with two binocular viewing heads. Roberts sat in the opposite chair and placed a glass slide on the viewing surface. "Here's low power. You see that?"

Peter looked at the purple and lavender splotches. "Looks disorganized."

"Yep," Roberts said. "See that sheet of cells? Pseudopalisade." He switched to high power. "And here. Mitoses. Giant cells. Hypervascularity."

For all Roberts' macabre bravado, he didn't say the diagnosis, focusing instead on the tissue description, as if avoiding the word *malignant* distanced him from the reality. Even Roberts, hidden in his windowless lab away from direct patient contact, knew the word was a vessel that carried only hopelessness.

Peter spared him. "Malignant astrocytoma. Grade IV. Nothing else it could be?"

Roberts lifted his eyes from the microscope. "Nothing else. That age right? Thirty-two?"

Peter met his gaze for a moment, sighed, and looked away. "Yes. Thirty-two."

"You want me to send the slides out? Get a second opinion? I could send them to Duke or Emory if you want."

"Sure. But it won't change anything, Bill. You know that."

Roberts nodded. "Supposed to rain tomorrow too," he said. "But then I hear it's going to be warm and sunny for the rest of the week."

Peter left him grumbling about the possibility of better weather. He thought about what he would say to Megan, how to deliver the worst possible news with something that might feel like compassion.

Just then, his phone buzzed. Dale Kelly, the hospital CEO, his boss—a call he couldn't put off.

"You got a minute?" Kelly asked. "Even if you don't, get up here."

Up here was the executive office suite on the eighth floor. Kelly wanted more than a minute.

Peter didn't need to guess why. "Sure. Be right there."

He had only a hundred feet of hallway and eight elevator floors to plan a defense. Then Kelly's administrative assistant waved him through the outer office and stood at the door.

"Come on in," Kelly said. "Have a seat over there." He motioned toward a small conference table. "Anything to drink? Coffee? Water? Soda?"

Peter shook his head, and Kelly dismissed his assistant with a head tilt. She backed out, closing the door behind her. Kelly took a seat on the other side of the conference table.

"This incident yesterday is a potential problem, Pete."

Pete. How friendly.

"More than potential," Peter said. "It's a big problem. I'm so sorry—"

Kelly's hand rested comfortably on the table, only one quick drum roll of his fingers conveying the tension. "Save it," he said. "Sorry is for sissies and the press release. It's not a big problem if we keep it contained. I've been around long enough to know that stuff happens. What we've gotta do is minimize the fallout."

"Fallout?" Peter tried to readjust to whatever Kelly was talking about.

Kelly grimaced as if instructing a slow student. "Yeah. The fallout. We've got to protect the reputation of the institution so we don't lose any other cases." He held up a finger. "That's the first thing."

Peter nodded.

Kelly lifted a second finger. "Number two, we have to protect you. You're an asset we don't want to waste."

Peter nodded again. He was an asset.

"I brought you on to modernize this neurosurgery program. I've got three years invested in building your career and reputation. I'm not about to throw that away."

Peter breathed a sigh of relief. He wasn't getting fired. "That's good news. Thanks."

"Sure. What are friends for, anyway? If we stick together, we all come out on the other side in one piece. We start sniping at each other? Then we all go down."

"I appreciate that, Dale. This has been hard on my family already."

Kelly's mouth tightened. "Yeah. I hear things. Even up here."

Peter's breath caught. "Like what?"

"Things." Kelly shrugged. "You know, a lot of exceptional men don't stay married. Not these days. Wives can't see the career challenges a man faces. They think this is a job you can turn off at 4:30 and take over childcare."

"We're going to work it out."

"Sure. Just saying," Kelly said. "Same thing is true about exceptional women. You know I like your wife. But I didn't mean to get off on that track. We've got a plan to contain the issue."

"Contain the issue?"

"Yes. Three points. First, we take care of this woman. What's her name?"

"Megan Kaiser."

"Yeah. Kaiser. I'm told this might be something malignant. That right?"

"Yes. She's got about a year with aggressive treatment. Sometimes more, sometimes less."

"Good. That works for us. I just sent Schafer down to talk to her. She's going to offer to write off the hospital bill and give her fifty grand. Only she can't go to the newspaper, can't sue us—and can't make a complaint to the Board of Medicine." Kelly eyed Peter and drummed his fingers again. "She'd be an idiot not to take it. Especially if she's only got a year left."

"Fifty grand?"

"I told Schafer to go up to a hundred if she bucked. Think she'll take it?" Now a sly smile seemed to cross his mouth.

Kelly seemed so pleased at Megan's malignancy, while to Peter it remained a tragedy he was only beginning to grasp. Kelly was reducing her life to problem containment and a financial transaction.

Peter felt dirty answering the question, but he had no choice. "Sure," he said. "More money than that would hardly help her now. And a lawsuit would never settle before her death. But I think—"

"Then," Kelly held up another finger, "there's you. The

Board of Medicine is going to want a piece of your ass. The bigger the piece, the more the publicity."

Peter clasped his hidden hands and felt a wave of nausea. He nodded. "I expect that. And deserve it, I guess."

"Here's what we'll do. We go to them. Preemptive strike, so to speak. We do a 'true confessions' presentation and offer to take whatever punishments they usually mete out over this kind of thing. Save them the investigation. Pay the fine up front. If probation, start now."

"How does that help me?"

"Publicity, Pete. We do it like this, and it's an obscure action by an obscure state agency. Chances are next to nothing that any newspaper will notice or, if they do, consider it newsworthy."

Kelly was right, but the dirty feeling didn't go away. "It's not something we can hide," Peter said.

"You're thinking about insurance contracts," Kelly said, leaning forward to put his elbows on the table. He pressed his fingertips together, tilted his head forward, and bored his gaze into Peter. "I'm ahead of you on this one, Pete. You might not like it."

"What?"

"I want you to see this as an opportunity. We can't go on as a one-man neurosurgery department forever. We've always planned an expansion."

Peter had talked with Kelly before about expansion but didn't see the connection with the current situation. He answered anyway. "Sure," he said. "But the numbers aren't there yet. Bell's practice still siphons a lot of cases away, but he's got to retire sometime. We're close, though. My numbers are big enough for one-and-a-half neurosurgeons now. We could start recruitment and have enough cases for the next guy by the time he gets here. Next year, even."

Kelly's gaze remained intense. "Imagine a three neurosurgeon department beginning next month."

"That would be great, but I don't see how it's going to happen. We don't have the caseload." Not to mention what a bureaucratic nightmare it would be to organize a group practice during the Kaiser case and his crisis at home.

Kelly sat back in his chair. "I've struck a deal with Bell. We're buying out his practice. He is now your partner. With both your practices combined, we can hire another neurosurgeon. We absorb Bell's insurance contracts with yours, so that even if there are some companies that drop you, the hospital's bottom line won't suffer."

Peter's voice rose twenty decibels and half an octave. "Just a damn minute here."

He tried unsuccessfully to calm down. "You hired me because you knew Bell was ten years behind the times. More like twenty, if you ask me. This deal condemns the hospital to a decade of mediocrity."

"Maybe." Kelly stayed remarkably calm. "But we can survive mediocrity. We can't survive scandal."

No, no, no—hiring Bell was like Adam and Eve hiring the snake to provide them with apples. Bell might have altered the schedule and consent form with help. He certainly had caused the late start.

"Hold on," Peter said. "Has Bell agreed to be the junior partner?"

"No," Kelly replied. "We offered him seniority commensurate with his years in practice. Twenty-five, I believe."

"He'll be my boss?"

Kelly nodded. "In a manner of speaking."

Peter stood and grabbed the table with both hands. "You can't be serious." His voice cracked with suppressed rage.

Kelly leaned back in his chair and looked up. "Deadly serious, Pete. This is for you as much as it is for the hospital."

Peter felt his face flush. "Well, I don't agree." His knuckles whitened on the table's edge. "I won't put up with it."

Kelly stood and put a hand on his shoulder. "You don't like Bell. I understand. But he is a power to be reckoned with. Especially now."

"What do you mean?"

"You know he used to be chairman of the Board of Medicine, and he still has friends there. His brother-in-law's on the Board now, too. Anyway, the point is we need that influence on our side."

"So why do I feel like I've been thrown under the bus?"

"Change is hard. You're in shock. As soon as you take the time to let it sink in, you're going to see what an opportunity this is for you."

Peter released the table, stood straight, and shoved his hands into his pockets.

Kelly gently ushered him to the door. "Think about it." He patted Peter on the back. "It's your only smart choice."

Stunned, Peter descended in the elevator. Heading for the ICU, he passed the small deserted chapel, the one room in the hospital he had never visited. He hesitated. He had zero belief in any religious nonsense, but now, more than ever, he needed a place to gather his thoughts.

After a furtive glance, he slipped into the deserted, dimly lit room. Four rows of short pews lined either side of a center aisle. A table, not an altar, stood at the front of the aisle. Centered above it was an artificially lit and abstract display of stained glass that gave the chapel the generic ambiance of a place of worship.

Peter sat in the back, folded his arms over the pew in front of him, put his head down, and closed his eyes. He let the past twenty-four hours wash over him. Kelly's distasteful deal was hard to refuse. Peter could either play ball or quit and face the Board of Medicine alone, unemployed and soon bankrupt.

He lifted his head and wished he had a god. He wished he could pray, give an offering, perform a ritual of some sort, so this god would turn the clock back twenty-four hours. Then he could do a perfect operation and show up for Ellen's counseling session.

"Difficult day, Dr. Jenson?"

Peter turned to find Charles Miles, the hospital chaplain, sitting in the pew behind him. He was a thirty-something man with thin hair and a round face that made him seem heavier and older than he really was. Peter had met him as he had consoled families in the ER and the ICU, but could never remember if he was supposed to title him *Mr.* or *Rev.* or *Pastor*.

He decided to skip his name altogether. "Didn't hear you come in."

"I didn't want to disturb your prayer." He smiled that chaplain smile, the one that said he was a nice guy, a human teddy bear walking around the hospital giving comfort to all the huggers.

"I wasn't praying."

The chaplain's smile didn't fade. "Doesn't hurt, you know."

"What?"

"Prayer. Doesn't hurt to ask for forgiveness."

So he knew about Megan Kaiser. Of course. By now, everybody did.

"You think I need *God's* forgiveness?" Peter demanded.

The smile persisted. "Amongst others."

Peter had always considered Charles Miles too inconsequential to think about. Now he was beginning to actively dislike him. "Listen," he said, "I made a mistake. I have to make it up to the patient, give the Board of Medicine its pound of flesh, make a deal with my wife. Me. Not some delusion in the sky."

Charles' smile began to slip away. "Do you think that will fix things?"

"Actually, yes. Living by the rules, paying the price when the rules are broken," Peter said. An image of Bell's smug face crossed his mind. "And making sure others pay up when they screw up. Accountability."

"Will you be happy then?"

"You think I'd be happier if I had God on my side?"

Charles nodded slowly. "The short answer is *yes*."

Peter got to his feet. Not many people challenged him, if that was indeed what Charles was doing. "I believe in the here and now," he said, pointing at the floor as if that represented the solid ground on which he stood, "and the facts as they can be observed. Science, Mr. Miles. That's what I believe in."

"Ah, science," he said. "A good way to find observable, reproducible facts. Little truths."

"What do you mean by *little truths*?" His voice was louder than he would have liked. He was a rational man, a scientist. But even if dismissive, his position on metaphysics was unassailable. He was sure of that.

Charles shrugged. "Don't limit the truth with facts, Doctor," he said. "You can define a mockingbird by size and weight and habitat, and by the shape of its feathers. You can even take photos of its colors and record its song, take note of the dominant harmonics if you wish. And you will have recorded some fine facts about the mockingbird, things that you can be certain are true. But, one day when you walk in desperation, searching for a sliver of meaning in this life, the mockingbird may sing to you with magnificent joy. He'll be sitting on the peak of the house, or the fence post, or the tree, always right at the top. And in that song, you will hear something of exquisite beauty, something that will give you hope. Then every fact about its weight and size and harmonics will shrink. Through its beauty, the mockingbird's song becomes hope. That can't be quantified. That's a big truth. That is the finger of God."

Peter stared at him, wondering if he was beyond delusional, insane even. But though Charles' words were uselessly abstract, something in them sounded right. Even so, he had no time for theological debates. A "big truth" was more than he could deal with.

He smirked at Charles. "I just wish this god of yours could turn back the clock twenty-four hours."

Charles smiled again, his standard, chaplain smile. "Sometimes He gives you something even better than what you wish for."

Peter gave him a wry look but managed not to roll his eyes. He even shook Charles' hand before he left, a gesture more of truce than gratitude. He had weathered an abusive father, an alcoholic mother, a cruel prep school, a cutthroat premed program, a demanding medical school, and a stressful neurosurgery residency.

Clocks did not run backwards; the only savior he believed in was himself.

He could weather this storm, too.

CHAPTER FIVE

MEGAN'S HEAD dressing was marked by a small, maroon bloodstain above her left ear. "Your buddy Lisa Schafer was just here," she said as he entered the room. "Free hospital care and fifty grand. All I have to do is sign this paper."

Peter nodded, looking grim. "You could get a hundred," he told her.

"Maybe more if I sue." She sat upright in bed, arms folded across her chest, head tilted slightly. "Seems being sick around here is a profitable venture."

Peter sat on the edge of her bed. "There's more." He thought about trying to hold her hand, but her arms stayed fully locked across her chest. "You might not have enough time left to collect on the suit."

She opened her mouth to say something before her face crumbled. She closed her eyes. "That bad?"

This conversation had started wrong. So wrong. He had wanted to be gentle and kind. Maybe he simply didn't know how.

"That bad," he said with regret. "Doctors have a couple of names for your tumor. *Grade IV astrocytoma. Glioblastoma* is the more common term. The operation you had buys time, but no matter how much is taken out in surgery, it always comes back. Sooner, if we don't do any other treatments. Later, if we do radiation and chemotherapy."

She turned toward the closed Venetian blinds. They both stayed silent. A single tear slid down her cheek. He wanted to comfort her, but he'd never comforted anyone before. He realized with unexpected shame that he didn't know how.

"So, this is how it ends," she said, still facing the blinds.

Peter searched for words but found himself rehearsing platitudes he was unwilling to utter.

Wiping the tear with the back of her hand, she faced him. "How much time?"

"Nobody knows. Not exactly." He bit the inside of his lip, wondering how much information he should burden her with now. "If we do nothing, the tumor will be back in about three months on average. Radiation treatment stretches the averages to twelve months. Adding drug therapy brings the averages to about fifteen months. That's about the best we have now. There are some experimental protocols, but . . ."

"Fifteen months."

"Sometimes people—especially young, healthy patients—do a lot better."

"How much better?" she asked.

"Three years. Sometimes four."

"And, those being averages, sometimes people do worse?"

Peter hesitated. Patients at this stage usually treated average survivals as guarantees and nearly always expected to do better. Apparently Megan was the rare stone-cold realist.

Finally, he spoke. "Sometimes, whatever treatment we use, nothing works."

"Worst case scenario?" Another tear slid down her cheek.

"Three months."

She fisted the tear away, angry, embarrassed perhaps.

"If nothing else goes wrong," he said, feeling vulnerable to the future, both hers and his. "I'm sorry."

She hid her eyes under her hands. The problem with a being a stone-cold realist is that grief comes unfiltered and raw.

Unable to heal or comfort her, Peter wanted to leave. More than leave, he wanted to run—out the door, down the street, to somewhere, anywhere.

Her shoulders trembled, and she sniffed. No longer trying to fight her tears, she slapped vainly at the tray table searching for tissues. He turned back and slid the box to her. She tore a handful of tissues free and covered her face.

Peter held the EMR tablet to his chest and glanced toward the door.

She blew her nose and covered her face again. She needed her space. But even as he told himself this and leaned to exit, he knew it was a lie. She didn't need space; he did. What she needed was contact. Close human contact.

He put the tablet on the tray table next to the cold cheese grits and reached out to hold her shoulder—an awkward gesture, but he wasn't very practiced at this comfort thing.

"I'm sorry," he said again.

Her hands left her face and clenched his arm. She leaned her head to his forearm. With his other hand, he touched her face. He found himself leaning into her, brushing her bandage with his cheek. His hands slipped to her back, and he held her in a clumsy embrace.

"I'm sorry too," she said, shuddering under his hands.

"It's okay," he said, but unexpected, unwelcome tears sprang from his eyes.

He held her until her sobs quieted.

"I'm not usually like this," she said.

Afraid to speak, he carefully disengaged, taking a tissue and hiding his face while he dried his tears. Then he picked up the EMR tablet and shielded his heart before he faced her.

"I'm tougher than this," she insisted. "Really."

He struggled to regain his composure, his mind racing. "It's hard news, Miss Kaiser."

"Miss Kaiser?" She sniffed. "You cry with me and can't call me by my first name?"

He wanted to deny that he had cried, but he couldn't. "Megan, then."

"Better." She nodded, tapped her index finger on the tray table, and looked thoughtful. No more tears. "So I'm going to die whether you botched the operation or not?" The stone-cold realist again.

"I'd give anything to do yesterday over." Peter studied his loafers before he continued. "I mean, today would be much the same. You would still have a malignant tumor, and I'd still feel bad. But I'd believe I'd done my best, and you'd believe I cared." He tried to meet her eyes but couldn't. He turned to the window with the closed blinds.

"Yes. And I'd have more hair."

In her comment he heard a quantum of forgiveness. He succeeded now in making eye contact. He even tried to smile, but the sad facts weighed him down. "For a while."

Her smile faded. "I know what I don't want."

Peter, feeling his hands shake, clenched the tablet tighter.

"I don't want to die alone."

Peter again fought the urge to edge toward the door.

Megan went on. "I never knew my father," she said. "I'm not sure my mother knew who he was. My mother . . . well, when I'm generous, I say she was sick and did the best she could. When I'm honest, I say she neglected me and left me vulnerable to a string of abusive men. Then I was in foster care for three years. I had better food mostly, but the same neglect and abuse. I ran away at fifteen and lived on the streets, using sex to pay the bills and drugs to keep me sane. Kind of sane."

She stared unfocused at the blank wall, appearing to recall something ugly.

Peter had heard more than he wanted to know, more than he had ever allowed another patient to share with him. Guilt, maybe? Driving this need to listen?

He didn't understand it himself, but he couldn't leave. He sat down, and she went on.

"Then I ran away from that life," she said, "and ended up in Jacksonville. Cleaned up a little, started working at Waffle House, started going to church, got my own apartment. Nothing big. But I have friends who are something like a family to me." She frowned and focused on her sheets. "Better than my blood family anyway."

"I'm sorry," he said. "Sounds tough."

Megan looked up as if remembering something. "Yes. But the point is, a life like that leaves scars. My friends are almost like family . . . but not. You know what I mean?"

Peter did not. He didn't speak to his parents and didn't know what to think about his wife and son. He didn't have any close friends.

Megan went on. "My friends are good people to talk to, good people to help when you need someone to cover your shift. But now? I'm going to need something else. Something . . . more."

Peter glanced at the door again. Where was she going with this?

"I don't know anybody I want at my side when I'm dying."

"Well, I can certainly arrange home care, even hospice, when the time comes," he said, but even as he spoke he knew this wasn't the answer she was looking for.

"When you talk like that, I hear 'Miss Kaiser' again." She

shook her head. "When I get sick, when I'm dying, I want to call you. And I want you to promise you'll come." She stared intensely at him, a challenge. "Not because I trust you any more than I trust anybody else, but because I figure you owe me."

He blinked and looked away. He liked being a surgeon because he could give orders that nurses carried out, and do operations on patients who were anesthetized. He wore gloves when he did a physical exam. He liked being a healer who didn't have to touch people. But he rebelled at being a caregiver. And this is what she was asking. Not to prescribe her medications, arrange her consultations, and call in hospice, but to be the one who dealt with the messiness of it all. Now he understood, all too well, what she wanted. And he wanted to say *no*.

"You owe me, Doctor," she said.

He had no idea what to say, but he had to do something. Anything. He put down the tablet and fished a bandage scissors from the pocket of his coat. "Your dressing needs to be changed," he told her.

"Fine," she said. "But you owe me more than that."

He sliced through the layers of gauze and took off the turban. Her head was bald in the front with an expanding mat of blond hair streaked with blood and antiseptic at the back. Symmetrical incisions closed with fine black sutures lined the sides of her scalp, both wounds shaped like question marks. He touched the left incision line gently, something he never did to fresh wounds. His mark of shame.

He *did* owe her. But how much?

Megan gently fingered her forehead, touching backward until she found hair and sutures. She put her hands down, picked up the mirror on the tray table, and studied herself, frowning.

"The rest is going to fall out with the radiation, isn't it?"

He shrugged.

She twisted her head sideways to see him. "I'll be okay until the end," she said when she caught his gaze. "If I'm not alone."

To replace the turban with a lighter bandage, Peter leaned in, close enough to feel her warmth. She was courageous, damaged, alone, and he owed her something. A better haircut, a better operation. A debt to care for her when she needed it most.

He made a promise he was certain he'd regret.

"I'll be there, then," he said. "Until the end."

CHAPTER SIX

Fluorescent light filtered down through plastic ceiling grids onto Peter's trembling hands. He couldn't think of what to do with them. They were a sign of weakness, even guilt, but pockets were out of the question. Doodling would be disrespectful. So he folded them, locking his fingers as if in prayer. The meeting room was in a mediocre hotel in Orlando, where the vague scent of dust and cleaning solution rose from a worn carpet. Peter sat at a table, a microphone in his face, while his lawyer, Jim Casey, sat silently on his left. Beyond the microphone, three long tables were arranged in a U-shape; behind the tables sat fourteen of the fifteen members of the Florida State Board of Medicine along with two lawyers and a transcriptionist.

Peter had resolved to follow his lawyer's directives. Appear patient and humble, polite. Show no anger or arrogance. Answer all questions concisely and completely. Do not try to make yourself look good—a lecture in the subtleties of neurosurgery would not be welcome, nor would excuses. The board had already decided guilt and negotiated a punishment. Arguing would only worsen the consequences.

Nonetheless, he was still aggravated about his cufflinks. When he first arrived at the hotel, Jim had met him in the hallway outside the hearing room and looked him over.

"Oh, great," he groaned. "You look like a million bucks. These guys on the board, they aren't surgeons. They're in primary care, or pathology, or dermatology. They want to hate you. They think you make way too much money, have way too much status. Oh, they'd swear it doesn't affect their decisions. But unconsciously, when they see you in your beautiful suit and gold watch—"

"The watch was a gift from my wife," Peter explained.

"And gold cufflinks, too?" Jim rolled his eyes. "Lose the cufflinks."

Annoyed, Peter slid the watch and cufflinks into a pocket, adjusting his sleeves to hide the loose cuffs. "I didn't know this was about fashion preferences."

"You've got to control the things you can. As things stand, this board can make your life miserable. If they want, they can revoke your license. Sure, some days you get lucky and they act like professionals. Most days, though, they want to make an example of someone. They want to feel like they saved Florida from some psychopathic doctor to justify all the time that they sit listening to banalities. Or maybe their spouse just ran off with their best friend, or they didn't get breakfast, or their shoes are too tight, and then the hearing becomes more like a lynching. Do not give them an excuse."

"But really, Jim? Watches and cufflinks? That's what matters?"

Jim's face reddened. He poked Peter on his tie with a manicured middle finger. "Maybe today they're looking to nail somebody. Half the time, they see doctors who are addicts but now say they're in rehab, and they feel obliged to give them a second chance. Or they're stuck with cases of sexual exploitation that are passed off as the poor doctor being seduced, or he just denies the incident—you know, he-said-she-said. So maybe they're hungry for something clear and provable. Like wrong-site surgery."

Peter didn't need to hear more. "Okay, okay," he said. "I get it."

But Jim kept talking. "The point I'm trying to make is that this is a good deal. Right now we have a consent agreement that costs you $25,000 and you agree to give some lectures to the medical staff about wrong-site surgery. Pre-tax dollars, too. I've convinced the board's attorney that you're a great surgeon, this is a first offense, that you're humble and remorseful. So look the part."

Now, facing the Board and tugging on his shirt cuffs, Peter did feel sorry, remorseful even. But also angry. Angry because he felt like he had been set up. Angry that Bell was taking over his practice. Angry that Ellen had left him.

The fifteenth member of the board made a late arrival. Like Peter, and unlike the other men on the board, he wore a neatly pressed suit and dress shoes. The chairwoman gave him a withering look as he slid into his seat. He returned her stare with a disarming smile.

She shook her head and called the meeting to order. "Case 2012-147, tab three. Dr. Jenson." She peered over her reading glasses. "Represented by Mr. Casey, I see."

"Yes, Doctor," Jim replied. "I think you'll find this a simple formality. The consent agreement is before you, and we don't want to waste your time."

She nodded with a wry smile. "So considerate of you. Still, if any of the board members have any questions of Dr. Jenson . . . ?"

Board members took their shots: *How could you? What will you do to prevent this in the future? What about the safety of our patients? Don't you care about the public's confidence in our profession?*

The questions caused knife-like pain, each a reminder of his failure and Megan's injury. But Peter kept his hands folded, his voice calm, his face passive, and his demeanor courteous.

The late arriving board member took the floor. "I see by your credentials that you have received a most excellent education, Dr. Jenson."

Peter heard a slight accent, probably Cuban, but no question. "Thank you," he said.

The doctor smiled and nodded, seemingly friendly and encouraging. Peter was relieved by the change of tone. He tried to see his nameplate but the angle was too acute.

"And a spotless record up to this point," the board member added. "This makes me think there must have been some extenuating circumstance that may have caused you to let your guard down."

Still not a question, just a statement. Peter glanced at Jim, uncertain of how to respond.

Jim pulled the microphone to himself. "Dr. Jenson takes full responsibility for his actions in this matter."

The chair spoke. "We want to hear from the doctor, Mr. Casey. Dr. Jenson, please respond."

Peter felt like he might be able to make them understand the pressures and frustrations of that day, but followed Casey's lead. "I take full responsibility."

The sympathetic board member took the microphone. "Yes, and we appreciate your cooperation. I was just curious as to what was going through your mind. An unexpected delay, perhaps? Some outside emotional pressures? Some complicity by another staff member? Some reason that such a fine surgeon should make such a surprising error?"

Peter had a momentary illusion that only the two of them

were having a conversation about what happened that day, that finally he could explain to someone who would understand.

"Well . . . I had a late start."

"A delay for an emergency?"

Peter could feel Jim tense at his side, but he answered anyway. "That I could understand. But I got bumped for a crummy lumbar disk surgery that could have been done anytime while I sat waiting to take out a brain tumor. It wasn't right."

Jim put his hand over Peter's forearm.

The board member, serious now, nodded. "An inconsiderate colleague. Anything else?"

"The surgery schedule."

Jim gripped harder, trying to get his attention, but Peter couldn't seem to hold back his compulsion to explain. "Somebody manipulated the schedule in the computer," he said, "listing the case for the wrong side. Maybe the same person who delayed me, but I can't prove it."

The doctor smiled again, but not so kindly.

Jim whispered in Peter's ear. "Not another word. You hear me?"

"So this wasn't really your fault?" the doctor asked. "Some bad doctor made you late for no good reason? Some boogie man sneaked into the computer and laid a trap for you?"

Silence filled the room.

"Dr. Jensen, please answer Dr. Umberto's questions," the chairwoman said.

Peter's carefully folded hands sprang open.

Umberto? That man was Bell's brother-in-law.

Peter rubbed his thumbs against his index fingers, but they were already starting to quiver. He closed his hands into fists and stole a sideways glance at Jim, who shook his head, almost imperceptibly.

Umberto didn't give him any time to answer. Instead, he

spoke directly to the chair. "I have heard of this man. Because of his fancy credentials, he is arrogant, treating his colleagues and staff with disdain. You see what he is. This consent agreement is far too lenient."

"I took responsibility." Peter's voice rose in protest. "I said I was sorry."

"Certainly," Umberto retorted. "To save your neck. All the while, in your heart you were blaming another."

"I blame," Peter said, nearly shouting now, "an incompetent and conniving old fool. An old fool who happens to be your brother-in-law."

Several board members spoke at once. The chair pounded her gavel.

Jim raised his whisper to a hiss. "Shut up, Doctor." He glared at Peter. "Or find another attorney."

Peter wouldn't shut up. "I apologized to the patient, the family, and to the board," he continued. "I could blame it on the schedule clerk, the OR team, or your brother-in-law. But I'm here accepting responsibility. So give me a break. Let's get on with it. Just don't insult me with your self-righteous hypocrisy."

Jim tightened his grip on Peter's arm and leaned his head to his ear. "Not another word if you want to leave this room with your license!"

Peter tore his gaze away from the smug Umberto to look at the other board members. The general countenance had changed from one of mild, bored concern to one of focused indignation.

Umberto continued to hold the floor. "I believe that we have heard enough from this witness. Clearly, he is without remorse, except for what consequences might occur to him. I move that we strike the Consent Agreement."

"Is there a second?" asked the chair.

Across the room, a hand rose.

"We have a motion and a second to reject the Consent Agreement. Is there any discussion?"

Peter was red-faced with anger, but he held back, sensing the threat. He knew what was on the line.

Jim raised the hand that was not gripping Peter's arm. "May I address the board?"

Umberto pulled his microphone close and opened his mouth to reply, but the chair stared him into silence. "I am sure we have no objections, Mr. Casey."

Jim gave his plea. "With the board's attorney, we have reached a Consent Agreement that takes into consideration that Dr. Jenson has no prior violations of the Practice Act and the incident occurred with extenuating circumstances during a time of high stress. In spite of my client's show of temper this morning, those facts are still in evidence. I believe the Consent Agreement to be fair. Perhaps Dr. Umberto would like to recuse himself because of his obvious emotional involvement at this time."

Umberto jumped to his feet. "Dr. Umberto would *not* like to recuse himself. I will not be intimidated by this arrogant bully!"

Whispering, the chair consulted the attorney at her side. Peter's anger morphed into confusion. He looked to Jim, who released his arm and said, "We talk later. Right now, not a word."

The chair addressed the room. "We are informed about the Consent Agreement. We also have the right to reject it and issue a new proposal. Is there any further discussion?"

There was further discussion, but no dissension from imposing harsher consequences. A new agreement was presented to Mr. Casey and Dr. Jenson: a $50,000 fine, two hundred hours of community service, and one year probation with Dr. Joseph Bell as the supervisor.

Jim took his arm and led him from the room. As Peter slowly realized his stupidity, his anger surged. "Two hundred hours of community service?" he said to Jim. "How am I supposed to come up with an extra five weeks this year? And Bell will crucify me before the year's end."

Jim heaved a sigh before replying. "Umberto is a genius at making himself look good and others not-so-much. You played into his hands. Fourteen docs are in there mentally patting themselves on the back for protecting the patients of Florida from the arrogant and dangerous neurosurgeon and thanking Dr. Umberto, who didn't let this one get away. And, in about two hours, Umberto will call his brother-in-law to tell him that they got you."

They exited to the hotel lobby. Jim stopped. "Or maybe he won't have to wait that long."

Joe Bell folded his newspaper and rose from a lounge chair. He walked toward them, smiling, his hand extended. Jim readily shook Bell's hand.

Peter knew Jim specialized in defending doctors at board meetings, that he'd probably had many encounters with Bell over the years. But that hurt, that handshake between his supposed advocate and his enemy. He held Bell partly responsible for the surgical error and fully responsible for the disastrous board meeting.

He pointedly jammed his hands into his pockets. "What are you doing here, Bell?"

Bell, in a congenial tone, replied, "As a former board chairman, there are times I meet with them for advice about historical issues." He nodded purposefully at Peter. "And, of course, I wanted to look out for my new partner."

Partner—a reality Peter could never accept. Heat rose to his cheeks and his hidden hands clenched into fists. He fought to control his voice. "What do you really want, Bell?"

Bell's smile remained frozen as he shook his head and turned to Jim. "Always a pleasure to see you, Mr. Casey. I mean no disrespect when I say that I hope we will not be needing your services again any time soon. Can you excuse us?"

"Certainly," Jim said. He glanced at Peter. "That is, if my client doesn't have any more questions?"

Peter's glare remained fixed on Bell. "Call me Monday, Jim."

Jim left. Peter's anger flared. "So what do you want?" he said to Bell. "Spit it out."

Bell's smile faded. "I want to be your friend."

"No. You don't. You set me up to do a wrong-side surgery." He jerked his thumb back over his shoulder. "And your brother-in-law ambushed me in there. This is friendship?"

"You cannot blame your mistake on me or a schedule misprint, and Dr. Umberto speaks for himself."

"Is this simply revenge for calling you out?" Peter asked. "If so, great. You got revenge. Now go gloat somewhere else."

"Oh, Dr. Jenson, please do not think of me as someone so small." Bell tried the smile again. "*Vengeance is mine, saith the Lord.* I believe that is what the good book says."

"So then what are you doing here?"

"I want your training and your skills, your reputation—as it was before this unfortunate publicity—and your referral network. I want these things working for me instead of competing against me."

So that was it. This old, barely competent doctor wanted to revitalize his practice with the knowledge, skill, and energy Peter had brought to the hospital in the last few years. What better way to get revenge than to get control?

"And if I say no?" Peter asked.

Bell held out his hands as if to demonstrate the obvious. "We are partners now, working for the hospital, and I am your senior. You are on probation, under my supervision. In your current situation, you will work for me or not work at all. Friendship is what we should have. Respect, in any case."

"Respect?" Peter replied. "Are you kidding me?"

Bell's congenial tone cooled. "Respect is a gentle term. You should fear me. You should believe that I have the power to make or break you."

"You are threatening me." But he knew Bell was right. A wrong word from him could lead to license revocation.

Bell gave him a smooth, superficial smile. "Think of it, Dr. Jenson, not as a threat but an invitation. Perhaps someday you will look back and see this moment as an opportunity."

Peter stared into Bell's cold, shallow eyes before he elbowed past, blind to any opportunity at all.

CHAPTER SEVEN

Peter laid his suit coat in the trunk, rolled up his cuffs, and folded himself into his Porsche. He jammed the car into first and squealed his tires as he left the garage. A red light stopped him at the freeway entrance. Usually the throb of the 3.6-liter engine could distract him with the illusion of power, but not today. Ellen would have understood. She would have listened, dissected the events, and said the words that would have made him feel better. He had trusted in only her, confided in only her, and now he had no one. Without Ellen, he was lost.

The car behind him honked as the light changed. He flashed his middle finger at the driver before squealing onto the interstate. His loneliness felt monstrous.

He accelerated up the I-4 ramp. The Porsche hit seventy, and he braked to merge into traffic. Weaving through commuter cars and tourist RVs, he finally got into an open left lane. He set the cruise control at eighty; speeding was not only his God-given right but a favorite distraction. But even when he pushed the speed to ninety, the board meeting kept replaying in his mind.

He cursed himself for being a fool. He thought about quitting. He had no savings, but the pressure to make a big income was less important now that his quarter-million dollar student debt was finally paid off. His other big expense was the mortgage on what was really Ellen's dream house. Now that he wasn't living there, meeting the payments didn't seem so urgent.

But he couldn't quit neurosurgery. He was forty-two and had a son, a wife, at least technically speaking, and no other marketable skills. Furthermore, he didn't want to do anything else. He was addicted to playing not god exactly, but at least the role of a hero snatching life from the jaws of death. Nothing else could give him that sense of satisfaction, that confirmation of his own self-worth.

He could relocate. No doubt he could get a new monitor for his probation if he moved. But with the recent board actions on record, he would have an uphill climb to establish a reputation and a practice somewhere else.

And he wasn't a quitter. He was bright but not brilliant; he got where he was by perseverance and hard work. He would rather deal with Bell than walk away and let him win. He would rather fight for his marriage and his child than give up. And then there was that vague promise to Megan, to care for her at the end, whatever that would end up costing. But the end could come anytime—a few weeks, a few months, even a year or two. By then, she might forget.

I can stay for six months, he told himself. *Try to adjust to Bell and give my marriage a chance. I can always leave, but I can never come back.*

As he approached Jacksonville, his dashboard screen signaled an incoming call from his answering service. He took it.

"We just got a call from the St. Luke's ER," the service said. "Can you take that now? Or should we give it to the covering doctor?"

Peter cursed himself. He should have never have committed

to being on emergency call today. He was in no mood to take care of a stranger. For the first time in his career, he thought about hanging up and turning off his phone.

Then he realized the sad truth: he had nowhere else to go. He called the ER.

"Dr. Jenson," the ER physician said. "Dr. Tito, here. I've got a mid-thirties white, maybe Hispanic, John Doe dumped on the curb, unconscious. Alcohol level of .380, abnormal LFTs, hemoglobin of seven, 30,000 platelets and INR of 2.5."

Peter knew what was coming. He had heard this introduction too many times before. Some kind of blood in the head.

"A CT scan shows an acute subdural hematoma," Tito said.

Peter pictured what had happened. An end-stage alcoholic whose blood couldn't clot due to liver disease had fallen down or been beat up. Now Peter was being asked to bring him back from the brink of a self-inflicted death.

Peter sighed, half-disgusted, half-resigned. "Give him two units of fresh-frozen plasma and a ten-unit platelet pack. I'll call the OR and be there in ten minutes."

Once he had lived for moments like this—the adrenaline rush, a life at stake, an opportunity to be a hero. He still got the adrenaline rush. A life was still at stake. But he knew there would be no accolades in a case like this. A drunk lived or died depending on a combination of how well he did his job and luck. But if the drunk lived, he would die soon enough by another cause. If he died, it would be easy for someone—family, a plaintiff's attorney, even Bell—to blame the surgeon. His only option was to provide the best care possible as quickly as possible, his fate bound now to a dying stranger.

Eight minutes later he left the car in a no-parking zone at the ER entrance, grabbed a white coat from the trunk, and ran through the ambulance entrance doors. He tossed his car key to the open-mouthed security guard and said, "Move it if you have to."

He saw the CT before he saw the patient, and the images confirmed the ugly reality he had imagined. A right-sided acute subdural hematoma compressed the brain. Midline structures were already shifted. The coma resulting from this injury might already be irreversible.

In the trauma room, a middle-aged man lay on a hospital stretcher, his black hair long and disheveled, his shoulders skinny, his abdomen soft and round. A crumpled white sheet had been thrown carelessly across his lower body in a half-hearted attempt to respect his modesty. His eyes were taped closed, a gastric tube taped to his nose, an endotracheal tube protruding from his mouth. Already he looked dead, at least brain dead, pale and still except for the rise and fall of his chest in rhythm with the thump-wheeze of the respirator.

Peter lifted the patient's eyelids and flashed a light into the pupils, then tipped the head back and forth to see if the eyes moved. Nothing. He knuckled the sternum to check for any response to pain, either purposeful or reflex, anything. Still nothing.

He stepped back, shoving his troublesome, trembling hands into his pocket, and contemplated the likelihood of John Doe's death. The man looked brain dead and possibly was. But the body temperature was ninety-five degrees and the blood alcohol level was near toxic, either one of which would suppress brain function. These facts prevented the most convenient diagnosis: brain death. Clearly, he was in a deep coma, and his body had suffered the ravages of years of alcoholism as well as the effects of this head injury. A prognosis for returning to a productive or even independent life was highly unlikely.

Peter closed his eyes and let his head droop. It was a tough call. He could declare further care futile and step away. The truth was that further care was probably futile. In America, every patient deserved every chance regardless of how expensive or how unlikely a good outcome. But no matter how much Peter wished for a next-of-kin to whom he could recommend early withdrawal from life support, he was obligated to give this unknown man his best effort.

John Doe's nurse bustled into the room with a sheaf of papers serving as his temporary chart. "OR is ready, Doctor," she said dropping the papers on the stretcher.

Peter stuffed down his ambivalence. If he was going to treat him, he had to do it quickly.

"You and me," he said to himself and John Doe, "let's do this thing."

"Let's go," he said to the nurse and respiratory therapist. The two women, already pushing the stretcher, looked puzzled until they realized from the pace he set that they all would be jogging to the OR.

Peter peeled off to the locker room to get into his scrubs. By the time he walked into Room Four, the patient lay stretched out on the OR table, and Archie Davis had him on the ventilator.

"Another drunk with no life and no chance, huh?" Archie said, as he checked his IV lines and monitors. "Looks like this one doesn't need anesthesia. Already came self-medicated."

"Funny you should be concerned," Peter said.

Archie looked away. Nancy raised her eyebrows.

Stupid to take out his frustration on Archie when he needed him at his best. Stupid to make a public reference to a private issue.

"I'm sorry, Archie," he said. "Just tired. I need you, buddy."

Archie remained silent.

While Peter shaved and positioned the patient's head, he answered Archie's question. "No, he doesn't have a chance, but we don't have a choice. Maybe he won't live with an operation, but he's not dying without one either."

Archie shrugged. "Hey, we're here. Why not? Just sometimes you wonder."

"You do," Peter said.

But the time for wondering was over. The time for action had come. He went out, scrubbed his hands, and returned. Carl handed him the scalpel. He checked the CT images and held the scalpel poised above the skin. Right subdural, right scalp.

"Carl. This is the right side of his head, right?"

Carl hesitated before answering. "If you mean *not left*, yeah. If you mean *correct*, you tell me. You okay?"

Peter caught Carl staring at his open, shaking hand. He took a breath. No time for hesitation. He took the scalpel, cut into the skin, and blood poured from the scalp. The incision swept in a large arc from the mid-forehead hairline backward, then descended and curved forward again to outline the top and front of his ear, like a huge, reversed question mark.

Peter pulled the scalp, underlying muscles, and tissue forward with no attempt to control the bleeding. As blood soaked the drapes and began to drip onto the floor, he used the power drill to make five holes in the exposed skull. Then came the power saw to connect the holes. The smell of blood and bone dust filtered through his mask. Now he removed a piece of skull that looked like a dirty white yarmulke. The *dura*, the fibrous cover of the brain, bulged from the hole in the skull.

Another incision in the dura and a blood clot squeezed through the hole like red currant jelly. Swiftly, he enlarged the incision and began his search for the bleeding points on the surface of the brain. His thoughts came in images and shapes; words became foreign intrusions, useful only to ask for the right instrument if Carl put the wrong one in his outstretched hand.

"Could you give me the name of the procedure, Doctor?" Nancy asked.

The question was necessary for some OR rule to tabulate the type of cases being done, but aggravating nonetheless. *Call it Johnny or Fred or Sammy the Surgery*, he wanted to say. Each operation was different, unique to the pathology and the patient. The name was always an abstraction.

"Call it 'An Exercise in Futility,'" Archie said.

Carl snickered.

Maybe, Peter thought. *Maybe not.*

"Ask me later," he told Nancy.

The scalp bled, the skull bled, and then the brain bled. Peter worked to protect the brain, by removing clots, by clearing the blood through suction or letting it flow over the drapes and onto the floor. Nancy threw towels, then blankets, to absorb the dark puddles.

Archie tried to keep up with the blood loss through transfusion, but the bleeding wouldn't stop until plasma and platelets arrived. The plasma was frozen and needed a half-hour or more to thaw. Then it had to be transported to the OR, identified as the correct units, and connected to the IV lines. Platelets weren't frozen, but were sometimes available only from the county blood bank or another hospital; they could take even longer. Every delay was marked by more suctioned blood, larger puddles on the floor, until finally the last platelet pack and the last unit of fresh frozen plasma went through the IVs.

Peter sucked the last clot from the surface of his brain. The hemorrhage from the surgical wound slowed, and then stopped. The room reeked with the metallic scent of blood, but John Doe was likely to survive.

Peter took a deep breath and allowed his eyes to blink. He scanned the pulsating landscape of the brain as if its appearance alone could tell him what the future would hold. But the brain's tan surface, with its map of tiny, bright red arteries and blue veins, kept its secrets. He didn't know, wouldn't know, until the effects of the anesthesia wore off, the alcohol metabolized, and the body temperature returned to normal.

His adrenaline high fading, he had just enough energy left to close the wound, fix the bandages, and take John Doe to the ICU. When they arrived there, his examination showed only that the pupils were pinpoint, consistent with the narcotic effects of anesthesia, and his arms remained unmoving. All that could be said for sure was that John Doe was not brain dead, an uncertain improvement since the ER. Still, Peter found himself cheering for him. He didn't know him, probably wouldn't like him if he did. But a potentially life-saving surgery created a certain bond. If John Doe died, Peter failed. If, by some miracle, John Doe survived and thrived, Peter succeeded.

On his way to the lounge, Peter checked the surgical waiting room. As expected, no one paced or sat wringing their hands for John Doe. Peter's eyes burned, his shoulders ached, and his feet were swollen. In the lounge, he collapsed into an overstuffed chair, images of the angry board and Bell's smug face washing over him, flowing like blood to the floor.

An hour later, he woke, stiff and groggy, struggled to his feet, and stripped out of the bloody scrubs. His socks, soaked with blood, went into the trash. Showered, he changed into his street clothes and headed out, longing for food and a good night's sleep. But this time, the waiting room wasn't empty. An older woman in designer jeans was perched on the couch, her well-heeled feet crossed at the ankles. She had the angular figure of a woman who either exercised religiously or suffered from an eating disorder, her designer tee tucked primly into her jeans. She wore bangles, a necklace chain, and stud earrings, all of them gold, and her short brunette hair was coiffed in a simple but precise style, with expensive blonde highlights.

He wanted to creep past, unseen, but she'd already spotted him. She looked him up and down, unsmiling.

He tried to smile anyway. "I'm Dr. Jenson," he said. "Can I help you?"

Her inspection complete, she stood and held out her hand on a weak wrist.

"Ann Alvarez," she said. "Yes. They told me in the ICU that I might meet you here."

"You are the mother?" he asked, hiding his surprise. Her eyes lacked the fear he usually saw in people awaiting the results of brain surgery, especially on their child.

"Yes." It sounded like a reluctant confession.

"Your son has apparently had an accident."

"Accident. Really. If you'd call it that," she sniffed.

"Not an accident?"

"Luis left the house three days ago. I can only assume he's been drinking again. Getting drunk is no accident."

"Yes, well. All we know is that a car dropped him off in front of the emergency room and drove away."

"He knows some bad people." She shifted the sleek leather bag on her forearm.

"He's been hurt badly. Maybe a fall, maybe an assault." Peter always gave the bad news in a heavy dose. "His liver and bone marrow have been damaged by his alcohol intake, severely enough that he isn't clotting his blood except by the transfusions we've given him."

She nodded. "Go on."

"He's had surgery to get the blood clot off his brain, but he still may have had severe brain damage. There is no guarantee he will wake up, and if he does, he may be intellectually damaged or paralyzed. Complications are more common with patients in his condition."

Realistic, even pessimistic, expectations helped to make the future tragedy more acceptable, but families often broke down at this point.

Mrs. Alvarez, however, nodded again, impatiently. "So when will you know?"

"You mean, if he survives?"

"Yes." No tears, no fears—she just wanted the facts.

He obliged. "The anesthesia and alcohol will have worn off by tomorrow. If another bleeding crisis doesn't occur, we should have a good idea by nine a.m."

"I'll be back then." She shouldered her sleek bag and walked to the exit. At the door, she hesitated and, in what sounded like an afterthought, said, "Thank you for your efforts, Dr. Jenson. As you may have assumed, I've been down this path before with Luis."

She strode away, her heels clicking on the tile floor. When she disappeared, a cold disquiet came to him. John Doe, now Luis Alvarez, hung in a delicate balance between life and death, but even his mother did not seem to care.

CHAPTER EIGHT

Peter walked through the ER to retrieve his car. Laura, the shift supervisor, stopped him to ask about the John Doe.

"A survivor," he said. "All I know for now."

"So good," she replied. "Did his mother find you?"

He nodded. "Also a survivor."

She looked puzzled, then added, "You've got another patient here."

Peter's low spirits sagged lower. "Another patient?"

"Yes. A woman with a brain tumor taken out last month. She came in tonight with some kind of seizure. Name of Kaiser, I think."

Of all days, of all patients. For a fraction of a second, he closed his eyes.

Laura noted his hesitation. "You don't have to see her. Dr. Garrison said her CT scan is okay, and her anticonvulsant levels were low. He gave her a loading dose of phenytoin, told her to increase her daily dose and call you Monday."

But he did have to see her. Not because it was necessary—Garrison had done all the right things. Not because it was smart—he needed to sleep. Because he owed her something.

But when he knocked on the open door of her exam room, a curtain was drawn around her bed.

He was about to retreat when the curtain slid open.

Megan wore ragged jeans shorts, a hospital gown, and a surprised look. Sadness washed over him. Through her gauntness and her scars, the fading shadows of her youth and beauty were still there.

"I didn't expect you to be here," she said, fastening a brightly patterned scarf around her head. "Your answering service said you weren't available. Dr. Ryan told me to come in."

He shifted awkwardly, one hand clutching the curtain. "Sorry," he said, "I . . . I had an emergency."

Her eyes scanned him, assessing the truth. Apparently he looked convincing. She nodded.

"But I heard you were here," he went on, jamming his hand into his coat pocket. "Anyway. I stopped by to make sure everything was all right."

"I'm okay. Scared is all." She swung her feet over the edge of the bed. "My left hand started shaking and wouldn't stop. I was afraid I'd have another seizure. But it's okay now. They said I could go."

She turned her back to him and shed the hospital gown, pulling a red t-shirt over her head. She slid toe-thong sandals onto her feet and faced him.

"You did the right thing," he said, "coming in."

She started to gather her purse, discharge papers, and the prescription that lay on the stretcher's rumpled sheets.

"I know," she said. "But I need a ride home. I better make a call."

She frowned at the wall clock, and then at the face of her phone. She seemed so small and alone.

He edged toward the door. He could walk to the security

guard, get his keys, find the Porsche, and drive away, his duty fulfilled. He could say goodbye and go.

But he didn't. "I'm just leaving," he said. "Can I give you a lift?"

She narrowed her eyes. "You're sure? You don't have to do this."

Already he regretted it. Acting like her friend, not her doctor, was crossing a line. But now it was too late to change his mind.

"It's no problem, really," he told her. "My car is right here."

At the security desk, the guard returned his key and told him where to find his car. "Anytime you want to leave your car during my shift, just let me know. Only, I might park it a long way away," he joked. "Like Oregon."

Peter thanked him and took the keys. When Megan tucked into the passenger seat, she fingered the leather upholstery. She said nothing except to give directions to her apartment. Peter realized that waitresses didn't often ride in Porsches; his car was an awkward, tangible symbol of their differences.

She directed him to a twelve-unit building on a busy four-lane thoroughfare with a supermarket, laundry, gas station, and Waffle House. Peter drove past this apartment building every day on his way to work and never thought about who might live here.

His closest experience to second-rate apartment living was in New Haven while he was in medical school. Even then, he and Ellen had lived in a duplex on a mostly quiet street, with neighbors who became their friends. Not only was Megan's neighborhood far from quiet, but the people on the street didn't look like anyone he would like to have as friends. His plan had been to drop her and drive off, but even he wouldn't walk alone here at night.

"I'll walk you to your door," he said.

"I'd like that," she replied.

In this sketchy neighborhood at midnight, they made an odd couple, the tall doctor in his white coat and the petite woman in her red t-shirt. He walked quickly, aware that if he were recognized, the situation could be misinterpreted. When he turned up the collar of his coat, she glanced at him and smiled wryly.

They climbed stairs up a breezeway to an apartment on the second floor. The veneer on the hollow door was cracked, the doorknob tarnished. A rubber mat picturing seashells lay before the entry. He felt like a high school kid taking his date to her door, embarrassed and uncertain. She dug a key out of her purse and shoved it into the lock. Just before she turned the key, she hesitated.

Finally, she looked up at him. "Thanks for the ride and all, but you look terrible. You want to come in, have a drink or something before you go? Maybe something to eat?"

He knew all the reasons he should say no. But he was hungry, he was tired, and he was alone.

"Dr. Jenson?"

He shook himself. "Yes," he said. "That would be . . . nice."

She nodded, turned the key, and led him in.

The kitchen was small, separated from the equally small living room by only a round table and four chairs. The room was clean and uncluttered, furnished with a tan, cloth-covered sofa, two beanbag chairs, and a small bookcase topped by a modest television. Yellow-orange floral curtains framed the single window, and seashells filled a foot-tall clear glass vase on the kitchen counter.

"My humble home." She gestured to the living room. "Make yourself comfortable."

He sat on the sofa beneath a framed color photo of a beach at sunset and leaned forward, resting his elbow on his knees. Instantly, his feet felt better, his lower back stretching gently.

He let gravity have its way with his head and hands, and he closed his eyes. It had been a long day.

A plate rattled in the kitchen, rousing him, reminding him where he was. He lifted his head and scanned the small bookcase—a Bible, a book called *Forgiving Our Fathers and Mothers*, another by someone named Max Lucado, some Beth Moore DVDs, and a couple of recent *People* magazines. Nothing familiar to Peter. He leaned back, resting his head while Megan clattered in the kitchen.

"Come and get it, Doctor," she called.

He must have dozed off. The smell of stir-fried vegetables and rice now filled the room.

He stood, stretching the back muscles that had already begun to retighten, and joined her at the small table. He picked up his fork then stopped, embarrassed, as Megan bowed her head and appeared to say a prayer.

"This is really nice," he said. "It's been a long day and this is the first food I've had. Thanks."

For the first time in weeks someone had given him a place to rest and a meal to eat. Simple pleasures forgotten. He felt like he had come back from a dark place into a warm light.

"Dr. Jenson," she said after a few bites, "the two times I came to your office, you didn't meet my eyes. And you sidestepped to leave as quickly as you could."

He stopped eating and wondered if she was right.

She pursed her lips, lowering her fork. "Do you hate me, Doctor?"

Peter coughed and studied his plate. "Of course not."

"You have to say that. But every time you see me, you must see a mistake." She shrugged. "Most of us don't like seeing our mistakes. We like to blame somebody for them."

"I don't blame you."

"Thank you. But that's not really what I asked, is it?"

"Fine," he said, but he would not meet her eyes. "I don't hate you."

"Okay," she said. "So . . . do I frighten you?"

He looked at his half-empty plate. The truth was that he didn't know. He would anticipate her next office visit, even rehearse it in his mind. Then he would see her name on his appointment schedule, his gut would knot, and he couldn't wait for her to leave.

"I don't know," he murmured.

"I mean, I got my money. I'm not going to sue you."

"No." He met her eyes. "I mean, sure, you could still sue me, and I would find it very unpleasant. But that's life as a neurosurgeon in Florida. We all get sued."

"So then why do I scare you?" she asked.

Because you are young, beautiful, and going to die soon, in a cold, merciless universe. Because I can do nothing to slow the inevitable. Because I should have done better, given you my greatest effort at the time of your greatest need.

"I don't know," he said. He couldn't meet her eyes.

"I need to trust you to do something for me."

He heard the insistence in her voice, the demand for eye contact. "Yes. I haven't forgotten." The debt he hoped not to pay. "Be with you at the end."

"I will need something special from you then."

"What?"

"I need you to kill me."

Peter put his fork down in disbelief and examined her carefully. Her pointed chin stuck out, and her full lips closed to a very tight line. Her deep blue eyes flashed as she held him in her gaze. She had meant every word.

He gave a careful, measured reply. "I can keep you comfortable," he said.

"I don't want to be 'comfortable' in a stupor for a month, a week, or even a day." Her voice rose. "I don't want to provide interesting and profitable projects for visiting nurses. I don't want friends sitting at my bedside knitting and sharing casseroles while I lay drooling on my chin and stinking in my shit. When I no longer know what's going on, when I can't care for myself anymore, I want my life to be over."

Peter leaned back in his chair and exhaled a little too loudly. So she wanted what horses with broken legs received. She wanted what sick dogs received. She wanted what everyone wanted: mercy.

"But I can't do that," he said.

Her eyes darkened. "You mean, you won't."

"I mean I can't. It's not ethical." He sighed. "Listen, I can give you drugs for pain or emotional distress, but I can't kill you."

She crossed her arms and glared. "But enough narcotics would kill me, right? So what's the problem?"

The easy answer would be to say there was no problem. He could give her enough drugs to keep her from complaining and himself out of trouble. But, no, he couldn't lie to her.

"The problem is intent," he said. "I can treat your pain but I can't purposefully kill you. It's not legal."

"You owe me."

The debt again.

He edged his chair away from the table. "You don't need me. You need Dr. Kevorkian."

"Kevorkian's dead. And I'm looking for personal passage, not public protest. I need to trust you when the time comes."

"And you don't," he said. "What do you want me to say?"

"You can't hate me. You can't look at me and see a mistake you can sweep away and never deal with again."

"I don't hate you."

"Then say you care about me . . ." Her voice caught. She

pounded the table gently with her small fist. ". . . enough to kill me."

She looked directly into his eyes. Tears rolled down her cheeks. "I want to trust you, either because of your guilt or your compassion. Or both." She wiped her tears and lifted her chin. "Can I?"

Peter got up and paced the few steps to the living room and back. He shoved his hands into the pockets of his lab coat. Ethics said he couldn't kill her; his mind said he wouldn't. But his heart talked.

"You can trust me," he said.

"So when I can't speak for myself, you'll care for me?"

"By *care for you*, you mean kill you?"

"Yes."

He touched her cheek to wipe away the last tear and edged toward the exit. His debt to her was to care, truly care, when she needed it most. She would be dead soon enough. Then he would grieve and be free.

"All right," he said. "Yes."

CHAPTER NINE

STILL IN LAST night's scrubs, Peter woke like a hung-over man, eyes swollen, mouth furry, face plastered to drool-damp sheets. Sunshine flowed through the open blinds, nudging him toward consciousness.

No alarm? Must be Sunday.

He blinked and rolled over, reached for Ellen, and found only cold sheets. Memories of the prior day washed over him—enemies, obligations, and an unsettling promise. He imagined that if Ellen were here, he would tell her about the disastrous board meeting, the ultimatum from Bell, the heart-pounding emergency surgery on the John Doe. In his fantasy she would listen and take his side.

Then he wondered if he would tell her about Megan and his grim promise. No, he decided. Not even in his fantasy could Ellen know.

His loneliness grew large and sat on his chest. Even breathing was painful. Moving seemed like a monumental effort. Without lifting his head from the pillow, he managed to grab his phone from the bedside table and call his wife. For the brief moments of the ring signal he kindled the faint hope she would answer.

"You have reached Ellen," her recorded voice said. "Please leave a message after the tone and I will return your call as soon as possible."

"We need to talk."

Come on, pick up.

A dull buzz was his only answer.

"Really," he continued. "I want to talk. Coffee or something. Call me."

He disconnected and stared at the ceiling. Fighting the inertia of loneliness, he sat up. Still gritty and dull, he sought a reason to get out of bed and came up with his obligation to the drunk John Doe he had saved the day before—Alvarez, Luis Alvarez, the guy with the ice mother.

He cleaned up and drove to the hospital, resisting the urge to drive by their house, Ellen's house now. No, he was not a stalker. Eventually, she would call. Certainly she would.

Luis had stabilized during the night. His pupils responded, and when his sedation was reduced, he moved all his extremities spontaneously and purposefully. But he still needed respirator support, and his vital signs showed that his pulse remained high, over 140, his blood pressure low, 95/58.

Nonetheless, the signs of neurologic recovery encouraged Peter. Perhaps everything he touched would not be a failure. The labs were satisfactory, too, except the hematocrit level, dangerously low at fourteen percent. This was easily explained by massive blood loss and easily remedied. He ordered two units to be transfused and went to the ICU waiting room. The first visiting hours would be at 9:00 a.m., but many times family members spent the night, especially the mothers. Ellen would have been there if Daniel had been injured. Maybe Mrs. Alvarez would be there now.

Indeed, she was waiting, pale and pink, coiffed as if each hair had a designated assignment from which it dared not stray. Peter could not tell how long she had been there, but she looked more like an early riser than an all-nighter. She rose deliberately, neither smiling nor offering a hand.

"He shows signs of recovery," he said, "and his CT scan shows no new bleeding. I can't be certain, but he could recover completely."

She frowned. "That will make things more difficult."

Peter hesitated, wondering how *signs of recovery* translated into *more difficult*. "He is still critically ill, of course. He'll need a transfusion and respirator support until he can breathe on his own."

"No, no, that won't do at all."

Peter cocked his head. "Excuse me?"

"I want it all stopped right now. No transfusions, no respirator." She looked at him, defiant, arms akimbo.

"I'm afraid you don't understand. Yesterday I thought he would likely be seriously brain-damaged and may not survive the night. Today he looks like he'll survive with supportive care. Even possibly get back to normal."

"Oh, I understand perfectly. I thought if I waited until today he might not make it, and this decision wouldn't be necessary."

"Decision?"

"My decision. To remove the respirator and all interventions. No transfusions, no resuscitation, nothing."

"If I do what you say, Mrs. Alvarez, he'll die."

She tightened her mouth and narrowed her eyes. "I know that. Do you think I haven't lived through this before? Five years ago in Baltimore he lay in a coma for six weeks, followed by months of rehab. Twelve hospitalizations for serious injuries in the past twenty years, always alcohol related. Plus five trips to alcohol rehab for in-patient care."

Peter wasn't surprised. "Yes. I'm sorry, but—"

She cut him off. "I told him when I took him in after his last accident that this was it. No more coming home to mom. No more leaving me to pick up the pieces. No more."

She turned away and dug a tissue from the purse she had left on the chair. Peter heard her sniff, but she turned back to face him, as fierce as ever.

"I am the next-of-kin, I am the designated healthcare surrogate, and I demand that all life-saving treatment stop."

"I can't do that," Peter said. "I won't do that."

She put her hands on her hips. "I am within my legal rights. If the hospital has an attorney, I wish to speak to him right now."

Technically, she was right. Treatment without permission was assault. Yesterday was an exception because she, as the next-of-kin, was unavailable, and Luis would have died quickly without treatment. Therefore, Peter and the hospital had been obligated to act in what he saw as the patient's best interests. But once Luis's mother was available, her wishes had to be followed.

Yet he couldn't let go of the life he had saved. "You can talk to whomever you like," he said, "but I still won't do it."

"I'll sue. I'll have a court order to have that breathing machine stopped."

She was a formidable force and likely had the law on her side.

He searched for common ground or at least a delaying tactic. "Will you consider meeting with the Ethics Committee?"

She looked doubtful. "Who's on this committee?"

Peter shrugged. "The hospital's attorney, the chaplain, the risk manager, the chief of ICU medicine, the director of nursing, and . . ." Peter hesitated, realizing who the last member of the committee was. "And the chief of surgery," he said. Bell.

"When?"

He calculated an answer that would be soon enough to prevent her from calling her attorney today. "Two hours. Maybe four."

She rubbed her chin. "Fine."

He nodded but wasn't sure Luis would survive another day without a blood transfusion. He needed her consent now.

He tried again. "Could we continue caring for him in the best way possible until the committee meeting?"

She narrowed her eyes. "You have made it clear that you won't remove the respirator without being compelled to do so. What else do you want?"

"A blood transfusion," he said. "Two units. Just enough to get him by until tomorrow."

"You don't get it, do you?" she said. "Let me explain Luis's situation in terms you might understand."

Peter, desperate, nodded.

"He has an incurable, terminal condition. Call it alcoholism. Call it addiction. Doesn't matter. If you called it cancer, we wouldn't be having this discussion. You would withdraw treatment and leave him, and me, in peace."

"But he doesn't have cancer."

She acknowledged him with a cold stare before continuing. "What he has is incurable. He has had it for twenty years and we fought it together in every way we knew. Now he has reached the terminal stages. Let him go in peace."

He understood her words, but he wouldn't accept her conclusions. "We all make mistakes—"

Mrs. Alvarez held up her right hand. "No more. Do not start with bleeding-heart platitudes. You have not walked in my shoes."

He hadn't walked in her shoes, but he had stood in her son's blood. He left with only her permission to convene the Ethics Committee, not to give the transfusion. Regardless, he went straight to the ICU, where Luis's nurse was at the bedside. She was young, maybe thirty, but she had the hard-eyed glint of a veteran. Her nametag read *Courtney*. He told her about Ann Alvarez and the Ethics Committee. If the sedation Luis was receiving to keep him calm on the respirator were stopped, perhaps he could wake up and make his own decisions.

"We need to try something, Courtney."

He asked her to turn off the propofol that was sedating Luis and to observe the results with him.

Five minutes later, Luis opened his eyes.

"Luis, squeeze my hand," Peter said.

He did.

"Hold up two fingers," he said.

He did.

"Can you understand me?" he asked.

Luis nodded.

"This is great," Courtney said.

Peter grinned at her. It was. Now that Luis could make decisions for himself, his mother's lethal intentions could be bypassed. Peter explained to Luis what had happened and where he was. He told him he needed a transfusion, that the risks were small.

"Can we give you the blood, Luis?" he asked.

Luis held up his right hand, mimicking a writing motion. Courtney got a pen and a pad of paper. Peter held up the pad as Luis laboriously wrote.

Peter smiled. If he could write, he was competent. He would be safe after all.

When he finished, Peter lifted and turned the pad. His grin faded as he read Luis's response.

Ask Mom.

CHAPTER TEN

"I HEAR you've got another little problem, Jenson," Bell said.

Peter had been waiting in the doctor's lounge for the committee members to arrive. He nodded deliberately.

"Tell me about it," Bell went on.

Peter presented the Alvarez case to him, concluding with the mother's lethal intentions.

"You know, of course," Bell said, "that the simple solution is to let the woman have her way."

"He'll die."

Bell shrugged. "He may very well die despite your best efforts. And he has made decisions that are less than life affirming."

"We don't treat people based on their good or bad choices."

"We don't?" Bell raised an eyebrow. "Maybe not, but choices always have consequences. Don't let his choice become your consequence. As in this case: if he dies, his mother moves on. Hell, she's already moved on. If he lives, he'll be a drain on our time and resources for weeks and will be dead in a year anyway. Nobody cares."

"Maybe he doesn't see it that way."

"Do the smart thing for a change, Jenson. Let him go. I'm telling you this as your partner." He paused. "And your friend."

Friend? The partner role was bad enough. "The Ethics Committee will decide," Peter said.

"Yes. But she's well within her legal rights."

"Rights don't mean right, Bell. He deserves another chance."

"You don't get to decide how many chances he gets. That's up to his mother."

Peter remained unconvinced. "Still. It seems wrong."

Bell gave him a wry smile. "That's the trouble with you, Jenson. There is no right and wrong. Those are just words. There is only success and failure. For once in your life, choose success. Let it go."

Peter knew that Bell could be a charming enough guy to the right people; it made him powerful—a board member at the Blues, a former chair of the Board of Medicine, the chief of surgery. Yet he was a mediocre surgeon, almost stubbornly refusing to modernize his techniques, dodging uninsured cases, and telling patients with difficult problems there were no solutions, when the truth was that solutions would require him to send the case to someone else. Still, Bell would effectively be his boss for at least the next six months, so the last thing he needed was another confrontation.

Peter waved him off to end the conversation. "I've got to go," he said. "I'll be back for the meeting."

Afterward, he went back to his apartment on autopilot, but the closer he got, the more he found the thought of sitting in that drab box oppressive. He turned and drove aimlessly, thinking about the unlikely chance of the Ethics Committee convincing Ann Alvarez to let her son live. In the distance, Sunday church bells beckoned the faithful. Megan would be in one of those churches. Doing what? Thanking God for giving her a brain tumor? Crying out to Him in anger? Pulling out her Bible and studying for finals? She would be having a face-to-face meeting with Him soon enough if He were real.

Her other doctor, Luke Ryan, would be in a church, too. As Peter passed Crossway Church, the place that hosted Ryan's free clinic, he wondered if Luke had found solace there after the tragedies that had split their friendship. On a whim, he swung the wheel and turned into the parking lot. His watch read 11:08, a few minutes after the posted service time, but he climbed out of his Porsche anyway and slipped into a back pew.

The auditorium was more like a movie theater than the churches Peter remembered from his wedding and the few occasions when Ellen had convinced him that this is what families did on Easter mornings and Christmas Eves. Here there were no windows, no organ, no altar. Dressed in street clothes, the choir and a guitar-keyboard-drum trio belted out something more akin to soft rock than hymns. The lyrics projected onto a screen, and a few hundred people waved their arms and sang along.

Peter shifted in his seat, listening. The song started with images of famine and fire, followed by a promise that the singer's first thought and last breath would be about *You Alone*. It sounded like a dark love song. *Save me,* the chorus repeated three times, and everybody sang along.

Only the *You Alone* possessed the words of life.

Peter wondered if the *You Alone* could save Luis Alvarez.

After the song, a middle-aged man with a mustache and thinning hair took the middle of the stage. He wore a checked shirt with the sleeves rolled up, a kind of studied casual look, like the cover of an L.L. Bean catalog. His slightly pudgy body rocking on polished shoes that seemed too small, he introduced himself as Pastor Nick and picked up a Bible from the lectern.

Peter didn't expect much. Pastor Nick looked too much like his eighth-grade social science teacher to be interesting.

"Today's lesson," Nick began, "is from the gospel of Mark, chapter three, verses one through five."

"Another time Jesus went into the synagogue, and a man with a shriveled hand was there. Some of them were looking for a reason to accuse Jesus, so they watched him closely to see if he would heal him on the Sabbath. Jesus said to the man with the shriveled hand, 'Stand up in front of everyone.'

"Then Jesus asked them, 'Which is lawful on the Sabbath: to do good or to do evil, to save a life or to kill?' But they remained silent.

"He looked around at them and, deeply distressed at their stubborn hearts, said to the man, 'Stretch out your hand.' He stretched it out, and his hand was completely restored."

Nick paused before continuing. "Jesus wants to heal a man's hand."

Must be nice, Peter thought. Tell the patient to stretch out the hand and it's healed. Touch them and the brain tumor is gone, or maybe the hematoma is out. Maybe, with one steely-eyed look, hemoglobin levels could be restored, and transfusions and respirators would be unnecessary.

"Why would the church leaders of those days disapprove?" Pastor Nick asked. "Who doesn't want to see a miracle?"

Good question—why would a mother not want to see a miracle?

"Understand," the pastor went on, "that those church leaders believed they were following the law of God that forbids work on the Sabbath. Jesus wasn't arguing the point.

At another place in the Bible he told the crowds that he was not here to abolish the law but to fulfill it, including the admonition to observe the Sabbath. 'Anyone who sets aside the least of these commands and tells others accordingly will be called least in the kingdom of heaven,' he said. So why didn't Jesus just wait until the next morning and heal the hand then? Schedule office hours, so to speak. The hand had been shriveled for a while; this was not a life-threatening emergency."

Peter imagined having mystical healing powers. Would he schedule office hours or charge fees? Would he advertise and build a mega-healing business?

"Jesus wanted to make a point. Not merely heal a hand," Nick continued.

Merely heal a hand? It was hard enough to heal *anything*.

"He wanted to give the church leaders an opportunity to embrace mercy, to recognize that there is a good that goes beyond the law. We mortals lay down laws for ourselves because we think we know the difference between good and evil. This is our original sin. I like to think that sometimes we get close. But following laws without following the underlying principles of love and mercy only makes Jesus angry.

"So don't think that because you have been to church on Sunday, placed an offering in the plate, shined your shoes and worn your tie, that you have been good. Seek first a relationship with Jesus that can lead you to a place of love and mercy. Then when you see suffering, you will not be silent like those synagogue leaders in the first century. You will pray for Jesus to heal that shriveled hand, and pray for it to heal now. Then you will not anger the one who created you."

Pastor Nick continued but Peter tuned out, thinking about Luis, whose fate now rested in the hands of a committee that would do the bidding of Ann Alvarez and Joseph Bell.

Everything would be legal. Peter would be silent. And Luis would be dead.

The choir started singing, repeating the same song. "Save me," they sang.

Peter edged out of his pew. He didn't really understand what they wanted to be saved from, but he knew what Luis needed to be saved from. Yet he had to admit that he took comfort in their myth: *God heals.* It made him feel less alone.

As he turned into the aisle, he saw Luke Ryan, his straw-colored curly hair shorter now, white at the temples. A serious-looking woman stood at his side, her expression blunting her natural beauty, thick black hair held off her face in a turquoise barrette, a chain of beaten silver around her neck.

Luke spotted him. "Jenson," he said, deadpan.

Peter hesitated, but then held out his hand.

Luke looked down, considered, and took it. "What are you doing here?"

Peter tried to think of an answer. "I was driving by."

Luke stared, waiting for him to continue.

"Megan Kaiser recommended it."

The woman's eyes softened. Luke grimaced. She nudged him.

"I forgot myself," he said. "Karen, this is Dr. Peter Jenson, my former chief resident. He's caring for Megan."

Her stoic mouth broke into a warm smile, and she held out a hand. "Thank you so much. Megan is a dear and beautiful friend."

Luke turned his gaze to Peter. "Peter, this is my wife, Karen. She runs the free clinic here."

Peter shook hands with Karen, a brief and light touch.

"We met at the Pine Ridge Reservation," Luke said. "I was working for the Indian Health Service, and Karen was the clinic social worker."

"Nice to meet you," Peter said.

"And nice to meet you. I've heard so much about you."

"Ah, thanks."

Which version had she heard about? The cold and unsympathetic chief resident Luke was working with when his first wife and son died? Or the almost capable doctor who took sloppy care of her dear and beautiful friend? Probably both.

He felt like a trespasser here. "Maybe I shouldn't have come."

Luke seemed to grimace. "No. Everyone is welcome." He paused. "Anything I can help you with?"

Despite these words, Luke's eyes slid away. Ten years was a lot of time for interest to accrue on bad feelings.

"No, I . . ." Peter started.

"Good. Well, come back anytime." Luke moved toward the growing crowd.

"Wait," Peter said. "Maybe one thing."

Luke stopped. "Yes?"

"I need two hundred hours of community service."

Luke gave Peter the full attention of a cold stare. "For the Kaiser debacle."

Not a question. He shrugged. "I thought you might know someone."

"I don't think so," Luke said.

Of course Luke wouldn't want to see him at the free clinic when every contact would remind him of Jane and Ethan. But he'd thought, wrongly, that maybe Luke would have a recommendation.

Karen tugged on her husband's arm, and Luke broke his hostile stare at Peter.

"What?" Luke asked.

"You know our needs," she said simply.

Luke and Karen exchanged a long look before he turned his attention back to Peter.

"Okay, we do need help, but I'm not sure we—"

Peter's phone beeped with the message that the Ethics Committee meeting was about to start. Congregants swarmed around them. Karen looked sideways at her husband's face, puzzled.

Peter, embarrassed, said, "I've got to go."

Luke looked relieved. But Karen reached out and touched Peter's arm.

"Call us tomorrow," she said.

CHAPTER ELEVEN

Peter arrived a few minutes late to the ICU conference room, where Dr. Ali Kamal, the director of the ICU, presided at the round table. The hospital chaplain, Charles Miles, bookish and bespectacled, flanked him on his right; Debbie Schafer, the prim risk manager, sat on his left. Sandra Doyle, the director of nursing, and Dr. Joseph Bell, chief of surgery, completed the hospital side of the table. Schafer announced that the hospital attorney had been appraised of the circumstance and was available by telephone.

Peter slipped into the one remaining chair next to Ann Alvarez. She flicked a floral print scarf across her shoulder, leaned back, and crossed her legs. Her dagger gaze rested only briefly on Peter before she locked eyes with Kamal, not the least bit intimidated by white coats and titles.

"Mrs. Alvarez," began Schafer. "I want to express the deepest sympathy of the hospital administration on the grave injury to your son and extend our heartfelt desire to act in his best interests. You do understand the purpose of this committee meeting?"

Anne regarded Schafer as if she had passed gas. An awkward silence followed.

"The patient," said Dr. Kamal in the sing-song rhythms of English learned in south Asia, "suffered closed head injury resulting in acute subdural hematoma for which he underwent craniotomy on the day of admission. He is two days post-op and remains on a ventilator. The course is complicated by underlying alcohol-related bone marrow suppression and liver disease."

All heads, except Ann's and Peter's, nodded, grateful the discussion was back on familiar ground.

"Mrs. Alvarez is the healthcare surrogate for the patient," Kamal continued. "She is requesting discontinuation of care on the basis of futility." He looked down at his notes. "This is correct, Mrs. Alvarez?"

She uncrossed her legs and leaned forward to put her hands flat on the conference table. "Let me be quite clear, Doctor. This morning I made a request. Now I am making a demand. Withdraw care. You have no right to prolong his suffering."

Murmurs came from Doyle, Schafer, and Miles. Bell frowned. Peter kept his eyes on Mrs. Alvarez.

Kamal, without changing his expression or tone, continued. "From a medical standpoint, he has an illness which is critical but treatable. Not what we usually consider futile. Dr. Jenson, would you consider his neurologic recovery of a futile nature?"

"No," Peter said, staring down Mrs. Alvarez.

"Luis is suffering from an incurable disease—alcoholism." She repeated the argument she had made to Peter earlier. "He has been in and out of treatment programs for twenty years. He has suffered multiple head injuries. I am his next-of-kin and his primary caregiver, and I swore two years ago that I would no longer consent to life-sustaining treatments as long as he still drank."

Kamal tapped the screen on an IMR tablet. "His alcohol level on admission was 0.380, significantly elevated, even life-threatening of itself."

"But surely you must have hope, Mrs. Alvarez," said Chaplain Miles. He smiled with his familiar air of calm assurance. "We all must hold on to hope in times of darkness."

"Dear Mr.—" She leaned in to see his nametag. "Miles. I have had hope in dark times for decades. I have held his head while he puked blood, driven behind the ambulances that carried him, prayed in waiting rooms, and taken him to his AA meetings. Now, you may think his case is not futile. But not one of you is willing to take him home, care for him and . . ." Here she tapped her finger on the table before pointing it at Miles. "And dare to hope." Her voice cracked. "Not one of you."

An awkward silence followed. Peter waited for someone to object. When no one did, he spoke.

"I think he deserves a chance," he said.

Ann sniffed. "I think you're a doctor who doesn't want to lose a patient."

Bell broke the ensuing silence. "Ms. Schafer, perhaps you could speak for the hospital's legal counsel who could not be here. Do we have any grounds for refusing Mrs. Alvarez her request to withdraw treatment?"

Schafer brightened, like a student with her hand up finally getting called upon. "As a matter of fact, I reviewed the case over the phone with Mr. Ramsey of Day, Brown, and Ritter. Mrs. Alvarez is quite within her rights. Unless the hospital wishes to petition the court to take over legal guardianship of her son."

Peter made the conscious effort to relax his shoulders, trying hard to imagine what circumstances would lead him to give up on his own son. Deep inside was a boy who wanted to run and cry, but that boy was buried under a mountain of manhood built by facing down adversity. Davy Crockett didn't cry; he went down fighting on the walls of the Alamo. Peter would go down fighting, too.

"And does the hospital wish to apply for guardianship?" Bell asked.

"Mr. Kelly has assured me that we do not," Schafer replied.

"Then I think we have nothing left to discuss here," Ms. Alvarez said. "Could you please stop torturing my suffering son with that respirator?"

"No," Peter said, certain only of his gut feeling. He twisted in his chair, Ann's face only inches from his. "One day you will be so sorry."

"My regrets are my own business, Dr. Jenson. Not yours."

Schafer smiled. "Of course you may refuse on the grounds of personal ethics, Dr. Jenson. Then Mrs. Alvarez has the option of requesting a different physician."

"Then," Bell continued, "I see no alternative. Dr. Kamal?"

"Yes, yes. Quite right. Dr. Jenson?"

Peter sensed defeat. The irony was not lost on him. If Ann had been in the ER before the operation, he would have agreed to withdraw care. Futile, they would have agreed, and Luis would be dead. But only Ann believed that now. Peter had made a commitment to save Luis's life if possible before the operation—before he even knew his name—and he was not about to quit now.

"I'll apply for guardianship," he said.

"I'll fight it," Alvarez returned.

"You can't be serious, Jenson," Bell said. "Give it up."

"This is just the doctor's delaying tactic," Alvarez said.

Kamal turned to Peter. "What is the period of time for making this application?"

"Noon tomorrow."

"Very well. One day does not seem an unreasonable delay in such a critical decision."

Alvarez picked up her newspapers and purse. "You will be hearing from my attorney."

Shoulders squared and with measured steps, she left without a handshake or goodbye. The room emptied until only Chaplain Miles and Peter remained.

Miles leaned over to pat Peter's forearm with sympathy. "A sweet gesture," he said.

"Or a stupid one," Peter replied.

He headed for the ICU where he found Luis sedated again, skin blanched, eyes taped closed. Except for the rise and fall of his chest driven by the respirator, he already looked dead. Oxygen saturations hovered in the low nineties; his pulse sped along at one-forty, blood pressure dipping into the eighties. If anyone wrote the order to discontinue the respirator at noon tomorrow, he had no doubt Luis would die before sunset. Even with the respirator, the tissue hypoxia from the anemia would kill him within a few days.

He had no chance to obtain a contested guardianship for someone else's child. Maybe, just to avoid the guilt, he could transfer the patient to Bell instead, and Bell could write the withdrawal of treatment orders. For Bell, Luis's death would be a simple solution to a messy and unprofitable case.

Peter, with no solution of his own, left the bedside, embracing the thin protection of procrastination, and did what he always did when he was desperate. He drove to the one place that had always granted him solitude and peace, the beach.

He preferred the nor'easter days of high surf, crashing waves, and cold winds. On those days he would have to expanse to himself. Today the mid-May sun had warmed the sand. The ocean remained too cool for Florida natives who waited for the tepid waters of summer, but a few people walked, some supervising their unleashed dogs. Under a blue sky punctuated by an occasional cotton-ball cloud, unhurried bikers, singly or in pairs, rode on fat-tire cruisers. Still, it was good enough.

This is where he came to think. Or more accurately, this is where he came to *not* think, to let wet sand massage his feet while the sound of the surf drowned out the voices in his head, and the breeze blew away his ghosts. This is where anger and grief seemed to shrink beneath the vast sky, near the broad sea.

He kicked off his shoes and rolled his pants to just below his knees. The waves were gentled by the offshore breeze, and the low tide expanded the beach to easily an eighth of a mile from seawall to surf. He strode to the edge of the water, then turned and marched south, taking his anger and frustration with him.

Each wave *shushed* as it curled onto the sand, until something inside him heard the advice of the sea and quieted. His shoulders relaxed, and his pace slowed to a meandering stroll. He allowed the waves to wash over his feet, to wash away his anger, the brooding that had filled him with *what ifs*.

What if he had started Megan Kaiser's operation on time? What if he hadn't botched it? What if he had made that 4:30 appointment? He would still be married, still see his son each day, still have confidence in his career.

But now he had made a promise he already regretted to a dying woman, worked for his arch enemy, and puzzled on how to keep a young man alive who everyone else, maybe even the patient, wanted dead.

He sat in the sand and looked out at the flat sea. In the distance, a container ship made for entry at the St. John's River jetties. A sailboat headed in the opposite direction, probably hoping to make St. Augustine as the tide turned.

Finally, emptied of thought and emotion, he stood and brushed the sand from his pants. He pulled out his phone and checked the signal. Reception here was unreliable. Only one bar, and he was still on call. Duty forced him to start walking back.

As he did, he counted his losses as if they had occurred in someone else's life, using the detachment that surgery had demanded of him. Like a surgeon, he asked himself to make a plan. What was he willing to fight for? His marriage? His career? His reputation?

Yes, but with no guarantee of success. But as someone had once told him, reputation was the shadow cast by the tree of character. He had no more control over his reputation than he did the sunshine. He could fight for his character only, and the outcome of the battle depended solely on him.

He checked his phone again. Three bars—back in range of the answering service, back on duty.

Hurrying now, he took to the hard, wet sand near the surf where he could get enough traction to jog. To fight for his character, he had to fight for his patients. Even if capable of monstrous mistakes like the Kaiser operation, he was also capable of great good, like saving Luis's life.

Better to save a life than destroy it—wasn't that what the preacher had said? Better to show mercy than observe the law. Terminal condition or shriveled hand, Alvarez deserved mercy. Maybe Peter didn't believe in God, but he was in agreement with this Jesus.

When he reached his beach club, he slid his still sandy feet into his socks, but the gritty sensation as he ran to the car didn't bother him. He set his course for the hospital, and once he arrived, went directly to the blood bank. Staffing for the quiet weekend left only one underworked technician on duty.

"You have two units of packed red cells set up for Luis Alvarez?" he asked.

She yawned, tapped some keys, and looked at her computer

screen. "They ordered the blood this morning, but then cancelled."

"But you have the blood?"

She looked over her shoulder with exaggerated care, then turned back to him, blank-faced and chewing gum. "It's a *blood* bank. Yeah, we got blood."

"For Alvarez. You have blood set up for Alvarez?"

She smacked her gum. "Not without an order in the computer."

"I'm here to pick it up now," Peter said.

She looked him up and down and smacked her gum again. "Not without an order."

He shook his head and walked away. He couldn't go back to the chart and reorder the transfusion. After today's Ethics Committee meeting the staff would be on high alert. The order would not be transmitted.

As he walked toward the surgeon's lounge, he tried to think of alternatives. And when he sat in the deserted room, in the same chair that Archie used between cases to watch the financial news, the answer came to him. He pulled out his cell and dialed Archie's number.

"Yeah, Pete. What's up?" Archie asked.

"I need a favor, and I figured you owe me."

Five seconds of silence. Then, a question. "What do you want?"

"You can order a blood transfusion on an ICU patient, right?"

"Sure."

"Without going through the ICU nursing staff?"

"The order goes directly into the computer, but the nursing staff still has to get the blood and administer the transfusion. You know that. Why ask me?"

"I need you to order two units of packed red cells for Luis Alvarez, the acute subdural from yesterday."

"You could do that yourself."

"No consent form. The nursing staff wouldn't take the order if it came from me. But if you ordered the blood and I picked it up and gave it, he'd have the transfusion before anyone knew."

Five more seconds of silence. "What's in it for me?"

"My undying gratitude. And what I'm already giving you: a break."

More silence.

"I want a prescription."

"No. No way."

"Come on, Pete. Cold turkey is hard. Make up a chart about me having chronic pain. Oxycontin. Start with forty milligram caps twice a day."

Peter knew he should hang up. No way did he want to become Archie's drug counselor.

"Just for a week," Archie said. "Then you could taper it over the next six weeks."

Peter hesitated.

"No script, no transfusion, Pete."

"Twenty milligram, not forty."

Now Archie hesitated. "Deal," he finally said.

"But only for a week at a time. And if you can't taper off in a month, you check into drug rehab."

"I'm ordering the blood as soon as I pick up the script."

Twenty minutes later, Peter was back at the blood bank. "Where do I sign?"

She shrugged, took his signature, and gave him the blood.

He carried the units to Alvarez's room in one of those reusable bags they sell for a dollar at the grocery store, bright green with *Publix* written on the side. At the bedside, he placed the bag on the visitor's chair while he looked over the monitors and held Luis's hand.

"Can I help you?"

Courtney stood behind him in the doorway, her hands on her hips, her jaw stuck out, one strand of auburn hair flopped carelessly across her forehead. Her eyes were hard; she'd been alerted to the discussion in the Ethics Committee.

"Yes," Peter answered. "I need IV tubing and blood filters."

"We don't have a consent form for the blood transfusion."

"I'm just asking for the tubing."

Courtney walked closer to the bed and looked at the bright green bag. "I don't know, Doctor."

"Of course you don't. If you knew he was getting a transfusion, you'd have to stop it and call your supervisor. But all you know is that Dr. Jenson came to see his patient at five in the afternoon and asked for IV tubing. Doctor's orders. You had no choice."

She shook her head. "I could get in a lot of trouble, you know."

He nodded. "Me too."

She stood still, breaking eye contact with him to look at the patient. Her expression gave away nothing,

"Courtney, look at me."

Her eyes, still skeptical, came back to his.

"You know what's happening here," he said. "You know what will happen if we do nothing."

Her green eyes narrowed. Peter waited without blinking. Finally, she pursed her lips and nodded.

Peter reminded himself to breathe. "You know what?" he said. "Sometimes doing something, even the wrong thing, is the only right thing to do."

She brushed the hair from her face, turned, and left the room. He waited, uncertain whether the stone-faced Courtney would return with a transfusion set or hospital security, trying to tell himself that he could be at peace either way.

When she returned, she dropped the tubing on the bed. "I found this transfusion set. I'm going to leave it here while I go on break. If it's here when I get back, I'll return it to storage. If I don't ..." She started to walk away, the soft soles of her shoes making a gentle padding noise.

She came back to the bedside. "But if you were giving a transfusion, you'd need someone else to double-check the numbers on those units. Standard procedure. We wouldn't want to risk the kind of attention a transfusion reaction might engender."

He opened the green bag. She checked the numbers on each unit as he read them off the blood unit. Then she walked to the door again, looked over her shoulder, and almost smiled.

Even when she closed the door behind her, he couldn't look away, grateful for her courage and her kindness.

CHAPTER TWELVE

The next morning, Peter didn't dress in clean scrubs for surgery. Instead, he picked out the pale mauve linen shirt and silk tie that went well with his windowpane-patterned grey suit. Today, he would need all the help he could get, even looking his best.

His first stop was the ICU. Luis's vital signs had stabilized: pulse in the eighties, blood pressure holding in the low hundreds, O_2 saturations 99%. He wrote the order to discontinue the respirator and went to the waiting room to seek out Mrs. Alvarez.

Folding her newspaper, she looked up silently to meet his eyes. She didn't stand.

"Luis is off the respirator," he told her.

"He should have been off yesterday." She raised the paper and shook it at him. "And I should have known not to give you one more moment to care for him."

Peter felt the heat rise to his face. He couldn't stop himself. "So it's care you want?" he asked. "Or something else?"

"As if you know about care," she retorted, unfolding the paper and pointing.

From the front page of the local news section, his photograph stared up at him. Above it, the headline *Local Neurosurgeon Censured for Wrong-Side Brain Surgery* was scrawled in bold script.

He gaped at the paper, speechless. It wasn't supposed to go down like this. As his gaze turned to Mrs. Alvarez's scowling face, he struggled to speak. Finally he said, "Luis is receiving nutrition and comfort medications. The staff understands that no resuscitation is to be done, if that remains your wish."

Her jaw tightened; her lips thinned. "I asked Dr. Bell to take Luis's case. He was very kind." She looked away. "Understanding, anyway."

Inwardly he groaned at the thought of the kind and understanding Dr. Bell comforting this pseudo-mourning mother.

"Yes, of course."

She likely would get the news within the hour, after Bell made rounds: short of actual euthanasia, Luis would live. But as he left her and headed for his office, Peter had little illusion that the transfusion would remain a secret. It was possible if nobody bothered to review the chart, which could happen as long as the patient did well. If questions were asked about the transfusion, though, Archie would rat him out and Courtney would put him at the scene. They would, without a doubt. Still, every obfuscation bought time, and the longer Luis had to recover, the less serious the illicit transfusion would seem, and the less likely he would be to suffer serious repercussions.

As Peter stepped off the elevator to his office, an elderly man with disheveled hair and a three-day growth of beard rose from a wheelchair. "Dr. Jenson?" he asked as he slowly straightened.

Peter reached for his elbow to offer support. "Yes. Can I help you?"

The man pulled an envelope from his jacket and handed it to him; Peter took it without thinking.

The grizzled face smiled. "You've been served, Doctor."

Peter stepped back, shocked, like he'd just taken an unexpected punch. The man, not so frail as he first appeared, pushed the wheelchair to the elevator, turned around and said, "Have a nice day."

He wasn't shocked anymore; now he was angry. Expecting nothing good—at best, a subpoena, at worst, a lawsuit—he tore open the envelope.

His knees weak, he leaned against the wall to steady himself.

Dissolution of marriage.

His vision blurred.

Ellen. Twenty years. One son.

All drifting away in a fog of legalese.

Irretrievably broken. Is that really what it was?

Almost stumbling, he felt his way along the wall to his office, let himself in through the private entrance, and collapsed at his desk. He dropped the papers in front of him, head in hands, waiting for the nausea and pain to recede. Then he reached for his cell and tapped in Ellen's number. From sad experience, he knew that her voicemail always picked up after the fifth ring, so he readied himself to hang up—a voicemail could never convey what he felt.

Then he heard her voice.

"You're calling about the papers," she said.

"You picked up."

"Only to tell you to stop calling. It's over, Peter."

The voice was hers but the words seemed to belong to someone else.

"No, we could do better," Peter told her. "We could do counseling."

"We did counseling."

Peter remembered the missed appointment. "No, we didn't."

"Exactly the point. Why would I expect the next twenty years to be better than the last?"

"We have a son, Ellen."

"*I* have a son. One who has been abandoned by his father."

"No, wait. That's so unfair. You know I love him."

"The currency of love is not pats on the head and birthday presents. The currency of love is time. You are cheap with Daniel, and you are cheap with me."

Peter's mountain of tough quaked. His heart sank; his eyes burned. "But I *do* love you," he told her.

"Listen, Peter, I picked up because I saw the news. But I'm sorry for my timing, not for the divorce. I'm sorry because I have ... *affection* for you. But that's not love."

The mountain quaked again. Peter heard his hoarse whisper as if it weren't his own. "I need you, Ellen."

"Need is not love," she said. "I'm sorry. Goodbye."

The connection broke. He let the phone drop on the desk, a foreign tear forming in the corner of his right eye. It rolled down his cheek. When another welled up in his left, he let the rest fall unchecked onto his desk, cupping his head in his hands. The little boy inside was kicking down the mountain.

"Dr. Jenson?"

Betsy, the practice manager, poked her head into his office.

He roused himself, grabbing a tissue. He turned his head, swiping away the tears.

She pushed her glasses up to the bridge of her nose and squinted at him. "Are you all right, sir?"

"Sure. Rough morning is all. I'll be okay."

She shook a stray lock of hair from her face, looking doubtful. "Well, we have patients in fifteen minutes."

"Yeah. I know."

He sniffed and wiped his nose. Could he pull himself together? In fifteen minutes, he would need to stuff his emotions down and listen with patient compassion to someone facing disability, pain, or death. Then give them good advice. Like every other day.

But not today. His great ability to separate what he felt from what he did had disappeared.

"I can't do it," he said.

Betsy stood in the doorway holding a schedule book. She nodded, eyes down. "We saw the news."

He nodded in return.

"I just want to say we're sorry." She finally looked him in the eye. "We—me and the other staff—think you're a good doctor."

"Thank you, Betsy," he said, and he meant it. This morning, he was grateful for any kind words.

"I'll reschedule the patients. Some of them have cancelled already."

He nodded again.

"We'll say you're not feeling well." She wrinkled her nose and tapped her glasses back into position. "This will pass, you know."

He found himself breathing again in the space Betsy had created. He sought out his cool, rational side, the side that had always guided him in the past.

"One more thing, Dr. Jenson." She had already taken a step back.

"What?"

"Mr. Kelly wanted to see you as soon as you came in."

Queasiness swept over him again. "About what?"

"Didn't say."

After Betsy left, he went to the restroom and washed his face. Examining himself in the mirror, he practiced a calm, stoic expression with little success. His suit and tie would have to be his armor. Luckily, Kelly was the kind of man who always saw the clothes and rarely examined the eyes.

He took the elevator up and entered the outer office.

The administrative assistant gave him a quick glance. "Go right in," she said.

Kelly had his back to the door, his hands clasped behind him as he looked out his window at the rooftops of south Jacksonville. He turned as Peter entered.

"Okay," Kelly said. "Let me start by saying I was wrong."

Peter managed a thin smile.

"You want coffee or something? Have a seat." He motioned broadly at the chairs before the desk.

"Sure."

Kelly flopped into his chair and took a sip from an already full cup. "It's over there."

Peter poured his own before sitting.

"I was wrong about the publicity," Kelly admitted. "I didn't expect the local rag to notice the board action and put your mug on the front page."

Peter tilted his head down and pretended to sip coffee.

"But these things pass. People forget."

So Betsy thought, too, but Peter had trouble believing it.

Kelly put his cup on the table. "But what I can't understand is this Alvarez woman calling to threaten me with a lawsuit about her son."

Peter's coffee sloshed over the edge of his cup. He set it down and folded his hands.

Kelly arched one eyebrow. "She's upset because he didn't die," he said. "Mad as a wet cat on steroids. She thinks you had something to do with it."

"I can't say I'm sorry," Peter said.

"She wants an investigation. She's threatening to sue," Kelly said.

"For what?" Peter muttered. "Wrongful life?" He knew a ten-minute EMR review and a couple of phone calls would detect his hand in the transfusion.

Kelly shook his head. "This is the kind of lawsuit that gets publicity simply because it *is* stupid. The people who want to know why man bites dog are the same people who want to know why mother sues the hospital because her son survives."

"So?"

"More publicity. In entertainment, any publicity is good publicity—in healthcare, not so much. People like to assume their hospital care is like their electricity. When they need it, they flip a switch and it shows up, nice and reliable. Your name in the paper again after the wrong-side surgery? Bad juju."

Peter felt his temper rising. "What do you want, Dale?"

"I want you to disappear."

Peter stared at him.

"Administrative leave. Six weeks." Kelly swiveled his chair sideways. "Do your community service thing, lay low, get out of town. Just don't get your name in the paper."

"I've got patients."

"Not today."

"But there are patients on the schedule."

"Bell can take them over."

Peter felt like a cold knife had slid between his ribs.

Kelly, responding to the silence, turned to face him. "I mean, it's only for six weeks. A guy's family breaks up, and he makes mistakes."

"My family didn't break up."

Kelly looked at him with a hint of pity.

"We're just separated, that's all."

Kelly's head did an almost imperceptible shake. "Take the time, Pete."

Peter stood, buttoned his coat, and pulled his cuffs out to his wrists.

Kelly stood and stretched his hand across the desk. "When you come back, you'll be a new man."

Peter hesitated, but then he shook Kelly's hand, wondering what it meant to be a new man. He would rather be the same old man in the same old pre-Kaiser life.

He walked to the Porsche, took off his coat, folded it neatly, and placed it in the trunk. Behind the steering wheel, he glared at the instrument cluster, finally faced with an object with which he could loose his wrath, a ridiculously expensive machine that could transport him anywhere at breakneck speed.

Except he had no place to go.

CHAPTER THIRTEEN

He cursed the Porsche. He had paid two months' salary, cash, to look rich and smart and fast. Now he only felt stupid—broke, fired, divorced, or at least sliding quickly in those directions. He wished he had the money back.

His wedding ring still encircled a finger that gripped the steering wheel. What had it cost? Five hundred, maybe? He didn't know, hadn't really cared at the time. Ellen's ring, the first one, he had financed out of student loans. After a year in practice, he had her diamond replaced with one more appropriate for a neurosurgeon's wife. He had thought she would be happier than she was. He fingered the watch she had given him: *Time is not money; time is love.*

Time. That was what Luke Ryan had against him. Peter had controlled the schedule when Ethan died. He hadn't given Luke enough time. Maybe now he could.

He turned onto the interstate and headed toward downtown. Toward the river, the houses had two stories with manicured landscapes, wide oak-shaded thoroughfares, and Audis parked in the driveways. A few blocks in the other direction, cinder-block houses squatted in small lots of scruffy grass, wooden power poles lined sandy roads, and pickup trucks rested in yards. But in the middle, century-old houses, too shabby for the rich, too big for the poor, had become renovation projects, multi-family units, or offices. One of those houses had a modest sign proclaiming the medical practice of Luke Ryan.

Peter parked in the shade of some stately live oaks and walked across a street spattered with sunshine so intense that the black pavement seemed lavender. Luke's office was a two-story house complete with a veranda and a white picket fence. It looked so much like a home that Peter hesitated on the porch to look for a bell before he pushed open the front door. What once might have been an entry hall, front living room, and sitting room had been converted into a waiting room. Two rumpled old men and a harried-looking young woman with a baby staked out different corners and different magazines.

A small window opened to a receptionist's desk. Behind the desk sat Luke's wife Karen, her face neither friendly nor hostile.

"Ah, hi. Karen, right? I'm Dr. Jenson. We met—"

"It was only yesterday," she said.

Already he regretted coming. What was he thinking? These people didn't like him. Had no reason to like him. Yesterday they were being only church-people polite.

"I was driving by and hoped to catch Luke."

"Thanks for coming. About Megan Kaiser, right? And the community service thing? Anything else?"

A dangling conversation. A lost friendship. Failure and recrimination.

"You know, this was a bad idea. Nothing urgent. I'll just go."

"No, you're here now. Have a seat. I'll pull Megan Kaiser's chart for him."

She closed the window, and he stood facing the frosted glass, uncertain whether to sit or run. He was retreating toward the exit when a door opened, and she waved him back in, gesturing toward the waiting room.

"Dr. Ryan needs to speak with a colleague first, but he'll be with you soon," she said. "Maybe fifteen minutes."

Fifteen minutes—at first, it seemed like much too little time, and then like an eternity. When it finally passed, he followed Karen to a corner office in the back that may have once been a bedroom. A rear window looked out onto a concrete driveway and a workshop. Except for the corner between the windows where Luke's diplomas hung, the walls were covered with bookshelves. Luke's desk was cluttered with a doctor's typical paraphernalia—a stethoscope, a reflex hammer, an ophthalmoscope, plus a small stack of manila-colored charts and an open laptop. Luke sat behind it, leaning forward on folded arms.

"Jenson," he said as a way of greeting, but he made no move to get up.

"Luke," Jenson said, pulling back the arm he was about to extend for the handshake. He glanced down at the two chairs in front of the desk, uncertain.

Luke had changed little in the past decade. His sandy brown hair had a few flecks of gray, and the lines on his face were a little deeper. But he still had the broad shoulders that marked his compact figure, and the sad, brown eyes beneath his bushy brows.

"You decided to drive across town to talk about Megan Kaiser?" Luke asked. "Like you want *me* to tell you it's okay?"

"Mind if I sit down?"

Luke made a small gesture toward a chair.

Peter settled himself and gripped both armrests. "It's not about Megan. Well, I guess it is . . . indirectly. The truth is, I really do need those community service hours."

Luke coughed and leaned back in his chair. "Your concern for the poor and downtrodden?"

Peter waited, uncertain again. "You said to call," he said. "I mean Karen . . ."

"You are the Jenson I remember," Luke said. "Ten years later I see you in church, and you walk in here the next day to tell me what you need and what I should do for you."

Peter looked out the back window and took a breath. "I screwed up. I'm sorry."

Luke leaned forward, elbows on desk, and steepled his fingers in front of his face. He nodded toward the ring on Peter's left hand, the one clenching the armrest. "How's Ellen?"

"Fine." He looked away, through the rear window.

Luke let his hands drop to the desk and let his eyes burn into Peter. "Good. I'd hate to think that the precious time you needed with your bride back then would be wasted now."

Peter tried and failed to meet his gaze. He folded his hands in his lap and studied them. "Yeah, well. I shouldn't have come." He started to get up. "I don't know what I was thinking."

"No. Sit down." Luke's voice was not inviting so much as demanding. "Do me the favor of figuring it out. What *are* you doing here?"

"Short answer? I don't know. I've screwed up a lot of things." He nodded at Megan's chart on Luke's desk. "Like that. I guess it made me think of you." He paused, trying to make sense out of himself before he spoke again. "I'm trying to set some things right."

"Ellen?"

"Got served with divorce papers this morning."

Luke didn't seem surprised. "Any kids?"

"One son. Daniel."

Silence filled the space between them, invisible, misty, brittle.

"You have a son." Luke's words, spoken softly, shattered the silence.

"I didn't know what it was like to have a son."

Luke's lips tightened. "Or lose one," he said.

"I'm so sorry about Ethan," Peter said. "And Jane." The words sounded too small and too late. "Now I can guess what that must have been like."

Luke's eyes stayed fixed on his hands. "You bring back dark memories."

Peter fidgeted, preparing an exit line.

Luke's eyes flicked to the doorway, where Karen had appeared.

"You need him," she said.

Peter twisted to see her. She stood, dark and serious, handsome more than beautiful, leaning on the doorframe, arms crossed.

Luke shrugged. "God will provide," he said to her.

Karen tilted her head toward Peter. "God provided him."

Luke shook his head slowly, but with certainty.

"Luke, you prayed for help," she told him. "You asked three doctors. Time is running out."

"Yeah," Luke said, "but this is Jenson."

"I know the stories. But God knows his heart." She stared at Luke, unmoving, unexpressive.

Peter started to get up, more certain than ever that he never should have come.

Luke held up a hand. "No, please sit."

Peter dropped back into the chair and gripped the armrest even harder.

"My wife," he said, glancing at Karen, "wants to know if you would consider going on an eight-day mission trip to Central America. We leave in two weeks."

Peter needed service hours, sure, but this seemed like more than he bargained for. "I don't know. I'll have to ask my attorney if that works."

"Karen thinks you were sent by God. And you have to check with your attorney?"

Peter resisted the urge to turn away. "Well, God doesn't talk to me."

"God talks," Karen said. "Few listen."

Peter was uncertain if this was an insult. He could only watch Luke's eyes examine her as if deciding something. Then his gaze came back to Peter.

"Okay," he said. "Two weeks from today, if your attorney lets you, I need you at the airport with your passport, a copy of your medical license, and backpacking gear. Can you do that?"

"Are you sure about this?" Peter wasn't even sure about it.

"No," Luke said. "I think it's a terrible idea. But I listen to my wife, and she listens to God."

Peter thought it was a terrible idea, too. He thought spending a few evening hours and Saturday mornings at the clinic would be difficult enough. Now to spend eight days in some backwater jungle with someone who hated him? Who had invited him only because his wife had the loony idea he was sent from God?

But, then again, he had the time, and he needed to fill it.

Peter stood. "See you at the airport." He held out his hand.

Luke hesitated, but then he leaned forward and shook it.

CHAPTER FOURTEEN

Two weeks and two days later, Peter struggled along a jungle trail, heading to some remote village. His backpack weighed thirty-five pounds and carried mostly his personal supplies—

clothes, sleeping bag and pad, toiletries, bug-spray, sunscreen, stethoscope, and ophthalmoscope. Indigenous porters carried the heavier necessities like food, stoves, propane tanks, medicines, and camp gear. Now, all he had to do was get himself and his pack up a long mud-slicked hill littered with logs and wet boulders.

He sweated and he cursed. He questioned his fitness. He questioned the mission's purpose. Most of all, he questioned his judgment. He doubted that he could have chosen a more difficult way to fulfill his community service hours. Jim Casey had appealed to the board to do the service hours outside the state of Florida. He had argued that Peter was serving his Florida-based church in a leadership position, a specious argument, but one the board lacked the interest and resources to check.

His consolation was that the mindless physical effort kept him from thinking about Daniel, Ellen, Joseph Bell, Megan

Kaiser, or anything at all. He was too busy concentrating on how to keep up with these religious fanatics.

Two days before, he and Luke had flown to San Jose where Luke's missionary friend, John White, had met them at the airport. John was a compact middle-aged man with closely cropped gray-blond hair. He spoke with the slow accent of North Carolina.

On the drive, they had their first run-in. John had given him a quick overview of the plans for the week: a two-day hike into a remote village, a three-day medical clinic and evangelism outreach, and the hike back.

Peter had made the mistake of asking, "Then what?"

Luke and John stared at him.

"I mean, don't they just keep getting the same diseases after we leave?"

John looked sideways at Luke, questioning. Luke shrugged.

"A clinic like this makes no sense if the only goal is to alter medical care for indigenous people in remote places," John agreed. "But this effort to make people feel better, even for a few days, tells them that we love them—and no one else in history has loved them. By extension of what we do, they understand that Jesus loves them. This is not ultimately a battle for health. It's a battle for souls."

Peter folded his arms and nodded with hooded eyes, trying not to roll them. He would put up with this for a week. Then John could feel good about the village, Luke could satisfy Karen's odd intuition, and Peter could have one hundred ninety-two of two hundred community service hours satisfied. Eight days times twenty-four hours—who would have guessed that this entire trip could count? He smiled.

"You're laughing, Doctor?" John asked.

Totally untrue. Nothing funny about the absurd. "No. I'm

just not a believer in any kind of organized religion. I think people should be able to believe what they want to."

For a few minutes, nobody spoke. The truck moved in the long line of traffic at the rate of the slowest vehicle. A rain cloud came up the valley; within moments they were in darkness as sheets of rain pelted the windshield. The truck slowed to a crawl and then stopped.

John turned from the driver's seat to make eye contact with Peter. "I should tell you right now that I don't accept that truth is something defined by one individual's belief, and I'm having difficulty understanding why an intelligent man like you would think so."

Peter wanted nothing more than to sit in his corner of the backseat and nurse his grudges, but he had to respond. "Truth to me is something that everybody can agree on," he said, "something that has facts that support it, something that stands up to hypothesis and experiment. In other words, science."

John kept his eyes on Peter as he spoke. The rain fell in sheets on the windows, turning everything outside into obscure, gray shadows. "Don't limit the truth with facts, Doctor."

Those were the exact words of that chaplain, Miles, a few weeks ago in the hospital chapel, right when he had launched into that soliloquy about the mockingbird.

Peter didn't reply to John. He did not wish to debate theology with a missionary. Ellen had broken his heart, he had jeopardized his career, and it seemed likely that it would take more than mumbo-jumbo about birdsong for him to recover. But for a brief moment, he envied John and Luke for their delusions.

The next day, they had traveled from John's home in the town of Bribri to the village of Bajo Coen. That trip had been enough of an adventure—riding in the back of a pickup truck to the river, sitting in a leaky dugout canoe with an incongruous outboard engine to get them upstream, and then walking over a flat, muddy trail for an hour behind horses that hauled their supplies. They slept in the earth-floored, bamboo-walled, thatched-roof home of Porfilio, a village chief of the Bribri tribe, as well as their guide and translator.

But yesterday was a breeze compared to today. Peter had been roused at dawn. By now, he had crossed two wide rivers in thigh-deep water, scrambled up and down muddy jungle trails, traversed an abandoned cane field, and waded through a swamp. Slick clay covered parts of a trail so steep that putting his hand out straight would mean touching the place his feet would be in three more steps, if he could hold his footing. He used roots and tree trunks, even thin branches, as handholds, always searching for snakes.

Unfamiliar trees provided a canopy from the brutal tropical sun, but the air remained thick with humidity. Along the way, he had refilled his water bottles at each river crossing, dutifully treating each bottle with iodine before drinking, but by the time he reached the small clearing on the crest of the hill, the last water bottle was empty. His lips were cracked, and his throat burned. As he threw off his pack, he noted with irony that everything on his outside was wet, and everything on his inside felt as dry as last week's bagel.

He collapsed in a small patch of shade next to John and Luke. After a few minutes he regained enough strength to sit up, resting against his pack. John offered him a half-full water bottle.

"Jesus Christ, White," Peter said. "This is a trip to hell and back. Tell me again why this is such a great idea."

"Language, Doctor, language," White said. "You're a representative of the church here."

Peter looked around. "Nobody here understands English except us. Who the hell cares?"

Luke stood up, towered over Peter, and clenched his fists. "I care. I care a great deal."

"Jesus Christ, Luke," Peter said. "Ease up."

"This is what I mean, John," Luke said. "This guy is such a self-centered ass that he's a danger to the mission. I say we send him back."

"Whoa, there," Peter said. "What did I say?"

Luke looked disgusted. "You said 'Jesus Christ.' And you weren't praying."

Peter lifted his hand to shade his eyes and tried to see Luke's face against the white-hot sky. "Calm down. It's just an expression."

"Not to me it's not."

John jumped up and put his arm around Luke's shoulder. "Walk with me, buddy," he said, and led him away. They talked softly beyond Peter's hearing.

This is a nightmare, Peter thought. *I'm in the middle of the jungle with a bunch of religious fanatics, and all I want is one hundred ninety-two community service hours so I can go home.* He felt a sudden ache in his chest. *If I had a home.*

Luke and John returned, and Peter stood to meet them. John studied the ground and cleared his throat before he met Peter's eyes.

"Dr. Jenson . . . I mean, Peter. We need to reach an understanding. I know God uses people without faith as his instruments—angels really—to bring his kingdom to Earth. But in a few hours, we will be entering a village that is a spiritual battlefield. Eternal souls will be at stake, and lives will hinge less on the medical care we provide than on the words that are said."

Peter doubted he was an angel and did not understand how words had more power than medicine, but he held up his hands in a gesture of peace. "I'll try to play the part."

John nodded but frowned.

Luke said, "John says we've got to work together, and we will."

Peter shrugged.

Luke stepped so close that the brims of their hats collided. His eyes were narrow with anger. Peter could smell his sunscreen, his bug repellant, and his sweat.

"And Jesus says I'm supposed to forgive you. So I will," Luke told him. "But I don't have to like you. In all the years I've known you, Peter Jenson cares only about Peter Jenson. But this time you need me to sign a paper certifying your community service hours." He paused to let that fact sink in. "If you screw up, I sign exactly nothing, and you're right back where you started." He jabbed his finger in Peter's chest. "Understand?"

Peter shoved him back. John stepped between them and put his hands up. Turning to Luke, he said, "Remember what Karen says. He is sent from God."

Luke and Peter stepped back. Peter believed that Karen had been wrong, and he was pretty sure Luke felt the same way.

They continued walking. The downhill slope was easier, with a stream at the bottom to fill the water bottles. But then they crossed another river, where the struggle against the cold current sapped the strength from Peter's legs. Porfilio carried his pack, walking patiently behind him and waiting while he rested. Even so, by midafternoon, he experienced a state of exhaustion he could not have imagined. He walked a hundred yards and sat to rest for five minutes. Then he walked another hundred yards. And rested another five minutes.

Mud dragged at his boots and tropical plants slapped at his face and arms. The rushing river he had stumbled through could still be heard off to his left. Finally, he shoved aside a vine and emerged into an unexpectedly broad meadow studded with coconut palms. Ankle-high grass replaced the jungle undergrowth, and cows grazed in the distance. Peter saw only a single structure: a thatch-roofed lodge built on stilts, the floor about four feet above the ground.

This is the destination, he told himself. He had made it. And if it wasn't the destination, it was as far as he would be able to go, no matter what.

When he reached the hut, John, Luke, and their indigenous team were already unpacking and setting up living quarters. Peter tromped up four stairs cut into a log that leaned against the floor. He dropped his pack and collapsed. The thatched roof extended beyond the floor by several feet on all sides, but there were no walls. Breezes from the surrounding mountain valleys blew across Peter's prostrate body, providing welcome relief from the afternoon heat. He closed his eyes and, in spite of the activity around him, slept.

When he woke thirty minutes later, Luke was sitting nearby on a camp chair. "I'm sorry about that outburst back on the trail, Jenson," he said. "I was hot and tired. We all were."

Luke's face was backlit by the setting sun that shone though the hut, so Peter could not see his expression. Uncertain of where this was heading, he felt weak and vulnerable.

"Right," he replied.

"When I look at you," Luke went on, "I remember Ethan and Jane. It took a long time to forgive myself. And I thought I had forgiven you . . . until I saw you. Turns out I just forgot about you."

Peter rolled onto his side, pushed himself up on an elbow, and considered whether he had regained enough strength to stand. He wanted to get up if this was going to be another fight.

"What do you want out of me, Ryan?"

Luke leaned back in his chair. "It's not about you. I'm trying to explain myself."

Peter took a long drink of water and considered whether he wanted to hear more about this old story that featured him as the villain, but his silence seemed to encourage Luke to continue.

"After Karen died, I lost myself in a bottle of vodka." Luke smiled ruefully. "More like a barrel. One morning I woke in some girl's room, no clue who she was, no clue how I'd gotten there. Big head of black hair on the bed. Looked like Jane. Startled me. I thought she was there, judging me."

Luke looked down at his feet. "That's when I cut and ran from Gainesville. Loaded up the truck and camped out all up the coast. I got to the Appalachian Trail, stored the truck, and started walking north. As long as I kept walking, I didn't have to think."

He made the same rueful smile. "I didn't have to feel."

This was a new narrative to Peter. He had never seen Luke after the funeral; he figured a guy with that kind of mess needed to disappear for a while. Anyway, he hadn't had time to care. The residency had sucked up every bit of empathy he had.

Luke went on. "Along the trail, I would rant. I'd talk to Jane. After a while, it was like she was real, a ghost. She started deciding when to appear, haunting me, tormenting me."

Luke's eyes looked distant, unfocused.

"One night, she came at me through the rain and mist, and I started yelling. Another hiker showed up. Maybe he thought I was crazy, but he didn't have anywhere else to camp in the dark and rain. So he stayed with me. Listened to me. Walked with me the next day." Luke paused and looked Peter in the eye. "He told me about Jesus."

Peter struggled to a sitting position. He had no idea why Luke was telling him all of this, but he tried to look understanding. He searched for a reply and came up short.

Luke sighed into the silence. "I know you're not a believer. You think I'm delusional, that this is some kind of prolonged grief response."

"No," Peter lied. "Nothing like that. I'm glad for you."

Luke shook his head. "I'm telling you it saved my life."

"Sure, I understand. I get it. I can play the part."

Luke scowled in frustration. "I know, Jenson. You get your community service hours, go home, and you think you get your life back. Because you think you made a couple of mistakes and you can fix them by—"

"Okay, okay. I said I was sorry."

Luke looked away, almost turned away, before swiveling back to Peter with frightening intensity. "What I'm trying to tell you is that what's killing you isn't about what you did. It's about who you are. Want to change your life? You got to change your soul. You have an opportunity here. Look around. Don't blow it."

Luke then stood and walked away, leaving the hut by the log stairs. Peter took another long pull at his water bottle. He wasn't going to judge. Luke had lost his family and his job. A guy could embrace any kind of delusion after something like that, even the Jesus thing. Whatever it took to keep going.

He needed Luke's signature. He needed to be respectful. But he didn't need to believe.

CHAPTER FIFTEEN

Peter woke to the sounds of pigs grunting beneath the floorboards. Dawn came with a gentle light, the sharp edges of the thatch canopy turning golden in the morning sun.

Luke, John, and Porfilio were already meeting with the local tribal leader and three men who served as village health workers during the long months between doctor visits. The health workers recorded live births and gave infant and child vaccinations through the first three years. The government paid for the vaccines, and the missionaries paid a small stipend to the health workers to compensate for the time they took away from their fields. John's mission also sent deworming pills for school-age children and prenatal vitamins for pregnant women.

Peter sat off to the side and watched the meeting. He did not understand the words, but he understood angry gestures, sharp retorts, and frowns.

"So what's going on?" Peter asked Luke afterward.

"The health care workers want to quit."

"They want more money?"

"No," Luke replied. "They don't want us to pay them."

"That doesn't make any sense."

"Makes sense to them. They don't want anybody to think they're Christians."

"Like they're embarrassed?" Peter asked.

Luke shook his head. "Scared. Last year we showed *The Jesus Film* here and had an evangelist who spoke their native language. One woman and her family professed their faith and became Christians."

"So that's what you want, right?"

"That night, her hut was burned to the ground and her pig was killed."

"Bad luck?"

"Yeah. Bad luck. Or, as the locals call it, evil spirits." Luke scowled. "I think the evil spirits that night carried matches and gasoline."

"What happened to the woman and her family?"

"They had to move to another village. There's a high cost to discipleship here. That's why the workers, even though they're not believers, want to quit. They want the government or someone else to pay them. Anybody but the Christians. Everybody wants free care for their children, but nobody wants their house burned down."

They broke off their conversation to start seeing patients. Luke saw patients with John assisting in Spanish translation, and Peter saw patients with Porfilio translating, an advantage since Porfilio also spoke the two indigenous dialects.

The women wore lipstick, rouge, and dresses with frills that were purchased miles away, each probably costing the proceeds from a day's work cutting plantains or bananas. This was a special occasion, and they were a proud people. School-age children wore white shirts and blue skirts or pants. Teenage girls wore hair ribbons and short dresses. The men often wore white starched shirts and slacks, but just as often came in ragged work clothes, sweating. Many carried machetes. Teenage boys differed from the men only in that their scars were fewer and their hands softer.

Dark-eyed, dark-haired, dark-skinned people looked at Peter expectantly, and Peter looked back. He panicked as his first patients sat down. He was used to seeing English-speaking adults who wanted an evaluation for a neurosurgical problem. Now he was confronted with people who did not speak English for problems he had not studied since medical school, if then.

He stood up from his stool and pushed aside the tarp that separated him from Luke's clinic area. "What am I supposed to do?" he asked.

Luke looked irritated. "Listen and try to help. Something new for you."

With no alternative, Peter nodded to Porfilio to ask the family what they needed. They spoke in Spanish, shyly, casting sideways glances at Peter while talking to Porfilio, then turning their eyes away and waiting. After a few minutes, Porfilio turned back to Peter and told him what they needed. But Peter had no ultrasound machines, no X-ray facilities, no CT scans or MRIs, and no laboratory tests to screen for disease or confirm clinical suspicion. Here, his diagnostic ability was less than that of a country doctor in the previous century—and at least those doctors had honed the skills of physical examination and observation over their lifetimes.

Peter had heard that the blind compensate for the loss of their vision with hyperaware hearing and other senses. He began to feel a similar shift as he perceived the people who sat on the stump in front of him. In America, his mind had formed possible MRI and CT scan images as his patients described their illnesses. But here, what he saw, heard, and felt were all he had, no filters. And because he had nothing else, this close, direct contact was intense, intimate, even frightening.

He was overwhelmed with a sense of inadequacy. What if

someone had cancer or heart disease? Could he do anything? What if someone had malaria or Chagas disease? Would he even recognize it?

He listened to the hearts of children beating in their chests and faced their wide brown eyes full of wordless questions. He looked in their ears and gently prodded their soft bellies. Never had he felt medical skills and knowledge were so needed, and his specific training so irrelevant.

One of the boys was ten, Daniel's age, fearless and strong, but skinny. A complex of scars and raw, oozing skin covered the right side of his neck; tiny insects buzzed on the oozing surface.

"What is this?" he asked Luke.

Luke came over and squinted through his reading glasses. "They call it papillamoya. I think it's cutaneous leishmaniasis."

Peter had no clue what Luke was talking about, and his face must have shown it.

Luke clapped his shoulder and said, "Fluconazole, 200 milligrams a day for a month, a week of cephalexin for super infection, antibiotic ointment for a week."

Peter nodded.

"It's not a standard treatment, but it seems to work." Luke smiled. "You just prevented a lifetime of facial scarring. You're a hero."

"I'm an idiot."

"True," Luke said, "but you're the only idiot they've got."

Peter's anxiety eased as he found that most ailments were simple, things that were treatable at the drugstore back home. A bottle of ibuprofen or short course of antibiotics gave comfort. Vitamins and antiworm medicines gave hope. Compared to brain tumors, the illnesses he was dealing with here were trivial. But families walked away with plastic bags of pills and ointments, satisfied and comforted.

After the first several families had been treated, Peter realized these people needed what patients everywhere needed. They needed to tell someone that they hurt and were sometimes afraid, that their children had coughs and fevers, that their lives were full of hard work and danger, that they feared dying before their children could care for themselves, and that their children would die before they could care for them. But what they wanted most was hope—hope that their children would grow strong and healthy, hope that they would be free of pain, hope that death would not come this night or the next.

As he worked, Peter looked out from under the thatch canopy to the meadow beyond the lodge. A middle-aged Bribri man in a cone-shaped hat woven from dried strands of grass scowled in his direction, his arms folded across his chest. The man stood fifty yards away and made no attempt to join his fellow villagers who were waiting to be seen. Four younger men stood around him, and the male leaders of each family group spoke to him as they came or left the lodge. They kept to the shade of the few trees in the meadow. But as the day wore on, whenever Peter looked up from his work, the man in the hat scowled.

When the clinic suspended operations at noon, Peter caught John's attention and asked about the scowling man.

"He's Reynaldo, the local witch doctor. He's watching us, and the other villagers are watching him watch us."

Peter gave John a quizzical look.

"The villagers see that we do good things for them and their children, and our services cost them nothing. Reynaldo doesn't want to come right out and denounce us, but he would love for us to make a mistake, do some perceived harm to someone, so that he could send us away forever."

"You're eroding his power and he resents you?"

John smiled grimly. "Oh yes. And you too, Doctor."

Peter shrugged. "Whatever. Us, then."

"He's a powerful man here. He collects tribute for their god, Sibú. He feeds off the people by threatening them with his curses. He will say to a family, 'Give me your pig.' And they will do so, because they fear his curses will make their chickens die, their gardens fail, or their children get sick."

"I can't believe they let him get away with that crap," Peter said.

"Don't underestimate the effectiveness of these curses. The chickens do die, the gardens do fail, the children do get sick. Houses burn down. Sibú and his pantheon are not nice gods. Sometimes Reynaldo demands the thirteen-year-old daughter for a week. No one dares say no."

Peter frowned. "But that doesn't seem possible."

"Not to you because this isn't your world. These villagers wouldn't understand the demons of your world, either."

Peter thought for a few moments about what he meant by demons. "Do their demons kill them?"

Luke answered. "If you ask them about the most common cause of death, the villagers will tell you it is the demon called *Tigre del Rio*, the River Tiger. Someone leaves his house at night and is found dead in the river the next morning with no marks on him. The River Tiger has taken him because he has lost the protection of Sibú."

"You don't believe this, do you?" Peter asked.

Luke tipped his head side to side and half closed his eyes. "Perhaps trying to cross the rapids at night after drinking a few cups of *chi-chi* might be another way of looking at the cause of death."

"Chi-chi?"

"Yes, a local brew made by distilling bananas. The point is not what I believe, but what they believe. And they believe in the River Tiger. Until the darkness that binds them is broken, the curses will hold them in bondage, and the River Tiger will kill them."

"Your spiritual battle?"

"Watch and see. Maybe your spiritual battle, too."

Early the next morning, an agonized cry cut through the white noise of the rushing river. Tangled in his sleeping bag, Peter poked his head out in time to see John and Porfilio run to the riverbank. Three Bribri carried a person wrapped in a sheet through the stream. Following behind, now entering the shallow rapids, a frightened-looking girl and a crying middle-aged woman guided the arms of an elderly woman. John and Porfilio leapt into the stream to help.

The men jogged up the path, the unconscious person now visible, a teen-age boy, blood matting in his black hair and the sheet of the makeshift litter. They dumped him on the floor of the lodge at Peter's feet.

John spoke rapidly in Spanish. A Bribri, possibly the father, bloody hands by his side, looked hard at him, as if great concentration could make the words more comprehensible. Porfilio interpreted, and the man answered in Bribri while the women wailed.

Luke straightened the boy and looked for other signs of injury. Peter, adrenaline rising, opened the boy's eyes and saw a dilated right pupil, a sign of intracranial bleeding, possibly an epidural hematoma—in his world, a surgical emergency. Here, sudden death. He used the razor from his personal kit to shave a strip of hair and identify the laceration, wishing vainly for a CT scan, a clean operating room, anesthesia, and a set of sterile neurosurgical instruments.

John summarized what the father had told him. "He fell

from a coconut palm this morning. Hit his head on a rock at the base. Out cold, the father says, but woke up and complained of a bad headache. Then he went unconscious, and they couldn't wake him up."

"How long ago did it happen?" asked Peter.

"After first light, but before the sun came over the mountain."

Peter calculated that the injury had occurred about an hour before. An epidural hematoma usually ran a four-hour course from the time of injury to the time of death.

"You're thinking he needs surgery?" asked Luke.

Peter nodded.

John said, "What are you guys talking about?"

Peter responded. "This kid needs to have an operation within three hours or he'll die."

John shook his head. "We've got no cell phone coverage here. The village has a radio for medical emergencies at a hut about five minutes away, though. I'll send Porfilio to radio for helicopter evacuation to San Jose."

"How long will that take?" asked Peter.

"Assuming a helicopter is available and the weather is good, an hour and a half each direction."

"That's cutting it close. He's got three hours. No more."

"It's the best we can do."

Porfilio ran to send the message while Peter and Luke cleaned the wound and stopped the bleeding. John explained the injuries to the father, uncle, and brother who had brought him in. The mother, sister, and grandmother wept and knelt at the boy's side after the doctors had bandaged his head.

Peter looked out of the hut and saw Reynaldo and his four henchmen approach the boy's family. The words were foreign, but Reynaldo scowled and waved angrily toward the Americans. Divine punishment, Peter guessed, for trusting those white devils.

He turned his attention back to the unconscious boy. Kneeling next to the mother, he opened the boy's eyes, and again he saw the dilated pupil and the fixed unseeing gaze. If he were in America, if this were Daniel, he would be in surgery in a few minutes, out of surgery in less than two hours, and on his way home in a couple of days. In this village, though, discharge home seemed an increasingly unlikely outcome. He tried to tell himself this was not his country, not his people, and not his problem. He didn't have the tools, anyway.

The mother grasped his elbow, fixed her deep brown eyes on his, and spoke rapidly in Spanish. He caught only her desperation.

"His name is Miguel," Luke translated. "She said, don't let him die."

Peter looked around the primitive hut, willing an operating room into existence, even a procedure room with a table, a few instruments, and good light. He wished he hadn't seen the mother's eyes, didn't know the boy's name.

"How much longer until Porfilio is back?" he asked John.

John shrugged. "Five minutes maybe."

"Do we have any tools here?"

"Why are you asking?"

Peter turned his head to look at John. "Just thinking ahead. If the helicopter is delayed."

Luke stared at him. "You can't be serious."

Peter returned the stare. "If that helicopter doesn't come, tell me how we could do worse."

Luke blinked, a hint of uncertainty.

Porfilio came running up the path. He spoke rapidly in Spanish to John and Luke. When he finished, John turned to Peter.

"No helicopter. Not today. The weather is socked in at the airport in San Jose. They expect it to clear by late this afternoon, but by then they expect thunderstorms in the mountains. Maybe tomorrow morning."

A full day too late. "He'll be dead by then," Peter said.

"Then we shall pray for a miracle for him and comfort for his family," John said.

Peter turned his back on the bleeding boy and faced John. "There is another way."

"What other way?" John asked.

"We have laceration repair kits with suture material. Each of those kits has a few simple but sterile surgical tools. If we could get some bone-cutting instruments of any kind—drills, saws, chisels. Even braided wire. I could get the clot out and stop the bleeding. It would be messy and risky, but it's this kid's one chance to survive."

Luke grabbed Peter's shoulder and spun him around. "You're a madman, Jenson. At the end of the day you're going to have a dead kid on the floor of this hut and a whole village that thinks we killed him."

John shook his head. "Luke's right. If we do something ghastly like that, something the people don't understand, and he dies? Well, then any missionary goodwill we've built up here for the last five years is out the window."

"Any other day since Miguel's ancestors settled in this valley, I wouldn't be here, and he wouldn't stand a chance," Peter said. "But you prayed for a miracle, and here I am."

"Oh, I get it. This is all about Peter Jenson's hero complex," Luke said. "Not about a dying kid."

John held a hand up to Luke. "Wait. Hear him out."

"I know you don't like me, Luke," Peter went on. " I know—"

"Sometimes you've got to let go," Luke interrupted, "and let

God take over. The stakes are too high for stuff you don't understand, like the church, the trust we've built here. Eternal salvation for a whole group of people."

Peter grabbed the front of Luke's shirt, pulling his face close. "Actually you're thinking about *yourself*, and what you and your church want," he said. "As doctors we have a duty to do our best for the patient. Even if no one else understands. Even if we get blamed for a bad outcome. Even if a whole village drives us out and goes to hell because of what we do. We still have to do our best for the patient."

Luke stared hard into his eyes and squinted, as if searching heart and mind were a visual task. Then he grabbed Peter's wrist and jerked his hand off his shirt.

He turned to John. "Get him what he needs."

CHAPTER SIXTEEN

PETER LOOKED AT HIS WATCH. Another hour had gone by. He opened Miguel's eyes and looked at his pupils. No change. Nauseated by anxiety, he stood with his hands tucked into his armpits to hide his tremor. If anyone detected the slightest hesitancy in his demeanor, the team effort would disintegrate, and the small chance of saving Miguel's life would evaporate.

John and Porfilio had browbeat a few men to ignore Reynaldo's deprecations and tear a hole in the thatch roof. With the thatch removed from the roof, Miguel's hammock was in direct sunlight, brighter than any operating room lights. But the shadows would be sharp, and darkness would hide anything except the most superficial anatomy.

Peter's operating room was ready. An ancient and stained cotton sheet covered a rough table normally used for meal preparation; the only flat surface available, it would serve as an instrument table. A sterile paper drape from a laceration repair kit partially covered the sheet. The meager contents of the kit—a forceps, small scissors, hemostat, needle holder, and a few sutures—lay on the drape. A stuff sack containing a claw hammer, the head of an adze, a two-foot length of braided wire, two forks, and a sturdy knife had been dropped in a pot of boiling water, plucked out, then tossed onto the table.

Miguel had been lifted into a hammock that would have to serve as operating table and hospital bed. The hammock was a net-like affair that effectively cocooned him. One person could immobilize Miguel by encircling his arms. Porfilio could steady his head.

As Peter scanned the tree line, looking for the messenger who was bringing the last necessary item for surgery, John approached him. "Reynaldo told the family that Sibú, their chief deity, is wreaking vengeance on them for allowing white demons to act as their healers."

"Not surprising, is it?"

"No. But he has 'cast the stones,' a ritual. And he has placed curses on us and the boy's family."

Peter turned his gaze from the tree line to John. "With all the real bullshit I have to worry about, now you want me to worry about a witch doctor's curse?"

John returned Peter's stare. "I'm just saying that curses have power here. You're not in Kansas anymore, Doctor."

"So you're saying we've been threatened."

John nodded solemnly. "Yes. Reynaldo will make sure there are consequences, either for us or the boy's family."

Peter was about to say something else when he saw the messenger, an eight-year-old boy, running toward him, triumphantly carrying in an upraised, honey-drenched limb, a beehive.

"The last piece of the puzzle," he said.

He drained the honey into a cooking pot and gave it to the boy as a reward for bringing in the hive. Then he washed the hive in filtered water with gloved hands and dropped it onto the ersatz instrument table.

"Luke," Peter said, "it's time."

Peter washed his hands with soap, dried them, used hand sanitizer, and donned one of their two pairs of sterile latex gloves. Luke, grim and resigned, donned the others. No gowns, no surgeon caps, no masks. One man, someone who had been a porter, held Miguel's arms by his sides and steadied the hammock. Porfilio held the head.

Under a shade tree fifty yards away, Miguel's mother keened, his sister cried, and his grandmother tried to comfort them. Beneath another tree, Reynaldo chanted and shook a leather bag of stones. The fire that cooked their breakfast and sterilized their instruments smoldered on a platform just outside the hut. Smoke drifted through the hut and formed a small cloud in the stagnant air. Peter's nostrils filled with the smell of burning charcoal and wood.

He swabbed antiseptic solution around the shaved scalp and laceration, draped the area with their last four sterile paper towels, and infiltrated the skin with their last few drops of local anesthetic. Miguel groaned as Peter enlarged the laceration into a skin incision large enough to expose the temporal bone. He handed Luke the two forks that had been bent at the tines to form primitive retractors.

"The harder you pull on these, the less it will bleed and the more I'll see," he said.

"Just get it over with," Luke said.

As Peter cut through the muscle layer, blood pooled over the exposed bone. He swabbed the blood away long enough to find the skull fracture. Using the adze as a chisel, he wedged it into the fracture and tapped it lightly with the hammer. Blood spattered in both surgeons' faces. The hammock moved as Porfilio twisted away.

Peter took a deep breath and levered the edges of the bone. A fragment broke free and a blood clot oozed from the opening. He wedged the adze into the cracks leading to the base of the skull and levered off another fragment. More old blood oozed out, and he wiped it away with a gauze sponge. The dura became visible beneath the clot.

Miguel took a deep breath and groaned. He started to struggle in the hammock, and the holders hugged him tighter. A good sign for his brain recovery, Peter thought, if only he doesn't hit the floor.

Bright red blood pumped in a pulsating stream from the base of the skull. Peter reached for the beehive and pulled off a small piece of wax. After rolling it into a pea-sized ball, he smeared it into the bone at the source of the bleeding. The pumping stopped, and the bleeding slowed, oozing steadily from the skin and muscle edges.

"Okay, Luke, take out the retractors . . . er, forks, and put pressure on the skin edges for about five minutes. I think the major bleeding has stopped."

Miguel kicked, and the hammock jerked away.

"Jesus Christ!" Peter shouted.

Porfilio held Miguel in the netting and kept him from falling.

"Language, Doctor," Luke said.

"Give me a break," Peter returned, feeling his face redden, stress morphing into anger.

Luke muttered, "Maybe you were saying a little prayer."

Bleeding from the open wound slowed with pressure on the edges. No bright red spurting streams came from the depths of the wound, and blood from the surface edges waned.

Tension drained from Peter's shoulders; the tremor left his hands. The worst was over.

"Right," he said to Luke. "A prayer."

They put a few sutures in the temporal muscle and closed the skin with running stitches. Miguel stirred, but without violence. He was easily held.

The operation had gone well, but the scene remained ghastly. Congealing blood covered Miguel's head; spatters coated Peter's and Luke's faces, their forearms stained. A slimy puddle dripped through the floorboards to the pigs that lived beneath the hut. They grunted and fought to lick it up. Outside, Miguel's mother continued to keen, and Reynaldo continued to agitate the villagers.

Luke brought a five-gallon container of water, and they washed Miguel first, then their own hands and faces, then the floor. As the water showered down, the pigs scattered. Porfilio and his assistants lowered the hammock to near-floor level so that Miguel would not fall if he thrashed about.

Peter opened Miguel's eyes and saw that the pupils were equal in size; they constricted in the bright sunlight, a sign that the pressure had been relieved. He almost smiled, daring to hope. When he looked up, he found Luke staring at him.

"Well?" Luke asked.

"Looks like he's going to live."

"Thank God," Luke said. "Maybe Karen was right."

Luke conferred with John and Porfilio, and the three of them brought the mother, sister, and grandmother to Miguel's side. Peter leaned against a post a few feet away and watched. The mother's tears streamed down her cheeks as she touched her son's face. She spoke to Porfilio in the Bribri language.

When she had finished, Porfilio translated. "She says this Jesus must be a powerful god and a loving god to listen to the prayers of a mother. She wishes to know more of this god of ours."

Peter nodded and smiled. Medical science had won a battle against ignorance and superstition. Let John celebrate the grace of God and the acceptance of the Gospel in this little village. Peter was going to celebrate a successful operation, metaphysics be damned.

Reynaldo disappeared. John and Porfilio directed a team of Bribri to reconstruct the thatch roof, vital to Miguel's recovery. Without IV fluids, he was undoubtedly dehydrated from the blood loss and the heat. In the sun he would die; in the shade of the reconstructed roof he would live.

Peter stayed by his side, taking his pulse and blood pressure every fifteen minutes, until an hour later when Miguel started opening his eyes. Cautiously, they assisted him to a near sitting position and, once they were certain he wouldn't vomit, coaxed him to drink a small cup of water. Peter examined the wound for swelling or bleeding, then redressed it. He glanced up at the already smaller hole in the roof, surprised that it was still light. The day had already seemed so long, but his watch told him it was only midafternoon—twenty more hours before they could expect helicopter evacuation.

Although the immediate danger of death had been mitigated by the surgery, dehydration, seizures, and infection remained risks. The sooner Miguel was in a real hospital, the more comfortable Peter would be with the outcome. He would stay at his side until the evacuation.

John explained that the family would also stay at Miguel's side, as per their tradition. The Bribri were not above seeking medical help, but the idea of deserting a sick family member to strangers was foreign and offensive. Tonight they would have a crowd in the hut. Even tomorrow when the helicopter came, family members would walk two days to the nearest bus stop, travel to San Jose, and stay at the hospital until Miguel was released.

Luke said, "You were right, I think."

"Are you apologizing?"

Luke shook his head. "Just saying. People will remember you tried to do a good thing here today."

"Only tried?"

Luke continued. "Another night, the River Tiger will return, and people will weep. But then they will remember the day the American Christians did a strange ritual—a terrible, bloody thing—and a boy who was dead to them came alive. They will know that they are not forgotten by the Christian God, that miracles sometimes happen."

Peter found himself wondering about the nature of miracles, like that story Pastor Nick had told about Jesus healing that guy's shriveled hand. That was supernatural. This was surgery. But his presence at this time and place *was* a miracle of sorts, the result of a series of odd events and encounters.

God's hand? He hoped it were true. For if Miguel was remembered by God and saved by a miracle, maybe God would remember Peter, too.

Their dinner that night, usually rehydrated trail food and some kind of reconstituted powdered drink, was supplemented by gifts of food from the village. They had red meat for a change, something the villagers had hunted and killed, and heart-of-palm, coconuts, and plantains. An old man brought a pineapple. He pushed it into Peter's arms, said something in Bribri, and disappeared into the darkness.

Porfilio told Peter, "He said you should learn to speak Bribri. Because how would you even know how to ask for a cup of coffee when you return?"

"You have been given a great compliment," John said. "In their creation myth, Sibú was roasting corn, but the corn burned. The good kernels became the Bribri; the burned kernels became everyone else. Their word for outsiders translates as 'bad seed.' Not many are invited back."

Peter regarded his gift, comparing payment in pineapple to payment by an insurance company. Today the pineapple seemed to be more than enough.

CHAPTER SEVENTEEN

As the cooking fire died down, they turned off the lanterns after one more check on Miguel. His bandage was clean and dry, but he was still confused when aroused. They moved him from the hammock onto a pallet made of burlap bags. His mother and sister curled next to him. Peter crawled into his sleeping bag and fell asleep to the sounds of the pigs beneath the floor.

He woke coughing. Smoke filled the hut, and flames raged in the dry thatched roof.

"Fire!" He shook the nearby sleeping bags of John and Luke. "Fire!" he shouted again.

Flaming ashes fell around him, and his sleeping bag started to smolder as he shook himself free. A flaming ash dropped onto Luke's shirt. He cried out in pain.

"Get out!" Peter yelled. "Now!"

He ran to the edge of the platform and leaped into the darkness. His feet hit the mud, and he fell forward, onto the grass. Luke flew out behind him and rolled onto his back to extinguish his flaming shirt. John and Porfilio followed.

A loud crack sounded from the fire. The roof beam bent in the middle, sending showers of sparks into the night.

"Where's Miguel?" Peter shouted.

But his question was answered as he saw the silhouettes of Miguel's family through the flames. Were they trapped in the fire? As he dashed toward them, a loud crack sounded. The central beam across the peak of the hut broke in two. The roof collapsed into what little remained of the structure.

Peter stopped in his tracks and screamed. "No! Noooo!"

He started to run again, straight toward the fire, but John bear-hugged him. He dragged him away from the intolerable heat. "You can't help them now," he said. "Stay back!"

Another pop sounded behind him, higher pitched and different from the sounds of the fire, then another, followed by the faint *clink-clank* of a round being chambered. A bullet slammed into a post of the burning hut, scattering flames.

"Somebody's shooting at us. Get down, now!" John commanded.

Peter dropped to the muddy ground, Luke beside him. "Luke, are you okay?"

Luke groaned. "I'll live. My back hurts like hell."

"Come on," John said. "We've got to get out of here, now. Grab your shoes if you can find them. Keep down."

Their boots, left outside earlier to dry in the sun, were visible in the glow of the fire. Peter crawled toward them through the grass while Luke, crouched on his knees, stripped off his burned t-shirt.

Another gunshot rang out. A pig screeched and ran into the darkness, sounding a decrescendo squeal. An ominous silence fell as Peter and Luke crawled after John. When they were in the darkness, too, away from the bright halo of fire, John stopped and listened. He risked raising his head. Another gun sounded, followed again by the faint metallic *clink-clank*.

John tried to guide Luke by placing his hand on his shoulder and was rewarded with a cry of pain. "Listen," said John, "the muzzle flash is from the river bank, upstream. We need to get to the cover of those trees, keeping the hut between us and them." A bullet whistled overhead. "Keep down. Stay quiet and follow me."

They crawled through the grass until they reached the tree line and a small gully. Porfilio was already there. The gunshots stopped. No longer exposed in the meadow, Peter could stand in the darkness. He peered through the brush at the flaming hut, now a funeral pyre for Miguel and his family. Rage filled him. He wanted to strangle the murderers.

John answered Peter's thoughts as if they were his own. "Not now," he said. In the distance, the flames outlined the shadow of a figure with a rifle. "Now we must run."

They moved in the direction of the trail that led to Bajo Coen, Porfilio's village, and the road home. As they jogged ahead, John said, "I just thought he'd try to intimidate the locals. I didn't think he'd come after us."

Luke grimaced in pain. "What are we going to do?"

They faced each other in the moon shadows of the jungle, the fecund smells of the gully displaced by the smoke drifting in from the fire.

"We'll split up," John answered. "Luke, take Peter. Cross the river and pick up the trail farther downstream. That way, they'll lose your trail, and you can move slower if you have to. I'll go with Porfilio on this side of the river and try to outrun them. Or we'll hide. The darkness is our friend, and no one knows this jungle better than Porfilio. We'll meet in Bajo Coen. We'll be safe there. Reynaldo won't dare go out of this valley."

Luke turned and spoke quickly to Peter. "Follow me."

"But you're hurt."

"Nothing that slows me down, and I'll be a lot worse if I get shot. Come on."

Peter tried to follow Luke's shadow. Branches slapped his face, and vines tangled his legs. A trickle of water ran through the bottom of the gully; rocks and mud sucked at his boots. Ahead, he heard the sound of small splashes, breaking twigs, and Luke gasping with effort and pain.

So this is how I die, he thought. *Buried in an unmarked grave in a jungle backwater that nobody gives a damn about.* A vine slashed across his right cheek. *And for what? For doing a crazy operation on some Bribri kid. And now he's likely dead with his whole family.*

He ran into Luke and grunted. To his right, he could hear voices, presumably from the men carrying rifles. Ahead, he could hear the sound of the fast-flowing Rio Coen.

"Where now?" Peter whispered.

"Stick to the gully. It'll take us to the Coen. Then we cross to the far side where they can't see us. I doubt they'd risk a night crossing."

Peter remembered how difficult that crossing was three days before, even with a guide, a hiking pole, and daylight. "Do you think it's safe?" he asked.

In the dim light, Luke's face was inscrutable. "Of course not. That's why we're doing it."

Peter crouched and walked as quietly as he could through the vine-tangled, muddy, rock-strewn ditch, listening for the river ahead and the men behind. He startled and froze at a sudden rustling in the underbrush near his feet—snake.

Luke turned back and caught his arm. "Keep going," he whispered. "They're close. Can't you hear them?"

"Snake."

"Just keep going. The snake's scared of you."

"Yeah. Well, I'm scared of him, too." But he crept forward, until he could see the moonlight glinting off the dark river.

They stopped together near a boulder at the river edge, their feet already in the cold stream. Ahead of them, black icy water rushed swiftly over submerged and ragged rocks, turning the river into a jumble of black pits and white waves.

Peter hesitated. A wrong step could send him tumbling helplessly downstream. Death by *Tigre del Rio* suddenly became real.

Luke seemed to sense Peter's hesitation. "Listen," he whispered. "I know it's risky. But if we make it across, they won't follow, not at night."

"You're sure?"

"Yes. It's dangerous as hell, sure, even worse for us gringos who don't know the river. But they lose every advantage by getting into the stream. They can't see us, they can't use their guns. They are vulnerable to something as primitive as a thrown rock."

Peter looked back at the flaming hut, and then nodded his assent. "Show me the way."

Luke pointed out a likely route. "Black water is bad. But those ripples from here to that big rock midway, they mark shallow water. Stick to that route, then tuck in on the downstream side of that boulder."

Peter did as he was told, holding both arms out for balance. His feet slipped on the rocks, and he staggered. The noise of the stream drowned out the sounds of the jungle and their pursuers. He reached the boulder and stepped into the hole on its downstream side. Water swirled up around his shorts, the boulder now at chest level. He leaned and clutched it with both hands.

Luke followed his route through the shallows, his white skin shining out against the dark jungle behind him and the dark water below. In a few moments, he too sheltered with Peter behind the boulder.

"Did you see anybody?" Luke asked.

"Nobody."

"Okay, good. Now, the next twenty yards will be hard. The water is deep and fast. We'll link arms and walk slowly. I'll go on the upstream side. Got it?"

Peter looked across the black water, unsure. The water was cold; if he released his grip on the rock he might be washed downstream. But he had no choice.

"After we get there," he said to Luke, "what then?"

He could just make out Luke's smile in the moonlight. "At least you said *after* not *if*," he answered. "A trail follows the river. We'll follow it downstream. In a couple of miles, it turns right and goes up the shoulder of a mountain. You remember that hill when we hiked in?"

Peter remembered. He remembered exhaustion. He remembered they had quarreled on the top.

"I remember," he said.

"Good. If we can find our way to the top of that mountain, we can find our way home."

"Home." Peter heard the doubt in his own voice. Home was an uncertain place in his heart, a distant place in his mind.

"Bajo Coen, anyway," Luke said. "There'll be people there who can help."

A long walk, even if they made it that far—two river crossings and a rough trail between the mountaintop and Bajo Coen. He was pretty sure he couldn't get there in the daytime, much less at night, but maybe Luke could. He had to know the way. Even if he didn't, they couldn't stay in the river much longer.

He linked arms with Luke. Together, they stepped into the current on the far side of the boulder. The water rose to Luke's armpit, swirling around his torso and pushing him downstream, but he broke the force of the flow so Peter could maintain his footing. Luke grunted with the effort of keeping his balance and fighting the current. Peter followed, carefully placing each foot forward.

Ten minutes later they reached some branches of small trees that overhung the far bank. The river became shallow, now with back currents and small whirlpools at their hips instead of relentless downstream force against their chests. Panting from exertion, they clung to the thin and bending branches. As Peter willed his weak and wobbling legs to take the last few steps to shore, a shout rang out from the distant bank. Against the moonlit shrubbery, three figures splashed downstream in the shallows, all carrying rifles. Behind Peter, Luke hung in the river, still clinging with both hands to the first branches he had reached, apparently too tired to take the last few steps to the shelter of the dark jungle.

"Luke," Peter whispered loudly, "hurry! They've followed us."

Luke's shirtless white torso stood outlined against the black night. Peter cursed the moonlight that had guided them this far. Another shout came, then a muzzle flash and a gunshot report, a *thwap* as the bullet flew through the leaves above his head. Then *clink-clank*, the sound of another round being chambered.

"Luke! Come on."

Luke struggled into the shallows, grimacing with exhaustion and pain. Peter stretched out an arm to him. In a moment they would both be in the shadows, invisible to the gunmen.

Another muzzle flash, another gunshot. But this time the bullet made a sickening *splat,* striking flesh. Luke fell into the water.

Peter lurched forward, seizing him. He dragged him to shore, heaving him onto a grassy opening between two tree trunks, his legs still dangling in the river. Luke muffled a cry of pain.

More bullets rattled the leaves above their heads.

"Where are you hit?"

Luke groaned and lifted his right arm, feeling his side. "Liver, I think."

Peter saw the small but steady black stream of blood running down his side. Another bullet hissed into the water five feet away.

"It could be okay," Peter said without conviction. The stream of blood was only a trickle. But if his liver was hit, a torrent of blood would be pooling in his abdomen now.

Luke took a deep breath and exhaled quickly. He felt the entrance wound again with his right hand, his abdomen with his left. "Nope. Not gonna be okay."

He took a few more deep breaths, looking silently up into the dark jungle canopy. The gunshots had ceased, but the three men were gathering on the far bank. If they made a successful crossing, Peter and Luke would be defenseless.

"Tell Karen she was the love of my life," Luke said.

Peter took his wrist and felt for the pulse, already fast and thready. Dehydration, burn, exhaustion, and now internal bleeding—his blood pressure was dropping fast. Luke could be gone in five minutes.

"Tell her yourself," he said, hoping his tone did not match his despair.

Luke shook his head. "She always thought it was Jane." He grabbed Peter's hand and turned to face him in the darkness. "You tell her," he said again.

"I'll tell her. I will."

The gunmen were not advancing into the river. Luke had been right. They wouldn't risk a night crossing. Not here. Maybe they would follow John and Porfilio down the main trail.

"Peter. I need to forgive you. My last chance."

"It's okay, it's okay," Peter said, still watching the shadows of the gunmen.

Luke tried to sit up, but fell back. "You were a jerk. A self-centered ass."

"I know. I'm sorry."

"I forgive you."

Peter felt Luke's pulse again. It was weak, barely palpable, very fast. Shock already. Without four units of blood right now, it would be irreversible, the outcome inevitable.

Luke was right. Peter had been self-centered and insensitive ten years ago. Even now he had used Luke for his own purposes.

"I'm sorry," he said. "I'm so sorry." His words seemed too small, too unforgivably late.

Luke grabbed his hand again with unexpected strength and looked intently into Peter's face. "Jesus loves you."

He fell back, releasing Peter's hand. Peter reached to feel for the carotid pulse.

Nothing. Luke was dead.

Peter had seen death more times than most men, but always in a clean, well-lit place, and never while the dying held his hand. He looked at his hands, now covered with Luke's blood, turning sticky and black.

He wondered about forgiveness from a dead man who had not been a friend in life. But mostly, he wondered why Luke had wasted his last breath to say that Jesus loved him—whatever that meant.

CHAPTER EIGHTEEN

Peter stepped into the shallows and washed Luke's blood from his hands. The gunmen were no longer visible. They had retreated or turned away to pursue John and Porfilio. He dragged Luke to dry ground and pulled three large banana leaves from a nearby tree to cover the body. As he pulled the last leaf up to cover his face, he closed Luke's eyes. He stood for a moment, thinking how inadequate his simple actions were to acknowledge the passing of this complex life. A prayer seemed appropriate, a few holy words perhaps. But he had no words to give.

Then Peter ran.

He pushed through underbrush, tearing branches from his face and kicking vines from his legs. His shirt tore; thorns clutched his ankles and calves. He fell countless times before he found the packed ground of the trail.

Once on the trail, he ran faster, only to find himself again in impenetrable brush. He backed up and started again, feeling more than seeing his way through the darkness. Stumbling, he caught himself on tree trunks, grasped at branches, until he fell again, lacerating his left calf.

He rolled onto his back in the mud and tried to catch his breath, letting the cut bleed. His body quivered with exhaustion. Despair crept around the edges of his consciousness. His legs barely had the strength to stand, much less carry him across the mountain and through the streams that led to safety. Maybe he would fall victim to the *Tigre del Rio* that Luke had talked about.

He waited in the mud for unlikely rescue or more likely death. Above, small patches of sky and a few stars showed through the forest canopy. The moonlight caused odd shadows in the tall trees, forming silhouettes around unfamiliar leaves. When the breeze blew, the shadows moved like demons hovering above him.

Peter closed his eyes and threw his arm over his face, heart thudding. His fear tasted like a copper penny. The blank stare of Luke's dead eyes haunted him. Gasping, he rolled onto his belly, pushing himself to his hands and knees. Panting from the effort, unable to stand, he folded his right leg and sat propped against a tree.

He wept. He wept because he hurt. He wept because he was going to die, his body never to be found, and no one would care. He wept until no more tears came, until his breath calmed, and his hands stopped trembling.

He reassessed his situation. The moon shadows still played through the jungle canopy, but were no longer demonic. Night birds sang strange messages, and a distant group of howler monkeys called to each other like a pack of wild dogs. But he heard no footsteps of men, no gunshots, and no River Tiger. Yes, he was alone and starkly aware of his solitude. But even though death was possible, it wasn't imminent.

He stood, testing his legs and balance. No longer did he hear his heartbeat or taste his fear. Finally, he walked on, simply because he was not dead and had no wish to die alone, unmourned and unloved.

He walked rather than ran, realizing that exhaustion was his enemy as much as men with guns. If he were to find his way through the jungle, over the mountain, and across the river, he would need to conserve his energy.

The trail was difficult to follow in the darkness. At one point it led into a marsh where it diffused into multiple muddy paths, some bridged with fallen logs, others trailing off into tall, thick grass. Other times he walked on a narrow path through dense foliage, only to find himself faced with impassable vegetation. Then he would retrace his steps and search again for the trail, sometimes on his hands and knees in the darkness.

The sound of the river guided him. He heard water rushing through cataracts and rapids, always on his left. Sometimes the river was loud and the ground muddy. Sometimes the river was distant and the ground dry and gravelly as it abutted the hillside. He stopped frequently and listened, never letting the sound of water disappear.

At last the trail broadened and opened into a small clearing. Moonlight revealed a fork with one path to the left into the river and another to the right, beginning uphill. From his memory of the hike in, Peter figured the path on the right led to Bajo Coen and on the left the river crossing led back to where he had come from. John White and Porfilio should have come this way. Reynaldo and his two companions may have come too.

Cautiously, he followed the path to the river, listening and watching. He hoped to find John and Porfilio, or some evidence his pursuers were ahead or behind. Once he was certain no one was in the vicinity, he washed the deep cut on his calf and the other superficial abrasions and scratches, wincing at the pain and wishing for bandages and antiseptic ointment. Then he put his face in the water and drank until he was full.

He rolled over, exhausted, onto his back. The patch of night sky between the trees was black, with no sign of the coming dawn. The moon neared the peaks of the western mountains, where it would disappear and plunge the valley into utter darkness.

The adrenaline had worn off, the need to sleep overwhelming. He moved to a flat rock on the riverbank. Sheltered by small trees, he closed his eyes, the sound of rushing water filling his ears, and he slept, suddenly and deeply. He dreamed that Ellen held her hand to his chest in a gesture of both intimacy and restraint, looked into his eyes, and asked, *Why?*

Because we have only a moment, he wanted to say. He tried to tell her, but now it was Megan Kaiser who nodded at him, as if she already knew.

He awoke to the sound of voices and the vague stench of human sweat. The moon was gone, the darkness profound. Just a few feet away, a shadow knelt and drank. Peter froze in position, moving only his eyes. The shadow stood, a rifle in the crook of his arm, and seemed to look directly at him. Peter used all of the self-control he had learned in surgery to suppress the adrenaline rush and refrain from running. The shadow turned and said something in an indigenous dialect. Then, not registering Peter's silent presence in the darkness, he walked away. With two other men, he waded into the river, his scent fading into the black curtain of jungle on the other side.

Peter began to believe he would survive. The gunmen were gone, headed back on the trail to the burned hut. The trail to Bajo Coen would likely be clear.

He left the river, slowly following the trail up the mountain, feeling his way, unsure of how much time had passed. As he climbed, the sky turned from black to gray and, by the time he reached the high point, pink.

With a clear view of the path and certain that his pursuers

had turned back, Peter felt a rush of confidence. If he remembered correctly, he had another three or four hour walk to get to Bajo Coen, starting with downhill to the river. After that would be another river crossing, and a few more miles. Then he would be safe.

Patches of gray mist rose from the valley and obscured the landscape far below. He started the descent, encouraged by the beauty of the deep green trees against the pink sky. His heart urged him forward toward safety, but his body rebelled. His quadriceps trembled with the effort of maintaining balance on the steep trail, his feet slipping constantly on mud or gravel. Hours had passed since he last drank, and his throat was dry, now more from thirst than fear.

When he heard the river, the sound gave him a precious seed of hope. It promised relief from thirst and represented the last barrier on the path home.

Encouraged, he picked up his pace, stepping over a log. The grass rustled as his foot hit the ground, and a sudden jolt of pain surged through his calf. His leg gave way. As he tumbled downhill, the fat body of a viper writhed and rolled with him. Yards down the trail, he slammed to a stop against another log. As quickly as it had struck, the snake released his leg and shot into the bushes.

Stunned, he lay still, wincing. Excruciating pain pulsed through his leg. Could he walk? He took a deep breath and gasped—a new pain, no doubt a broken rib.

He pushed himself to sit against the log and inspect the wound in his leg. He found only the innocuous appearance of two fang marks. But he knew that within an hour it would be red and swollen; in four it would turn purple, and in eight, the skin would break down. In twenty-four hours, if he survived, a gaping hole in his skin would expose the dying muscle beneath. The snake had looked like a pit viper of some sort, probably the dreaded *fer-de-lance*. If it had released a full dose of venom and he did not receive antivenin within six hours, he would die.

Closing his eyes, he calculated. He needed to move, even if he had to crawl. He struggled to his feet, limped off the trail, and sought a stick. He broke a young tree, little more than a shrub, to form a crude walking stick. As he limped back to his log, he looked down the steep trail. The sound of the river called to him, its song of hope now a cry of desperation.

He stumbled and slid down the mountain trail, his calf muscle already burning from the local spread of the venom. The sun was above the horizon by the time he reached the river, but the sky still held the pink and gray of near-dawn. On his knees, Peter drank several swallows of water. Immediately, he retched, the effects of the poison spreading through his system.

He leaned back and dangled his legs into the river, letting the cold water wash his wounds as he tried to think. Soon his mind would cloud; his heart would fail. He could walk no farther. Dehydration, exhaustion, and leg wounds factored against him, even before the snakebite. But if he stayed where he was, by evening he would be dead.

Facing death, his choices were limited. He could rest in the warm sun and the cool river, accept his fate and seek peace. Or he could refuse to accept it, wage war against oblivion.

He had seen patients choose either course at one time or another. Some called hospice and took the drugs that facilitated peace. Others screamed their defiance until their breath failed.

At last he decided. Luke had died trying to save him; he owed Luke the struggle to survive, to attempt to carry his last message to Karen. He staggered into the stream, his sandals sliding on the gravel beneath, and scanned the cataracts for the dark water that marked the deepest channel, the dangerous current that might yet carry him to safety. He slid into the protected pool behind a boulder. His legs quivered from the effort of wading. He hoped that the tingling in his fingertips and lips was due to cold water and not the effects of the venom. Giving up his last contact with solid ground, he threw himself into the black water, keeping his feet downstream and his head up.

Bright blue sky and a white hot sun replaced the soft, pink dawn. He was flotsam in dark water. As the river flung him side to side, he could only hope the rushing current would carry him to help. Thrown against a rock, his side flared with pain from his fractured rib. He tried to protect himself by using his legs to push off downstream rocks, but each time, the pain was excruciating and his muscles failed. More than once, the current swept him into an undertow, and he emerged coughing, sputtering and paddling, frantically trying to regain control.

Shivering, his strength waned in the cold water. When his feet hit the next rock downstream, his legs folded. His body collapsed into a ball against the boulder, and then tumbled left, out of the main current. Finally, he came to rest on a rocky beach, half submerged. Mind drifting, he gazed at the azure sky, his body spent.

No part of his body was pain-free, but his right leg burned like it had already gone to hell, his allegorical one foot in the grave now a literal reality. His lips and face tingled and flamed as the venom spread. His tongue swelled. The sky grew bright and faded to gray. He had a moment of clinical observation, a flash of looking down on himself as a patient, and what he saw were the last moments of his consciousness. *He's going out*, he would have said if he'd seen a beached, derelict form like his on a rocky shore.

He took comfort only in knowing that he had tried to stay alive, tried as hard as he could. He waited for death, more exhausted than afraid, filled with regrets for loves lost and wrongs not set right. He mourned Luke Ryan. He apologized to

Megan Kaiser. He said goodbye to Ellen and Daniel, and closed his eyes against the blue-white sky and merciless sun.

Pain woke him up, tearing his leg and stabbing his side. Somehow, he was moving; he was being dragged across the rocks. Noise, voices maybe. He fought to open his eyes and speak, but even that required too much strength. Before darkness overcame him, he thought *I'm not dead yet. Dead men feel no pain.*

CHAPTER NINETEEN

Peter woke, vaguely aware of rough cotton sheets and white curtains blown by a cool breeze. A ceiling fan turned slowly as he realized that every part of his body ached.

"Welcome back to the land of the living," a voice drawled.

He turned to make out John's figure sitting at his bedside. A sharp chest pain reminded him of the broken rib. Memories flooded back—the cold river, the snakebite, the night of terror in the jungle. Luke.

"Where am I?" he asked.

"San Jose. A hospital called Clinica Biblica."

"What day?"

"May twentieth."

Peter tried to remember when they fled the jungle.

"You lost three days," John said, making the calculations easier. "One of Porfilio's men found you in the river. We didn't think you were going to make it, but we threw you in a canoe and hauled ass for the boat landing at Shiroles. Porfilio radioed for an ambulance to meet you and take you to the Home Creek clinic where you used up all the antivenin in the province. They transferred you here the next morning for the operation on your leg."

Peter became aware now of the thick gauze dressing on his right calf.

"They said you'd probably lose the leg if they didn't operate. I told them to go ahead. Hope you don't mind."

Peter sat up, gasped once at the rib pain, and touched the bandage on his leg. Nothing seemed real, including the fact he was alive. The last thing he remembered was giving up.

"Luke's dead," he said.

"I know. The police found his body." John paused, but then continued, his voice husky and breaking. "I called Karen. She's . . ."

"Is Miguel dead too? With his family?"

John shook his head. "No. We found them and hid them until morning. They are safe at the mission in Bribri now."

"Thank God for that," Peter said. "They arrest those bastards?"

"The tribes don't talk much to the police. And the police are happy to let them settle differences themselves, even when it leads to years of blood feuds—as long as it stays on the reservation. The current theory is that Luke was a victim of a hunting accident."

Righteous indignation at the injustice overwhelmed Peter. Luke had not been a friend, exactly, but he a good man. His death should not go unpunished. "They were shooting at us. I was there. It was cold-blooded murder."

"The police have my statement and will want yours, of course. They'll want you to identify the shooter."

"I know it was Reynaldo."

"But it was night. I couldn't see any faces," John said.

"Neither could I. But I know it was him."

"So you, as a foreigner, are going to tell them that some

people you couldn't identify shot at you in the darkness, and you're sure it's a guy you saw the day before, and you don't know his last name."

"So you're saying I shouldn't say anything?"

"No," John replied. "You can tell them everything you saw. Just don't expect them to do a lot about it. This will be an impossible case for them unless someone from the tribe comes forth."

Peter stared at the fan as he absorbed John's words. So Luke was dead, his own leg was injured to an unknown extent, and the perpetrators would likely go free. And for what? So a couple of dozen indigenous people could feel a little better for a week?

"Was it worth it?"

John paused before replying. "Yes," he said simply.

"Luke's dead, Miguel and his family are refugees. How is that worth it?"

"In all things, God works for the good of those who love Him. Luke loved the Lord, so regardless of what my eyes see and my mind tells me about the tragedy of it all, I've got to believe that it was worth it."

"You'll forgive me if I take a different point of view."

"I've got to believe Jesus sent me to these people," John insisted. "I can't abandon them to the darkness."

Peter was incredulous. "You can't be thinking of going back."

"Absolutely."

"You'll be killed," Peter said. "Like Luke."

John shrugged. "Maybe."

"You think one dead American isn't enough?" Peter asked. "Two will change things?"

"I think death comes to all." Here John paused, appearing to puzzle out how to frame what he would say next. "But darkness comes only to those who choose it and those who don't know there is a choice. As one of our great leaders once said, only light can drive out darkness; only love can drive out hate. Going back is bringing light to the darkness, matching love against the hate."

Peter wanted to tell him he was wrong and stupid and wasting the few precious moments of this life. Peter's life had been dedicated to medical science, and what was medical science if not the great struggle against death?

But John was right about one thing: death is inevitable. He had been so certain he would die that he was surprised to be here. Maybe John was right about the rest of it, too. Maybe love could change things.

"I need to talk to Karen," Peter said.

"I hope you can."

"You're saying I might not make it?"

"Naw. The doctors say you're out of the woods. It's just that . . ." John paused and studied Peter. "How well do you know Karen?"

"Met her twice, about five minutes each time."

"Yeah. Well, she carries some baggage."

"What are you talking about?"

"Nothing. I shouldn't have said a darn thing. Out of place entirely."

"You can't quit now. Come on."

"No. I didn't mean anything. Really. You just go talk to her when you get back."

The conversation went silent. Peter lay back on the bed, tired from the effort of sitting and talking. He tried to absorb the recent events, still feeling his "real life" was somewhere else. American suburbia. An air-conditioned Porsche on an open road. A well-equipped hospital and a clean operating room. Safety.

But those familiar things now seemed more like a setting than a goal. He had a wife and a son to love. He had a promise to keep to Megan Kaiser. He had a message to take to Karen

Ryan. America was only the frame around the story he needed to be in.

Peter traced back the path that had brought him here and came to a single name—

Megan Kaiser. Everything since her operation was some form of atonement for that failure, and he still owed her. Now he owed Luke, too.

When Peter woke a few hours later, John was gone. A note said he had returned to his mission in Bribri. He would be back in two weeks.

Alone, weak from his injuries, and separated from most of his caregivers by language, Peter slid toward depression. His call to Ellen went straight to voicemail. At least she would know that he couldn't take Daniel the next weekend, but a voice message couldn't come close to saying all he needed to say to her. He also called the hospital to tell them where he was and when he would return. Kelly's administrative assistant let him know that his suspension would be over in three weeks, and he would be expected back in the office. Peter imagined her holding the phone with her fingertips, taking care not to damage her nail polish as she pushed the button to disconnect.

He slept sixteen or more hours each day. His waking time was spent in therapy, dressing changes, and thinking about home. When he was a child, home meant that house in Philadelphia where his father, the philosophy professor, lived with his mother, the socialite and drunk. He had become aware at a young age that he was an unwelcome accident, something to be managed, not someone to be loved. He began to feel more comfortable at the various boarding schools and camps his parents sent him to. But on the few weeks that he visited their house, his hope for love faded; every year, his sense of isolation grew.

When he met Ellen in college, he had hoped that their love would create a home. When they decided to have a child, he vowed that his son would have a home where he felt safe and loved, a home he'd never had. In this, he admitted to himself, he had miserably failed.

To push away despair, he held onto his new mantra—going back was love. He had a family. He had a promise to keep. He had a message to deliver.

Two weeks later, John came back from Bribri to give him a ride to the airport. He'd been released to fly home.

When they pulled up to the airport, they rolled to a stop between two minivans and were quickly boxed in by a taxi.

"You could come back with me instead, Doc," John said. "You'd be welcome."

"Don't hold your breath."

John pulled the bag out of the trunk as Peter struggled with his new aluminum cane.

"Just saying," John went on. "We need a doctor. And here you got into a mighty struggle between good and evil. Sometimes you get home and all your daily battles start seeming small. Then you want to get back in the big fight."

The need for a "big fight" seemed unlikely. He was going back to fight for his marriage, for his son, for his career. None of those battles seemed small. Yet, maybe now he believed there *was* a battle for good over evil, not just a battle for the sake of winning.

"I'll think about it," he said.

John smiled and handed him his bag.

Back in Jacksonville, Peter retrieved the Porsche, sliding his hands over the leather-covered steering wheel. He turned the key, hearing the purr of the finely tuned engine. But his bag had to occupy the seat next to him because the trunk was too small. He tried to think of a single reason to keep this ridiculous street-legal racecar. Nothing about it seemed real anymore.

The next day, he drove his new Honda Civic past the stone pillars, manicured lawns, and marble fountain of Daniel's school. A security guard looked suspiciously in his direction.

Daniel sat on a bench, his backpack secured with both straps. He didn't smile, and he didn't join the other boys who were shoving each other, shouting, and running in tight circles. He was a silent, unremarkable student, and the last chosen for any team. Peter feared for him in a world of predators—the bullies on the playground now, the Joe Bells and Reynaldos later. His instinct to protect him battled with his desire to make him fierce.

Daniel looked blankly toward the arriving cars, expecting the Porsche. Peter lowered the passenger side window and waved at him, but he seemed oblivious. Only the security guard noticed. "I'll have to see some ID, sir," she said.

He handed her his driver's license. The guard checked her list and handed him his license. "Thank you, sir."

She turned and called to Daniel. He looked up, surprised, then made his way to the car. He sat down in the front seat, his overstuffed backpack on his lap.

"What happened to your car?" he asked, fitting the seatbelt between his chest and the bag.

"The Porsche was too stupid. Too small." Peter pulled away from the curb. "I'm glad to see you, son."

Daniel peered across the car to his father's foot but only said, "Okay. Same hotel?"

"No. I got an apartment. But I just got back last night, so it's a little sparse." Peter felt barely visible. Like a chauffeur. "I missed you, Daniel."

Daniel stared ahead as the car turned onto San Jose Boulevard. "Where'd you go?"

"Central America. On a mission trip. Remember? I told you about it?"

"Yeah, but after that? Why were you gone so long? You were supposed to have me last weekend."

"I was in the hospital, Daniel. Didn't your mother tell you?"

Daniel shrugged. "She said you were gone, that's all. Like she didn't care if you came back or not." He turned to look out the window, so Peter barely heard him add, "Now, she's like, 'Fine. Free babysitting.'"

Peter glimpsed the same abandonment he had felt as a child. "Your mother loves you."

"Like you'd know," said Daniel, his face still turned away.

Peter felt like a ghost; he was dead to Daniel. He wanted to know the magic words that would bring him back to life, to create a real relationship. But he had nothing.

Rain slowed the traffic as he turned onto University Boulevard, a four-lane undivided street that bisected miles of strip malls, tire stores, and restaurants like Waffle House.

He stopped for a light and turned to face the back of Daniel's head.

"I love you, Daniel."

"Whatever," Daniel said to his rain-streaked window.

At the apartment, he dropped his backpack in the entryway. Peter wanted the apartment to be like a home for Daniel. He envisioned his clothes in the closet, his sports equipment in the hall storage space, and his books open on a desk in his room. But for this hastily planned reunion, Daniel had neglected to bring clothes, pajamas, or even a toothbrush, and Peter had neglected to provide a desk, food, or even the means to cook.

Daniel walked around, looking at the beige walls and rented furniture: a single twin-sized bed in Daniel's room, and a queen-sized bed and side table in Peter's room. The third bedroom, "the study," was bare. No pictures, no decorations, no mementos.

"You got a TV?" Daniel asked.

"A fifty-inch flat screen and DVD/Blu-Ray player. Just no cable until Wednesday."

"PlayStation? Internet?"

"No PlayStation. I'm using my iPad for Internet access."

Daniel slumped on the side of his bed. "Jeez. What am I gonna do here?"

Peter felt as if he were walking in the dark, searching vainly for the right words. "Your homework for starters," he finally answered. "I've got to get off my leg. Then we'll go get you some clothes for tomorrow, a toothbrush, and something to eat."

"Jeez," Daniel said again, this time to the carpet. Then he brightened. "Could I use your iPad? Or your computer?"

"For a video game?"

Daniel shrugged.

Peter sighed. "Tell you what. You finish your homework, we run our errands, then you can teach me a video game of your choice."

At least they'd be doing something together.

Daniel shrugged and didn't meet his eyes, but he muttered, "Deal."

An hour later, they drove to the nearest Target to get what they needed—three sets of underwear and socks, khakis, and some polo shirts and tees that would get them through the night and the weekend. Then they could figure out how to stock Daniel's closet more permanently.

Peter ordered takeout from the country club. Since the club charged a minimum for food he never ate, this was like a free meal. He made a mental note to himself to cancel the membership. They had joined the club so Ellen could play tennis, Daniel could use the pool, and Peter could someday learn to play golf. None of those fantasies seemed likely or vital.

The rain had stopped by the time they reached the club, but the clouds hid the setting sun and darkness came early. Peter limped to the club entrance, his leg aching again. Daniel slumped along beside him. Just inside, the club dining room was separated from the entryway by an indoor window. He glanced into the dining room and was stopped by the sight of Ellen.

At the far end of the room, she sat at a table with a man he couldn't identify from behind. Peter first imagined it was Joe Bell, if only because of the level of hostility he immediately felt. But it wasn't. Someone taller, younger, with a better haircut. Familiar . . .

She looked up to see him staring. With cold indifference she brushed a lock of hair away from her forehead and turned back to her companion.

Peter, his spirit freeze-dried by the single glance, turned and followed the hallway toward the kitchen, where his order had been left on a side table below a dark painting of red-coated men on horses. Daniel, his attention focused downward, remained unaware of his mother's presence. Peter envied his ignorance.

He fled, limping, Daniel carrying two Styrofoam boxes and a cardboard flat with two chocolate malts. They threw the boxes into the back seat, and Daniel balanced the malts on his lap. Peter slammed his door and struggled to get the keys into the ignition. He gripped the steering wheel with white knuckles and glared at the darkening parking lot.

Daniel looked at him. "Are you okay?"

Peter inhaled deeply, exhaled slowly. He reminded himself of the mountain he had climbed, one step at a time. "I hope so, son."

He drove to the apartment, distracted by the aching in his chest. When he slammed on his brakes, nearly missing the turn into the apartment complex, Daniel shouted, struggling to keep the malts upright.

Before running to his room with his backpack, Daniel ate three bites of cheeseburger, two fries, and one gulp of his malt. Peter had lost his appetite. In what could have been no more than ten minutes, Daniel returned, proclaiming that his homework was done and demanding the iPad.

"Man, it's like you've got no games at all on this thing," Daniel said, swiping through the available apps.

Peter shrugged. "I never play games. It's a tool."

Daniel looked at him, puzzled. "Yeah. But why not? It's fun."

Fun didn't get recognition. Fun didn't get money. Fun didn't get love.

Fun didn't make your son fierce.

But a deal was a deal.

"Okay, then," Daniel said, "we'll have to start you off slow. The big games are, like, *Assassin's Creed* or *Grand Theft Auto*. I think you need to start on *Angry Birds* or *Sniper*."

"Whatever you think, son. You're the expert."

"Okay. We'll start you with *Angry Birds*. Everybody likes *Angry Birds*."

In a few minutes, Peter was flinging angry birds across the screen at smug pigs. Daniel laughed at his incompetence. Peter forgot about Ellen, Bell, Kelly, and Megan's brain tumor. He knew he could kill even more of the smug pigs with a little practice. Soon, he wasn't satisfied to clear the screen with one star; he wanted three stars.

Daniel took his turn. Peter looked at his watch. "Jesus. It's after nine. You've got to get to bed."

"Yeah, but you had fun. Right, Dad?"

Daniel had called him *Dad*.

"I had fun, son."

"Okay. How about I download just one more game in case you get bored with *Angry Birds*?"

"Sure. Go ahead."

Daniel tapped on the screen until a new game appeared. "Okay," he said, "this is called *Sniper*. I'll just show you once how it works so you know."

"Then straight to bed. And brush your teeth."

Daniel showed him the screen. A black figure appeared on a simple street scene. Daniel tilted the iPad until a red dot centered on the figure's head. Then he tapped the screen. A gunshot sounded, followed by the metallic *click-clank* as the game rifle reloaded. Red splattered on the wall, and the figure dropped to the pavement. A red pool spread from his head to the sidewalk.

At the sound of the *click-clank*, Peter vision went dark; pain pierced his abdomen.

"See, it's easy, Dad," Daniel said. "Dad? Dad? Are you all right?"

Without looking, he took the iPad from Daniel and turned it off with trembling fingers.

"Go to bed Daniel." He added, "Now."

Daniel's face crumpled, puzzled, then hurt. He ran silently to his room.

Peter stared at the empty kitchen wall and saw Luke's body, a hole, and a stream of oozing black blood.

CHAPTER TWENTY

Friday afternoon he picked up Daniel from school for their first weekend together. That night they went to eat at a burger joint, and Saturday morning he learned to make pancakes. They went to the zoo, but he had to cut the trip short because his leg couldn't take it. They played *Angry Birds*, but Daniel steered Peter clear of any other games.

They cautiously learned to know and trust each other, step by baby step. Fatherhood was turning out to be hard work. Each evening after Daniel went to bed, Peter recounted every word of their sparse conversations and imagined how he could have done better. Then he would fall asleep and the nightmares would come. Black jungles and black rivers, fire and blood. He woke in a cold sweat at three a.m. each morning, took a pain pill, and drifted off until dawn.

Kelly wanted to see him at nine o'clock Monday morning. No doubt he wanted to lay down some rules about the return to practice. Peter walked through the main lobby, feeling unexpectedly alien in the hospital where he should have felt at home. His clothes, too, the tailored suit and linen shirt that had seemed so natural a few weeks ago, now seemed like a costume.

As he crossed the lobby he saw Ellen standing, her head down, concentrating on a sketch. Surprised, he stopped and stared. She looked up as if she felt his presence, almost like she was expecting him.

"What are you doing here?" he asked.

She wrapped both arms around her sketchpad. "Dale hired me to redesign the lobby."

He let his hand drop to his side. "Kelly?"

"Yes. Dale Kelly."

"Why you?"

"You think I can't handle it?"

"No, not that. I'm just surprised."

"Don't be. I've got a son to support and a business to run." She turned back to her pad. "And no husband to count on."

"Come on, Ellen. I'm trying."

"Someone's got to pay the bills. You haven't worked for six weeks. I hear you conned the board into letting you take a vacation to Costa Rica for 'community service.'"

"It wasn't a vacation, Ellen. People died. I almost died."

Her eyes narrowed, questioning, judging. Then she looked away and sketched a few more lines. "Tell me why I should care."

"Because I want you to understand. Because I love you."

The pencil stopped. "Once I thought you knew what that meant," she said quietly.

He stepped closer. "I'm not sure I did. But I know now."

She shook her head, keeping her gaze on the sketchpad. "I won't feel sorry for you. I can't do this again." She waved the pencil vaguely.

"We need to talk, Ellen."

"No. We don't. It's over, Peter." She spun away and walked out the door.

Peter started after her, but his limp brought him up short.

"Ellen," he called to her disappearing figure. But what did he really have to say that he hadn't already said and she hadn't already ignored?

He climbed into an elevator and slammed his fist into the button for the eighth floor.

When he stepped off the elevator, Kelly's assistant, all polished nails and high heels, waved him into his office. Peter wondered, as he did every time he saw her, what she really did to earn a salary.

Grinning, Kelly jumped up from his desk and gave Peter a firm handshake. "Pete! Long time, no see. You want some coffee or something?" He gestured toward the coffee pot.

Peter shook his head. "No, thanks," he said through gritted teeth. "But it's good to be back."

"Yes, yes. Sooner or later, work is better than golf, right? I mean, hey, you can only play so many rounds."

Peter grimaced. "I wasn't playing golf."

"No, of course not. Didn't mean to say so. Community service. Very admirable. Very good publicity. Good strategy at this point."

"I saw my wife in the lobby."

"Ellen?" Kelly seemed surprised by the sudden change of subject. "Of course. Very attractive woman. Talented, too, I understand. You're separated? Divorced?"

"Separated."

"Sure. Hope you don't mind I'm using her for some of the renovations."

"Yes. I do mind that you're using her."

"Well, yes. It could be awkward. New relationships and all."

"You take her to dinner last week? Maybe at the country club?"

Kelly held his hands up. "Strictly professional. She had a design presentation to make."

"So she paid?"

Kelly looked uncomfortable. "Nothing serious, I assure you. Everything above board. Nothing that should inhibit our working relationship."

Peter stared at him.

"Really. Let's talk about work. We can't let the interior designer interfere, even if she is your ex. You don't have to interact with her at all."

Peter calculated the costs of beating the insipid smile off Kelly's face and finally decided it would not be a positive step toward the restoration of his career or his family. He forced a nod.

"Good. Bell assures me you will be assigned your fair share of new patients, and the Board of Medicine has approved him to be your supervisor for the— what do you call it? Probation? Should be a rubber stamp. The neurosurgery section should become a great profit center for hospital operations."

Profit center? Was this the great struggle against pain, disability, and death?

Peter tried to remind himself of the promise he'd made— give it six months. Try to smile.

But all he could think of was Ellen. "She's not my ex," he said.

"What?"

"Ellen. She's not my ex. We're not divorced."

Kelly stared at him. "Right. I thought we'd moved on. The point is, are you ready to come back to work?"

"Sure," Peter said. "Except for my leg. Can't stand for more than an hour or two. I'll have to go light on surgery for a couple more weeks."

"Bell assures me that he can cover for you."

He will love stealing my patients. "Of course," Peter said.

"We've set up your offices on the fourth floor. Your secretary

—Betsy, is it? She was a great help with making an easy transition."

So Betsy still had her job. "And the other staff?"

"Well, Joe told me there were some efficiencies to be gained by combining staff, but I don't know the details."

Peter had no trouble imagining the details. But if he wanted to save his career, he would have to be compliant. A team player. And even though his plan to salvage his marriage and family was still vague, he felt certain it involved having a practice in Jacksonville.

"Can't wait to get started," he said.

Kelly glanced at his wristwatch and stood abruptly. "No time like the present, then. Just keep your head down. No newspaper stories, okay?" He smiled and held out his hand.

Betsy showed him to his new office and desk, the inbox piled high with charts, messages, and mail. He limped to his chair and reconsidered whether he should have brought the cane to work. He had thought the cane made him look even more vulnerable than he felt, but now he could hardly wait to sit.

"It's not the same," Betsy said.

"No," he agreed. "Something you want to talk about?"

"Bell's an ass-grabber." She pulled her reading glasses from their precarious perch on her nose and brushed an imaginary strand of hair from her face.

Peter noticed, not for the first time, that she was an attractive woman who disguised her figure with baggy scrubs, her face with glasses, and never wore makeup, not even lipstick. Harassment would not sit lightly with her.

"You could file a complaint."

She nodded. "I need this job."

"We work for a big corporation. They have a human resource team and grievance procedures."

"Yeah. But they need this neurosurgeon more than they need an 'administrative assistant.' Put my word against his, and who do you think they'll believe? I might not get fired. More likely I'll get offered a 'lateral transfer' to someplace in Tennessee, and I can't do that."

Peter wanted to reassure her and tell her he'd take care of it. But he was as vulnerable as she. "I'm sorry," was the only thing he could say.

The tower in the inbox had diminished only slightly by ten o'clock but he left it, put on a white coat, and limped down the hall to see Megan Kaiser. She looked thin and tired. Dark circles underscored her eyes. Instead of a wig, she wore a colorful patterned scarf to cover her scalp. Seeing Peter enter the room, she slipped off the scarf so he could see her incisions. Patches of blond fuzz did not obscure the accusing double scars.

"How are you, Miss Kaiser?" he asked.

She smiled thinly. "*Miss Kaiser* is it?"

"Megan, then," he said, clutching her chart.

"I'm about as well as could be expected. Tired, worried, weak. And so slow. Takes me forever to do anything, even clean my apartment, and you've seen how small that is, Doctor."

"I think you can call me Peter."

"No." She smiled. "I can't. But, on the bright side, I found out smoking weed takes care of the nausea. And I get a little buzz. You should try it."

Startled, he looked at her and realized she was not joking.

"Did I shock you?" Now she was almost laughing at him.

"No," he lied. "I'm just . . . tired."

"You look like hell. And you're limping. What happened?"

"I feel like hell. I . . ." Words failed him. He had too many things to say, too little time to say them, and the setting was inappropriate.

"Don't worry," she said. "I'm the one person you can really talk to. I won't be around long enough to throw your words back."

He looked into her eyes, no longer seeing the dark circles or the sallow skin or the scars. He saw humor, courage, and loneliness. He put his hand out and grasped hers as if she were not a patient but a friend. She lowered her head and leaned in, then lightly covered his hand with hers. She smelled of soap and perfume, and the faint odor of death.

He released her and stepped back. "I've thought a lot about you," he said. "And the promise I made."

"I've thought about it, too, Doctor."

He nodded. "You went back to work?"

She frowned. "Yes, but no one treats me like I'm okay. I'm invisible. Or they treat me with exaggerated courtesy, like I might break and bleed. It's lonely. You know what I mean? It's hard to feel alive when everybody treats you like you're already dead."

"I understand," he said.

Because he was here instead of buried beside some river in Costa Rica, he had a new appreciation for how thin the line was between the dead and the living. They were both survivors, at least for now. Only he struggled with the meaning of his uncertain life while she seemed at peace with her certain death.

She nodded. "Come to the Waffle House. I'm working Wednesday night. You could give me a ride home."

Peter had never been in a Waffle House. "Maybe," he said. "Let's get your MRI tomorrow, and I'll see you Wednesday morning for the results."

Peter moved on, continuing to see patients and working

through lunch until Betsy interrupted him with a phone call from his attorney.

"Now what?" he asked Casey.

"I talked with the compliance officer from the Board of Health, the one who signed off on the Costa Rica mission to fulfill the community service requirements."

"And we're good? The hours are taken care of?"

"Not so good," Jim said. "A board member, presumably Umberto, asked about your community service and objected. Instead of approving the trip for the whole two hundred hours, they're giving you twenty."

Peter went silent. A month of his life, a life-threatening injury, and Luke's death all traded for what? Twenty hours of community service.

"Didn't we have board approval before I left the country? I would never have gone for twenty stinking hours."

And Luke would still be alive.

"Changing approval after the fact is not fair, but it's legal. They figure to give you credit only for the hours spent in hands-on medical care. And I need this Dr. Ryan to sign off on those hours."

"He's dead."

Now Casey was silent. "Sorry. He was a friend, right?"

"Not really."

But because of his last words, he seemed more like a friend in death than he had been in life.

Casey, apparently taking his answer as permission to continue, said, "This complicates things. Without a signature, you get no credit."

"That sucks."

"I'm just the messenger here. I'm filing a protest but don't count on a reversal. Umberto has it in for you."

Peter disconnected and put his aching right foot back on the desk. He rubbed his face with both hands, hoping to dispel the weariness that oppressed him. Then he looked at the stacks of paperwork, thought of doing another month of community service, and restarting his practice under Bell's seniority. Every problem in his life had been solved by working harder, but now the hard work came with no great likelihood of success. Furthermore, he was beginning to think that the restoration of his career held little promise of joy.

Not even hard work could get him through the day. By 3:15, the stacks of paper on his desk were diminished but still sizable, and he had seen a few, but not all, of the scheduled patients. His heart wasn't in his work. And when the work involved human beings who trusted him with their lives and their hopes, they deserved a doctor whose heart was in it.

Wondering if he would ever feel passion for his job again, he told Betsy to reschedule the remaining patients. He had always believed medicine was the highest calling, and neurosurgery the ultimate medical specialty. The climb to the mountaintop had been worth the effort, for he had gained the power to heal the most dramatic of human illnesses and injuries, and received the acclaim that went with that power. But now, like Sisyphus, he needed to push the rock back up the mountain.

Unlike Sisyphus, though, he had a choice. He could quit. But he would lose everything. So he had to work with Kelly and Bell, whose primary passions were maximizing the number of profitable cases while minimizing the necessary time and effort. Once, he had been a physician; now he was a provider. Once, the hospital had been a center for healing; now it was a center for profit. Once, caregivers had provided charity; now they provided "uninsured care," a necessary overhead cost to be managed, like janitorial services or laundry. The only humanist the hospital had was one chaplain of negligible influence, and he was there only because the Joint Commission required it.

And, if Peter was honest with himself, these were the same principles that had driven his own practice.

Up until Megan Kaiser.

Now he wanted to return to the career that let him be a healer. The profit centers could take care of themselves.

CHAPTER TWENTY-ONE

OF THE CHALLENGES he faced coming out of Costa Rica, delivering Luke's message should have been sad but simple, yet he was getting nowhere. His calls to Karen Ryan went directly to voicemail. His many messages and texts on Monday went unanswered. Finally, he checked the church's website for a notification of a memorial service for Luke, but to no avail. That night, like most nights, he slept poorly, his dreams punctuated by images of blood. Certain a gunshot had sounded, he woke in the darkness. Then he couldn't return to sleep due to the pain in his leg.

Tuesday, he moved through the office feeling slow and detached, as if underwater. He placed another futile call to Karen. Patients' problems seemed distant and abstract. Decisions were difficult. The office staff irritated him, and interruptions made him furious.

At noon Betsy called through the intercom. "Dr. Bell is here. Can I send him in?"

Peter's heart sank. He thought about the back door and the fire exit stairs, but his leg hurt. The confrontation was inevitable.

He put his leg on his desk and steeled himself. "Sure," he said.

Bell wore a dark shirt, white tie, white belt, and a smug look. His lab coat flapped at his sides like a cape.

"Welcome home, Dr. Jenson," he said as if he meant it. His thin lips curved into a smile.

Peter remained seated. "What do you want, Bell?"

Bell continued to smile. "I see you've been injured. So sorry." He looked around. "Mind if I have a seat?"

Peter waved at the nearest chair.

Bell sat down and crossed his stubby legs. "I have a business proposal for you, my friend."

"We're not friends," Peter growled.

Bell nodded and continued. "We have not been friends," he said, fixing a serious look on Peter. "But the past, though it must influence the future, may not necessarily replicate itself."

Peter was already tired of this evil, little man. "Get to the point."

"Okay, fine. I want you to transfer to Panama City," Bell said. "You have, shall we say, a limited future within the Jacksonville system. But with your ex-wife and child living here, Jacksonville is probably still your first choice of locations for future employment. And Panama City is within driving distance." Bell almost smiled. "I am prepared to offer you a position within the hospital network. The salary's admittedly lower than your current income, but with the possibility of a production-based bonus beginning next year."

Peter closed his eyes to shut Bell out. "She's not my ex. We're separated, not divorced." He opened his eyes. "And why would you be so generous?"

"We haven't gotten on well, but that doesn't make me blind. And, despite recent unfortunate publicity, you've got talent, Doctor. Sure, after you called me, what was it, 'a self-centered liar and manipulator, an incompetent'—I believe those were your words just before your infamous Kaiser case, right? After that, I did consider destroying you completely. But I thought I could use you. Now I think maybe not. But I can profit by making you disappear. Oh, and there is a small finder's fee, thirty grand, for locating a new neurosurgeon to the Panama City hospital."

"Uh-huh," Peter replied. "And why would I agree?"

"Ah," Bell said, "I thought you would have seen. Mr. Kelly will give you ninety days' notice once he hears from the board that you are not meeting the requirements of your community service and probation, and your license is likely to be revoked. He may prefer you to stay; he likes you. And he hired you. Your failure reflects on him in the corporate world." Bell smirked. "He certainly would prefer your wife to stay. But he will have no choice."

"So you're saying, move to Panama City or lose my license."

"Ah, and I was beginning to think you had become slow."

Peter said, "I'm not going anywhere."

Bell stayed seated. "Perhaps I was right. You are slow."

"I'd rather rot in hell."

Bell shrugged. "As you wish." He stood, straightened his lab coat, and walked to the door. There he turned back. "You're making a mistake, Jenson. I might not get my paltry thirty grand, but you won't have a way to make a living."

"Get out."

Bell smiled and gave him a look of near pity as he left.

Peter wanted to punch Bell, just once, to wipe the victory smirk from his fat face. But the satisfaction would be short-lived, and his leg hurt. He leaned back in his chair, briefly wondering if a new start in Panama City wasn't really the smart move. The old Jenson, the smart one, would have played his cards better. Maybe he'd refused only because Bell had wanted him to do it.

Maybe he should have taken Bell's offer, so he could expedite his divorce and get on with his life.

But he couldn't. Wouldn't. He wouldn't give up on Ellen and Daniel. Not yet.

And he had a message for Karen—if she ever would answer her phone— and a promise to Megan.

Yet all of it was hard, hard enough to make him long to escape, to go some place safe, where he was loved. To go home, to *have* a home, a real home. He had miles to go before he could sleep—a family problem, a widow problem, and a patient problem. But he would start with the problem he could deal with today.

"Betsy!" he shouted.

Betsy appeared at the doorway, pushed her glasses up, and wrinkled her nose to keep them there. "There's an intercom, you know."

"Ask me if I care. When is Kaiser's MRI?"

"Kaiser? Today, I think. They gave her a slot this morning."

He let his foot drop, tested his weight on it, and stood. "I'm going to have a look at it. What time do afternoon patients start?"

"Two o'clock."

As he limped past her, he waved over his shoulder to acknowledge he had heard.

The neuroradiology reading room was a small closet with a large computer screen at which gazed the neuroradiologist, Dr. Kyle Norton, a thin man with curly, dark hair. His spectacles reflected the images in front of him, his fingers flying from keyboard to mouse and back as he manipulated Megan Kaiser's MRI.

Peter crowded into the closet, and Norton pushed himself into a corner to share the view.

"Been awhile, Peter."

"Been out of town. Long story." He found himself already irritated. "What've you got on Kaiser?"

Norton used the mouse to point out the images on the screen. "The MRI from this morning is on the right. The one on the left was done six weeks after surgery, at the end of her radiation therapy. You can see the surgical excision site on both images, but on today's image we have this three-centimeter contrast-enhancing mass."

"Could it be radiation necrosis or post-op artifact?"

"Not likely. Looks like a recurrent tumor."

"Kind of early for recurrence," Peter said, objecting not to the truth of Norton's observations, but to the injustice, the end of hope.

"It happens." Norton's voice reflected the small sympathy of a man who is grateful that *it happens* to no one to whom he has to deliver the news.

But Peter felt those two words stab into his gut. Nauseated, his knees started to buckle.

Norton shot to his feet and shoved Peter into his chair. "Are you okay?"

This was not the first time, nor was it likely to be the last, that Peter learned a patient was about to die. He had the duty to be the messenger of doom. The old Peter, the one before Costa Rica, even took a secret pride in his skill at delivering the blow cleanly and clearing the way to prepare for death. And he knew logically that Megan's tumor would eventually recur. But he had hoped that the treatments would push her to the far end of the survival curve.

"A little leg injury," he told Norton. "I'm fine. Like you said, it happens."

He had fueled his hope with his own personal desire for her survival. But now he knew that he had hoped in vain.

Norton looked skeptical. "You don't look too good. Let me take you to the ER."

Peter gave him a wry smile. "What ails me is not something the ER can fix." He pushed himself to his feet and took extra care not to limp. "Thanks for your help."

As soon as he got to the hallway, he leaned against the wall and called the office, telling them he was sick, which was not really a lie. He was sick and tired and alone. And whatever purpose he had to his life seemed to elude him. Reconcile with a wife who has already moved on? Give a message to a grieving widow who didn't want to be found? Tell a woman she was dying soon? Try to resurrect a career in a profession that didn't seem to want or need him?

He limped out to the Honda and drove to Jacksonville Beach, parking in a public lot. He didn't feel like passing through the well-heeled clientele of his beach club, but he was drawn to the ocean, the closest thing he had left to sanctuary.

He left his coat and tie in the car and stepped onto the warm asphalt, rolling his sleeves up and breathing in the stink of tar, gasoline, spilled beer, and tobacco smoke, all muted by the promising scent of saltwater meeting the shore. He made his way to the oceanfront walk and leaned on his cane. In the past, when he had lost patients or failed in any other way, he had gone to the beach and run until the beating of the surf, the beauty of the sky, and the sweat of his brow wiped conscious thoughts from his mind, and all that remained was a primitive sense of breathing heavily in rhythm with the waves of the sea. Then he would walk back to where he had started, the power and infinity of the ocean and the sky making whatever sorrow he'd felt seem manageable and finite.

Today, however, he couldn't run. Before he reached the

sand, he turned away, already tired, and searched for a place to rest. He picked a bar with an ocean view, ordered a sandwich and a beer, looked across the sand to the sea, and sought infinity.

The tide was out and, across a vast expanse of sand, the surf rolled in, gently flattened by an offshore breeze. Above, the pastel sky of summer was broken by white clouds that appeared as if painted by an illustrator of children's books. Sea gulls swarmed in distant flocks and conga lines of brown pelicans skimmed the rolling breakers.

Peter was not the only one to seek something at the beach. Men and women of all ages ran in jogging shorts, sleeveless shirts, and baseball caps. Grizzled men with blanket rolls sat near the dunes nursing bottles in paper bags. Fishermen in wide-brimmed hats made their way across the sand with five-gallon buckets, coolers, and short heavy poles. Teen girls and aging women lay on chairs facing the sun with their eyes closed, striving for the perfect skin tone.

They all wanted something. Beauty, excitement, health, peace. And love. Peter wondered if any found what they needed. Or would these players on the beach hope today and die tomorrow, still searching? Then other players would take their places. In each, hope would rise but whether they found their way home or not, death would follow, forever.

He drank another beer and felt numbness begin in his lips. The alcohol lubricated a slide from hopelessness and grief toward apathy. All of it seemed so tiresome.

But apathy was not comfort. There was a choice. There was always a choice.

Slowly a dark plan emerged as he looked into the middle distance of the bright seascape. He waited until he could feel his lips, then drove to his apartment. Heading straight for his bedroom, he removed his Beretta from the drawer of the bedside table. On a shelf in his closet was the key to the trigger lock and a fresh box of 9 mm shells. He unlocked and loaded the pistol. Leaving the safety on, he lifted it up and down, judging heft and balance. It was heavier than he remembered.

He recalled from the dusty memory of some college humanities course that Albert Camus once wrote that suicide is the central question of all philosophy. Peter hadn't followed the argument well, but as he recalled Camus had asked why any sentient adult *wouldn't* commit suicide. The answer was, improbably, inertia. The habit of continuing to breathe.

Now, on the edge of his bed twenty years later, his inertia had run out. His practice was sliding away. His family had already left him. The person he owed something to was dying too quickly. He couldn't even deliver a dead man's last message to his wife.

Yes, in theory, he could start over—a new city, a new practice, a new lover. He was only forty-two. Yet, the effort seemed monumental, and even a successful journey back would lead to only fragile joys. Twenty more years of hard work and good luck might bring him only to where he was now, to have it all crash down again. A momentary lapse of concentration, a flash of anger, another mistake, and the imaginary new life would disappear. So much work for so little hope.

Inertia once carried him on. But now he had lost momentum, stopped dead. Now inertia paralyzed him. But he had an alternative, an easy exit from the expectations of others and his own desires. He could squeeze the trigger of a well-aimed handgun and, without even hearing the gunshot, step into the unconsciousness that lay beyond biologic life, into darkness, oblivion, and, perhaps, peace.

When hobbyists at the gun range pulled triggers, they imagined home intruders suddenly falling in clean, quiet heaps like the countless deaths they had watched on film. But Peter knew the destructive power of the handgun better than most. Death by gunshot was never quiet, rarely clean, and frequently not sudden. Many of his patients had simply missed. Bullets glanced off the skull, leaving only a shallow fracture. Pistols discharged into the mouth, aimed at the brain but merely fracturing jaws and damaging ears. Worse, a nonfatal shot could lead one to life as a turnip. Using a pistol to cause a lethal gunshot wound to the head required knowledge of anatomy, the correct procedure to load and aim, and the discipline to squeeze the trigger steadily.

He sat on the bed. He needed to think this through carefully. He had only one chance to get it right.

CHAPTER TWENTY-TWO

His phone rang. He laid the Beretta on the bed and dug the phone from his pocket. Karen Ryan—she was finally returning his calls.

He looked back at the pistol. He forced himself to answer.

"This is Peter." A silence greeted him. "Mrs. Ryan?"

A quiet voice answered, "Karen, yes. You left a message."

Peter, staring at the pistol, made himself go on. "Yes," he said. "I want to tell you how sorry I am about Luke."

"That's the message?" Impatience edged her voice.

Peter hesitated. "Luke wanted me to tell you something."

She laughed mirthlessly. "Don't forget to pay the life insurance?"

"Much more personal," he said, nonplussed.

What was wrong with her? First, she wouldn't answer her phone; now, she made sick jokes. Perhaps he should spit out Luke's dying words and hang up, go back to the Beretta.

He took two breaths to decide. Something better seemed to be required.

"We should meet."

She hesitated, maybe for two breaths, before replying.

"There's a Starbuck's on the corner of University and Beach. I can be there in thirty minutes."

I have time, Peter thought, *as much or as little as I want*. He hefted the pistol, the late afternoon sun slanting through the window blinds. "I'll be there."

He concealed the gun in a holster under his sport coat, grabbed his keys and headed for the parking lot. As he approached his car, three crows scattered away from a discarded McDonald's bag. They fled to the top of a stunted live oak where they met the wrath of a pair of audacious mockingbirds. The much smaller mockingbirds harassed the crows, trying to drive them away from their roost.

Distracted by the micro drama, Peter paused to follow it to its conclusion. When the crows finally gave up, the mockingbirds started to caw in soft syllables. Then, as Peter opened his car door, they sang another set of melodies, maybe from the wrens or the cardinals. Somehow the whole of their song was greater than the sum of all the borrowed melodies.

Amazing, he thought. Then he remembered Charles Miles' words about walking in desperation and searching for a quantum of meaning. He looked up, located the birds in the pinnacle of the tree, and wondered about what Miles had called "something more." The fatalism that had given him the illusion of peace loosened its grip.

When he arrived at the coffee shop, Karen was already seated at a table for two near the back, a cardboard cup steaming in front of her. Her black hair combed carelessly into a ponytail, she wore no makeup, a wrinkled off-white blouse, and jeans. Turquoise-silver earrings were her only jewelry.

Peter ordered a latte and sat opposite her, the holster on the back of his belt forcing him to edge forward. He probably appeared more attentive than he intended.

"I tried to call," he said.

She nodded.

"Several times."

A long blink and a shrug. "And you want to know why I didn't pick up? Why I wasn't so eager to hear the details of my husband's death?"

"I'm sorry."

"So you said." She folded her hands around her cup, gazing into the steam. "He didn't want to take you. I forced him."

Peter felt guilt well up. "I meant him no harm."

"Nor did I." She lifted her cup to her lips and gave him an accusing stare. "Yet, he is dead."

Peter wanted to tell her the events were unpredictable, that others, evil ones, were responsible. Not him and not her. But she wasn't wrong. If she had not said what she'd said, if he had not done what he'd done, Luke would still be alive.

"Yes," he said. "He is."

She put the cup back on the table and regarded him with a flat expression. "You have something you wish to tell me?"

Actually, he wished to return to his room and his pistol, but he had come this far. With this promise fulfilled, perhaps he would find it easier to pull the trigger without guilt.

So he spit it out. "He knew he was dying, and he asked me to carry a message to you."

Tears welled in the corners of her eyes.

"He said to tell you that you were the love of his life."

She sniffed. "No, it was Jane."

"He said you would think so. He wanted me to tell you it was you."

The tears rolled freely now. She blotted them with brown napkins and hid her face.

Her pain was contagious. Peter stopped thinking about the Beretta and ached for her loss, their loss. He awkwardly took one of her hands.

She sniffed again and wiped her nose. "Thank you," she said. "I know it wasn't your fault."

"Nor yours." He waited through another minute of quiet tears. "What will you do now?"

"I don't know," she said. "What I have been doing is this." She pulled her hand away and retrieved a brown paper bag from her purse. It clunked onto the table.

"And that is . . . ?"

"A bottle of death. Suicide, one shot at a time. A means to step into the arms of the angels."

"Poison?"

"Bourbon."

Peter was silenced, shocked by her weakness. Somehow, he had expected her to be stronger than he was.

"The curse of my people, the Lakota," she explained. "I met Luke when I had just been released from inpatient treatment and had started working again. I was a social worker at the medical clinic on the Pine Ridge Reservation. He was my rock." She paused, wiping the last of her tears and crumpling the napkin. Her hands went back to the paper bag. "Only ties of love allowed me to live sober. Now . . ."

"That's why you didn't take my calls."

She shrugged. "Your calls harassed me enough to make me think about getting help. First time since I moved to Florida I called AA. With Luke at my side I didn't feel like I needed anyone else."

"John said something . . . but I didn't know."

"Yeah, well, no way you could have. That's why the second *A* stands for *anonymous*. I didn't really want anybody to hear about the real me."

"The real you? Really?"

"I haven't been to a meeting yet, but they assigned me a

sponsor, a real veteran of AA coming off a relapse himself. He says he knows you."

Peter raised his eyebrows.

"The rules say I shouldn't tell you who it is. But when he heard me complain about your calls, he said I should call you back. I wouldn't have, except for the story he told me."

Peter shifted in his chair, the Beretta a constant, uncomfortable reminder. "The *A* is safe with me. I don't have a clue who you're talking about."

"Luis Alvarez."

The name stunned Peter. He hadn't had any contact with Alvarez since the day of the transfusion, didn't even know if he'd survived. Or if he knew who his doctor had been.

"You're like Jesus Christ to him. Literally." Karen's eyes now bore into him, as if she challenged him to answer an accusation. "He says you brought him back from the dead."

He lowered his eyes. No way did he feel like anybody's savior, especially as he faced Karen Ryan.

"Just doing my job," he said. "Long story. I'm glad he's doing well."

He looked up to find Karen's eyes still holding him, still waiting for a better explanation. Or a better excuse. He decided that silence would be his best option.

She crinkled the brown paper wrapping with both hands. "I've been sober for twenty-four hours," she said, "so I returned your call. Now I have to arrange Luke's memorial."

"I was wondering," he said.

"Maybe a service next week. The body is being shipped. Apparently the church carried travel health insurance that covers return of the remains." Her eyes stayed on the bag. "They say it was a hunting accident. He was mistaken for a wild boar."

"Lies."

"Of course," she said. "I want you to promise me something."

He was wary of another promise. "What?"

"You'll speak at the memorial?"

He remained silent. One hand went behind his back to feel the Beretta.

She stared and waited.

"I don't know if I'll be here," he said.

She frowned.

He looked around the shop. No customers were nearby. He slipped the pistol out of the holster and laid it on the table between them.

"What is that?"

"Death," he said. "Suicide, one shot at a time. A means to step into the arms of the angels."

She stared at him.

"If there are any," he said.

"Oh, there are angels for sure," she said, shaking her head. "And demons, even more certainly."

They faced each other silently for a minute, Karen's hands wrapped around brown paper, Peter's covering cold steel.

"You want me to promise I won't kill myself," he said.

"And you want me to promise I won't drink," she said. "But I can't."

"Nor can I." He thought of the next twenty-four hours, especially of telling Megan she was about to die. "But I can make it one more day."

Two coffee cups cooled between them as they examined each other and the bargain they had just made. They both nodded, as good as a handshake to confirm their agreement. He holstered the gun, and they left the shop together. At the door, Karen dropped the bag into the trashcan. She winced at the sound of breaking glass.

"Did he say anything else?" she asked.

Peter went back to that night by the black river. "Jesus loves me," he said.

"I guess," she said. "Sometimes that's all we've got."

That, he thought, *and mockingbirds*.

CHAPTER TWENTY-THREE

On Wednesday afternoon, Betsy appeared in the doorway to his office. "Two more patients. The next one we have listed as Dr. Bell's, but he insists on seeing you."

It had been a long day. His leg hurt and despair fluttered around the edges of his thoughts. A sense of duty and a deal with Karen were the only things that kept him focused on the tasks at hand.

"New patient or follow up?" he asked.

"Says you saw him in the hospital."

"What's his name?"

"Alvarez. Luis Alvarez."

The second time he had heard that name in as many days. Only he couldn't let Alvarez know anything about his conversation with Karen, that she had named him as her sponsor.

Alvarez was skinny and sallow, black stubble and a Braves cap hiding his scar. He stood when Peter entered, shaky and uncertain, glancing sideways before meeting Peter's eyes.

Peter gestured for him to sit again.

"I heard what you did," Alvarez said.

"I was on-call. Any surgeon would have done the same."

"Maybe. Except this time you did it for me. So thanks."

The weight of the Beretta on his waistband had not left him, though the pistol was in the trunk of his car. He felt like Death walked behind his left shoulder at all times, and it would be easy to stop and turn to him at any moment. Now, as Luis Alvarez stood before him alive, he who would have been dead, Death took a step backwards.

"I think I might have done it as much for me as for you," Peter said.

Luis cocked his head and raised an eyebrow. "I don't know about that," he said. "But what happened with my mother?"

Peter didn't know how to answer. "What did you hear?"

"Nothing. That's the problem."

"What do you mean?"

"My mother sued the hospital and the hospital settled by writing off the balance of the bill."

Peter hadn't known that, but it sounded like how Kelly would have spun it. "Mistakes happen," he said.

"Yeah, but what mistake? Here I am." He splayed his hands at his side in demonstration.

"What did your mother tell you?"

"Nothing. She don't say much to me anymore. I got to live at her house as I ain't working, but it's like I'm not there. She sure don't like you, though, and I can't figure why not."

"Sometimes I'm not very likable." It was the only honest answer he could give.

Luis looked away. "No, me neither. But I got another chance now." He held out a tremulous hand.

He took Luis's hand and held it, perhaps too firmly. Luis seemed to flinch. "I hear the Waffle House is hiring," Peter told him.

When Peter sent Luis on his way, he headed to his last appointment, the one that he dreaded.

Megan was huddled in a chair beside the exam table. She did not appear relieved to see him. "Well?" she asked.

He sat down at the computer screen and tapped a few keys. The images of her MRI scan appeared. He motioned with his hand, inviting her to examine the screen. She looked at the black and white abstractions for three seconds before she fixed her gaze again on his face.

"Well?" she asked again.

Peter swiveled his chair to face her completely. Unable to meet her eyes, he looked down at his folded hands. He had hoped that the office setting, the white coat, the quasi-official chart, and the technologic display of computer-generated MRI images would make a recurrent malignancy into something clinical and distant. Instead, it felt raw and close.

He glanced at her face before swiveling back to the screen. "I've selected three images to show you," he said. "The scan on the right shows your tumor before surgery, and the scan in the middle shows your scan after surgery and radiation."

He looked over his shoulder at her before continuing. Her eyes now focused on the computer screen.

"And this," he said, pointing to the last image, "is the scan you had two days ago. As you can see . . ."

"Cut the doctor crap. I see butterflies and storm clouds. Just tell me."

He couldn't risk turning around. "Your tumor came back. This is it, right here." He gestured at a cauliflower shape on the last image. "It isn't as big as it was on your first scan. But it was gone at six weeks and now it's back at twelve."

"Meaning what?"

He swiveled to face her, forced himself to look her in the eye, and shook his head.

She searched his face. "How long have I got?" she asked quietly.

"There are options, of course. We could try a different kind of chemotherapy. Medical centers at Gainesville, Duke, Mayo, MD Anderson all have promising experimental protocols."

"Knock it off. Talk to me. Not doctor to patient. Friend to friend. I need to trust you to give it to me straight."

He looked at his hands again, unfolded them, and turned the palms up. "Six weeks. No more. Maybe less."

Silence filled the small space. Peter turned back to the computer, blocking himself from her pain with the contrived need to log out. But grief weighed him down. Losses built upon losses—Ellen, Luke, his practice, and now Megan. More than at any time in his career—no, more than any time in his life—despair closed an icy grip on his heart. Only his deal with Karen kept him from reconsidering the option of the Beretta.

Then he felt her hand on his shoulder.

"It's okay," she said. "We knew this day was coming. Don't feel bad."

But he did feel bad. He thought he knew how to tell patients difficult truths; it had gotten easier as the years went by. But now each hour of each day seemed precious. Everyone chose life until life was no longer a choice. Almost everyone, almost always, even Luis Alvarez.

"Will you pray with me?" she asked.

Pray. The word was more familiar now, the concept better known, but the practice was still foreign. In the past, whenever a patient would make this request, he would excuse himself by appealing to the privacy of each individual's beliefs. He hadn't even prayed over Luke's body.

"I . . . I don't know how," he said, still facing a computer screen that he no longer saw.

"It's easy," she said. "It's just talking to God, telling Him what you feel, asking Him for what you want."

"I've never done it."

"We'll give it a try. I'll pray. You fold your hands and close your eyes so you're not distracted. Then you can add something if you want."

"Okay," he said and closed his eyes. He took a breath and tried to think of nothing, especially not of the cauliflower shape on the last MRI. But he could not ignore the small, warm hand on his shoulder.

"Father God, I'm frightened," she said. "I know you tell us not to be afraid of death and that someday we will live with you forever, but I'm still scared. Help my unbelief. Give me courage. Keep me from pain. Send the right people to help me. Thank you, Jesus."

Silence followed, and after a few seconds Peter realized this was his turn. He hesitated, embarrassed and uncertain. Then, trusting Megan more than God, he spoke.

"Ah, God, if you're there, and I'm beginning to think you are, heal Megan. Just heal her. Nobody else has ever been cured of this kind of tumor, but if you're God, you can do it." He paused, unable to think of anything else to say.

"Amen," she said.

"Ah . . . amen," he said.

He opened his eyes and swiveled his chair around. She had stepped back to lean on the exam table. Her arms crossed, she was smiling, looking peaceful.

"That wasn't so hard, was it?" she asked.

"The prayer thing?" He shrugged. "Not so hard, I guess. You think it helps?"

She nodded. "Ten years ago, I was trying to kick a cocaine habit and get off the streets. I'd gone from hit to hit, and trick to trick, since I dropped out of high school and ran away from home. I figured I'd die and was afraid I wouldn't. I prayed, and He sent people like Luke and Karen. I got a life. Maybe not much compared to what you got, but a life."

Peter nodded, thinking how wrong she was about his life.

"So I had ten good years. And time to plan for the end of this life before I go to heaven. So, yeah, I think it works. I think God sent you."

Peter wasn't so sure. Karen thought God had sent him, too, and look how that turned out. And if God had sent him to Megan, maybe He could have kept him from screwing up the operation in the first place. His prayer seemed likely to go unanswered.

"You need a ride home?" he asked.

"I've got an Uber account."

"You mean, yes. You do need a ride home."

She smiled. "I mean, I would enjoy a ride home if you're not too busy."

Busy he was not. His practice was dying, strangled by Bell. He dictated a short note and walked her to his car.

"New car?" she asked.

"The old one didn't seem to fit anymore."

She sat in the passenger seat. "Yeah. A lot easier to get into."

He started the car. "Can I ask you something?"

"Like I'd have anything to hide now?"

"This is personal." He pulled out into rush hour traffic.

"I'm dying," she said. "And you're helping me, so, yes, you can ask me anything."

"So you believe in those prayers?"

"Even Jesus prayed not to die, but he trusted his Father in heaven to do his will. I believe God loves me."

"What do you think happens after you die? Angel wings, harps, flitting cloud to cloud?" He didn't want to discourage her, but he wanted to know. The only thing that made sense to him was enduring unconsciousness. The brain stops, consciousness stops, the body decays.

"The ones who have touched the edges of heaven," she said,

"those with near-death stories, talk about light and a feeling of going home."

"You seem so sure."

"My life—the last ten years, anyway—is a miracle. Seems natural that my death would be a miracle, too."

The Beretta was in the trunk, its presence haunting him. He thought of it as a tool to obliterate the unpleasantness of life, not to unlock the passageway to paradise.

He stole a quick glance at her. "But you don't think suicide would keep you out of heaven?"

She stared forward, stoic. "Jesus loves me. He sent you to guide me to Him."

He wanted to tell her that Jesus hadn't sent him anywhere to do anything, and the last time someone thought like that people died, perhaps needlessly. But he owed her, and she was dying. His objections could wait. So could the Beretta.

CHAPTER TWENTY-FOUR

THE NEXT DAY he sent Karen a text: *I'm still alive.* She replied —*Me 2*—and Peter wondered if she was also still sober.

The following morning she called. "Luke's memorial will be next Friday at ten o'clock."

"I'll be there," Peter replied.

"I asked you to speak because I wasn't sure I'd be sober. I'm still not."

"I said yes because I wasn't sure I'd be alive."

A pause, long enough to remember the deal, their one-day-at-a-time non-suicide pact.

"You don't have to if you don't want to," she said. "Pastor Nick could do the eulogy."

"Your call," he said, hoping the pastor would be her choice. "We had a long history, not a long friendship."

"Yes, but you were there when his heart broke. You were there when he died."

Peter didn't kill Luke's wife and child. But he also didn't do anything to prevent his grief from overwhelming him. Peter didn't kill Luke. But he insisted on doing the operation that incited the murderous response from the shaman. Those didn't seem like good qualifications to do a eulogy. On the other hand, he couldn't say no to her. Not today.

Each day he texted her: *Still alive.* Each day she replied: *Me 2.*

It was a thin thread to hang onto, just one other desperate person who shared despair and kept on waking up and walking and talking and pretending they were alive. But it was enough to get by. He never unloaded the Beretta; its availability was never far from his consciousness. He expected Karen thought the same thing about her nearest drink.

Then, on the day of the memorial, Peter woke up and exchanged the same texts and wondered if they would do so again the next day, if there would be some sort of closure, whatever that was, or even more despair. He put on his blue suit, the one he hated because of where he always went when he wore it. He wore it on the days he had to do an operation with a high chance of a bad outcome. He wore it to borrow money. And he wore it to funerals. Today, he matched it with the dark blue tie with thin red stripes. He needed to look like he was giving a eulogy to a friend.

As he knotted and adjusted the tie, a knock interrupted his musings. No one ever visited, except Daniel, and he didn't need to knock; Peter always picked him up. He went to the door expecting to see something like two Mormon missionary kids in white shirts holding a handful of tracts. A repeated series of loud knocks convinced him that Mormons, whatever else they believed, were not big on patience.

He jerked open the door to find Ellen, red-faced, red-knuckled, and dressed for business in a gray pantsuit and white silk blouse.

"I need you to take Daniel," she demanded.

He hadn't seen her in weeks and, for a moment, wondered

what it was that he had missed about her. Daniel cowered behind her hip.

"Good morning," Peter said.

"I don't have time for that. Here's your kid."

"Hey, Daniel. I was planning on picking you up at four o'clock."

"Study day," Daniel mumbled.

"What are you talking about?" Peter asked.

"Finals next week," Ellen said. "No school. It's on the school website if you ever bothered to look at it."

"And that explains what?" he asked. "You want to come in and explain this?"

"No. Listen, I should have sent you a text."

Or called, he thought.

"But I called your office and they said you have the morning off."

He stuck out his chin while he opened his palms. "For a *funeral*."

She had incredible hutzpah to show up here and pretend this was his fault. About to meet her anger with his own, he looked at her and saw something else. Not panic exactly, but some kind of frantic anxiety. Fear.

"Listen," she said, "I came because I didn't want to give you a chance to say no."

He took in the clothes and guessed. "You have an appointment."

"I've got twenty minutes to get to a design presentation for the contract of the new First Coast Country Club."

For a brief moment he wondered if he should say no or at least make her say please. But then he saw Daniel, still cowering behind her, the bystander, the real victim.

"Sure," he said. "No problem."

Her expression relaxed. But she didn't say either please or thank you before she turned and walked away.

"I'm not your enemy," he called after her.

She hesitated, then stopped and looked back. She stood for a moment regarding him before she hurried away.

He closed the door, a myriad of emotions roiling within—love, anger. Hope, maybe. Hands shaking, knees weak, he leaned against the door and breathed. When he opened his eyes he found Daniel staring at him, backpack still attached, an overnight bag by his feet. He was wearing khaki shorts and a faded t-shirt.

"You don't happen to have a blue suit along, do you?" Peter asked.

Daniel shook his head, puzzled and nervous. He was at an awkward size, too little to hug and too big to pick up. But Peter picked him up anyway and hugged him. He put his head in Daniel's mop of curly, brown hair and breathed in. *I'm still alive*, he thought. Suddenly the despair that had made the Beretta seem like such a good idea became distant and absurd.

"Hey! Lemme go!" Daniel squealed.

Peter put him down and squatted next to him, keeping his hands on his shoulders. "I've missed you, son."

"Hey," he said, "I was just here last week. No big deal."

Peter hugged him again and let him squirm. Because it *was* a big deal, and he didn't have the words to explain why.

He found a collared shirt and some long pants for Daniel, good enough that he wouldn't be a distraction, not good enough if his mother had dressed him for the same occasion. Daniel had never been to a funeral before, and perhaps this was the right introduction—someone he didn't know or love.

The coffin stayed closed. A few days in the jungle would not have been kind to a corpse. It didn't matter to Peter. He didn't need to see the body to remember a montage of Luke through the years. The eager, young resident. The anxious father. The grieving widower. Then a blank screen until the angry family doctor appeared. The reluctant partner in the mission. Then a dying man on a dark night, his black blood pooling in a cold river.

Daniel sat next to Peter and nudged him. "Was he your friend?" he whispered.

Peter tried to think of a quick response that a child would understand, something that would be true. "He did me big favor."

"So maybe he was your friend," Daniel said.

Peter leaned in to whisper, "He didn't like me."

Daniel didn't say anything for a few seconds. Then he asked, "Can I use your iPhone?"

Peter muted the phone and handed it over. It seemed disrespectful to allow him to tap on a screen, but at least he would be quiet. Peter didn't really expect him to pay serious attention to the funeral.

By then, the church was nearly full. Peter recognized a few doctors and nurses. Lots of churchy-looking people surrounded Karen, hugging her and drying her tears. While they waited for the service to begin, wordless music that Peter did not recognize played over the muted voices. In the front of the church stood the closed oak coffin, a poster-sized photo of Luke mounted on top.

The clergyman—Pastor Nick, if Peter remembered correctly—entered from a side door and stood above and behind the coffin in his black robes. He welcomed the congregation and announced the "celebration of life," a choice of words that Peter considered ridiculous. This was a recognition of death, a time of permanent farewell, a time to mourn and acknowledge the presence and power of chaos. A good bar is a place for celebrations; a church is a place for funerals.

A soloist sang a sad song, after which Pastor Nick read some Bible passages. Next, he gave a mini-Easter sermon about the dead rising and seeing our loved one in heaven. *Uh-huh*, Peter thought, *the things we tell ourselves to feel better*. Then it was his turn to "say a few words," "deliver the eulogy," or whatever they wanted to call it. To him, it was just atonement for his part in causing Luke's death and a favor to Karen, his part in their day-to-day survival bargain.

Peter left Daniel engrossed in his video game and walked to the lectern. He faced the church crowd and shuffled his three-by-five cards. For the first time, he noticed a few scruffy stragglers filling the pews in the back, perhaps free clinic clients, and amongst them, Megan. The black Waffle House uniform with the matching black headscarf made her look even more pale than she had appeared the week before in the clinic.

He should have expected her, of course. Luke and Karen had befriended her and made sure she got treatment for her tumor. But somehow her presence surprised him, as if someone so close to death herself should not be expected to spend any of her last precious days near coffins and graves.

He paused, shuffled the cards again, knew he wouldn't look at them, and started talking. He didn't lie, not exactly. After all, a eulogy was supposed to be the "true word." So he talked about how Luke had been a hard worker and a loving father. How he suffered great tragedies with grace. He skipped over Luke's bitterness and anger, his long, drunken binge and disappearance after Jane's death, the way he could bear a grudge for years with strength and commitment. Then he told them what they all knew, and what they wanted to hear: Luke was passionate and compassionate, even at the cost of his life. He was faithful to his

God and loving to not only his fellow man, but to his friends and his wife.

Karen wept and mouthed, "Thank you."

Megan was too far away to see. Daniel kept his head down, concentrating on his game, frenetically tapping the screen. Peter came back to the pew and sat down.

Daniel handed him the phone. "He *was* your friend," he said.

CHAPTER TWENTY-FIVE

Another week went by. The daily texts continued. *Still Alive . . . Me 2*. On Wednesday Megan called, unable to work with a headache and drowsiness.

"Why do you care, anyway?" he asked her. "You can't need the money."

"It's how I prove to myself that I'm still alive."

Dying people want to be normal. He knew that, but somehow thought that Megan would want to do something more significant than wait tables. "Come in this morning for some labs. Maybe the anticonvulsant levels are too high or your sodium is too low. Stop by the office and I'll have a prescription for pain pills."

He had thin hope that the labs would find something easily corrected. But he didn't think there would be much risk in starting narcotics for pain; it was too late for that. She was nearing the end.

Two days later, Peter looked at normal lab results and knew the only explanation for her symptoms was tumor growth. Narcotics were the only drugs likely to help. He went cold as he realized it was time to fulfill his promise: to be with her at the end, to be sure she could end her life on her own terms. But he didn't want to do it, not alone. He had already tried hospice. They could not see her before Monday. He needed someone who knew Megan and knew about death and dying and mourning.

I'm alive, he texted. *Can I call?*

His cell rang a moment later. "I'm alive, too," she said.

"Megan Kaiser," he replied.

"I remember."

"She's dying."

"You knew this, though. Right?"

"I don't mean sometime. I mean she's dying now."

Silence. "Are you there?" he asked.

"Yeah. Just a lot of dying lately."

"You're okay?"

"I'm sober, if that's what you mean."

Exactly what he meant. "I can't get hospice until Monday. I'm going over to see how bad she is."

"And you're telling me, why?"

"I don't want to face her alone."

"I don't want to face her at all. I'm tired."

"Megan needs you."

Silence.

"I need you." He waited in the continuing silence, uncertain whether he would hear her voice or the click that signaled a disconnect.

"Pick me up in twenty minutes," she said. "I'll be ready."

Together they rang the bell at Megan's apartment and waited. Then rang again and knocked. Then rang again and pounded.

Peter had already pulled out his cell to call 911 when a bedraggled Megan opened the door.

"I'm sorry." She stepped back unsteadily and bumped into her table. She leaned on it, and then fell into one of the chairs.

Karen hurried in and sat beside her. "Are you all right?"

Megan put her elbow on the table and leaned her forehead against her hand. "The headache is okay. The pills, though—they make me groggy. I can't keep my eyes open."

"You don't have to, honey," Karen said. "Let's help you back to bed."

Peter helped Karen usher Megan back to the bedroom, then went to the living room and sat on the couch. The order and cleanliness that had given this place charm was gone. Dust balls floated in the corners, a crumpled napkin lay under the table, and the sink overflowed with dirty dishes.

She had, at best, a couple days before she would become confused and bedridden. Even if hospice could come today, they would only give her good nursing care and adequate pain medications. She would linger in confusion and a coma for days, possibly weeks, before the end.

That was specifically what she had not wanted. That was specifically what he had promised to stop.

He paced around the small room, knowing he should have planned for this moment. So what was he going to do? Put a pillow over her head in this sad little apartment? He looked at the beach photograph above the sofa and the glass vase filled with seashells on the kitchen counter. He got the beginnings of a better idea—or at least a better setting.

Karen came out of the bedroom. "She's sleeping. What now?"

"I'll get her some steroids. That might help. Then she needs to go to the beach."

"She needs a bed and a quiet place and someone to care for her."

"She's going to a quiet place for a long time," he said. "She'll want to see the beach again."

Karen looked back at the closed bedroom door. "Does she know?"

Peter nodded.

"She did love the beach," Karen acknowledged. "You want me to stay with her?"

"I promised I'd be with her at the end. But I can't do it alone. So, yes."

"Okay, I'll be there. You okay here for now?"

"I guess."

"Fine. I'll take an Uber home, pack a bag, and meet you wherever you take her. Call me."

Peter reserved an oceanfront room on the ground floor at a Ponte Vedra resort, called in a prescription for steroids he could pick up on his way, then called the office to tell them to reschedule his patients.

He kicked off his shoes and stretched out on the couch to think. By tomorrow, perhaps Megan would be in heaven. That's what she believed, anyway, and that's what she wanted. And Peter hoped it was true. If heaven were real, she belonged there.

But she also expected him to do what was necessary to get her there with the least amount of indignity and suffering. He didn't think she intended that he should murder her, only that he provide her with the means to do it herself. Assisted suicide was the euphemism for the almost acceptable, almost legal, practice.

He ran a list of potentially lethal prescriptions through his head. Narcotics, sedatives, even blood pressure medications were potential candidates, but the nausea, vomiting, slow absorption of the drugs from the stomach, and unpredictable timing of death were all problems. Anesthetic drugs would be best, delivered through an IV, but he didn't have access to that today.

He was still musing when he heard the shower running; shortly after Megan emerged from the bedroom. Her hair was but wisps of yellow, the thick blonde curls he had shaved from her scalp a distant memory, and her scars were angry red lines. But her eyes were blueberry-hued and warmly open, her face smooth and young. She wore ragged denim shorts and a light-blue t-shirt. She raised her hand as if to brush back the hair that no longer fell in her face.

Pleasantly surprised at her recovery, Peter found himself hoping he was wrong about her inevitable, impending death. But then again, MRI scans didn't lie.

"You feel better?" he asked.

"Yes. Much better. Headache is barely there, and the dope wore off." She paused and frowned. "But I'm not taking any more of that. I'd rather hurt."

Peter stood. "Would you like to go to the beach?"

She looked around the small refuge she had created for herself, perhaps also taking in the increasing disorder, and turned back to Peter. "Absolutely."

"I have a reservation for a beachfront room in Ponte Vedra for this afternoon. It should be ready right now."

She smiled, a kid offered an ice cream cone, but then the shadow returned. "This is it, isn't it?"

His silence conveyed the truth.

"Okay," she said, "let me rephrase that without the question mark. This is it. I don't want to hurt, and I don't want to be drugged. I want to go to heaven before the next bad headache."

He wanted to say no, but put his arm around her shoulder instead.

The room had two double beds and opened onto a small patio and patch of grass. On the grass, two white Adirondack chairs faced the ocean, and beyond the grass a narrow sidewalk ran along the inland side of a low seawall. Beyond the seawall lay an expanse of sand and beyond the sand lay the Atlantic Ocean. Above the ocean hung the evening sky, deepening purple streaked with pink and yellow, a dark cloud looming in the distance. A few degrees above the horizon, the moon cut a small crescent slit in the sky.

Megan put on a black swimsuit that hung loosely on her wasted frame and tied a blue bandana around her head to hide her scars. Peter took her arm to steady her as she walked across the sand to the surf. She opened her arms as if to embrace the beauty of the dying day. A wave crashed at her feet, and she stumbled. Peter reached out again to catch her. She laughed and hugged him.

He flinched, startled by the warmth. Getting close wasn't the plan. He was trying to say goodbye. But she leaned into him, and he relaxed. *This is only one night*, he told himself. *I can give comfort for one night.*

He led her back to their room. She covered herself with a resort robe and collapsed into the Adirondack chair.

"Thank you," she said, "for all this." She waved a glass of ice water, toasting the evening sky.

"My pleasure," he said.

The beach had always been his refuge. This was where he had built sand castles with Daniel and—years ago, it seemed now—had walked with Ellen, holding hands. If he had ever felt at home, it was here. And somehow Megan's presence seemed exactly right.

His phone buzzed in his pocket. When he pulled it out, the

number from St. Luke's emergency room stared up at him. He debated with himself before answering; he wasn't on call, and it could only be trouble. But then, maybe it was personal. Maybe it was Daniel. Or Ellen.

He swiped to take the call.

"Dr. Jenson, this is Dr. Tito from the ER."

"Dr. Bell's on call today."

"That's just it, Dr. Jenson. Dr. Bell's the patient."

Peter sat down on the other chair, dimly aware that the colorful sky was fading to darkness. "What's wrong with him?"

"He's been beat up. He says it's an old patient and her boyfriend wanting drugs or something. Looks like he's got a spinal cord injury. The radiologist says he has jumped facets at C5-6 on his CT, and a disk herniation on his MRI at the same level. He's wiggling his toes but he doesn't have much of a grip."

Peter ran this description of the injury and images through his mind. Bell would need an operation at the earliest opportunity to have any chance of not being crippled.

"Not really my problem," he told Tito. "I'm not on call, and I don't think he wants me anyway."

"But he does want you. He asked specifically for you."

"You can send him to Shands in Gainesville."

"Well, I can. And I've already called. There's a Dr. Kirby there who's willing to accept him in transfer."

"Dr. Kirby?" Peter asked. "Are you sure?"

Peter knew Kirby. He was a well-respected and experienced pediatric neurosurgeon at the University, but had no expertise in spine-related conditions in adults.

"Yeah. He said he was the only one on call, but he had plenty of residents to help him."

Peter understood. The American Association of Neurological Surgeons annual meeting had started today in San Francisco. Everybody from the University who had a paper to present would be at the meeting. Most of the neurosurgeons in Jacksonville would also be at the meeting. Bell understood this, too. He knew he needed surgery and didn't want the least experienced spine surgeon at the university supervising a trainee resident for an operation that would make the difference between whether he could feed himself or not.

He thought about Bell sabotaging the OR schedule, gloating over his Board of Medicine censure, smirking as he suggested relocating to Panama City. He felt his anger rise. Let him take his chances on a hundred-mile helicopter ride, the pediatric neurosurgeon and the junior resident.

Then he envisioned Bell lying on an ER stretcher gasping for breath, unable to make a fist, to sit up or roll over, no way to commit suicide even if he wanted to. Pity crept into Peter's anger, and the guilt of being a doctor eroded his resolution. *I could go see*, he told himself. *My obligation would be fulfilled*.

He told Tito he would come, but not to cancel the transfer arrangements. Not yet. He called Karen and gave her the room number. Then he told Megan he had to leave.

Her eyes narrowed and her mouth thinned. "You promised."

"Karen will be here in a few minutes."

"You promised," she repeated.

"I will be back as soon as I can."

She looked doubtful.

"Hey," he said. "I haven't forgotten. Until the end. I owe you."

CHAPTER TWENTY-SIX

IN THE ER, he found Bell on a stretcher loosely covered with a hospital gown and a sheet, an IV in each arm and an oxygen cannula in his nose. Peter hesitated, thinking that maybe pity would replace the repugnance that welled up, but his wish was not fulfilled. He stepped forward to speak to Bell as an act of will, not an act of compassion.

A soft cervical collar encircled Bell's neck and five-pound sandbags lay on either side of his head. Abrasions covered his nose, chin, and left forehead, and swelling nearly closed his right eye. Peter walked around the stretcher to where Bell could easily see him despite the restraints around his neck.

"Dr. Bell," he said.

"Peter. You're a sight for sore eyes, my friend. I'm in a pickle here."

My friend.

Peter gritted his teeth. "What happened?"

"I want you to know I always liked you. Respected you. That thing about your boy, Alvarez? Why, that worked out fine. Your job, too. It's secure. I was just messing with you. I was."

"Right," Peter said, shaking his head, "but I asked about what happened to you."

"And that nasty business with the board. That's going to be behind you in a flash. I'll do everything I can to help."

Peter grimaced and pushed on. "Bell, listen to me. I need to know what happened to you if I've got any chance of helping you. You need to act like you're a patient and I'm your doctor. If you can't handle it, go to Shands."

"No, no. I'm not stupid. I need my cord decompressed and my spine stabilized now. By the best person available. And that's you."

"I'm not on call and I'm not your friend."

"Peter. Think about it. I can help you. You know I can."

Peter could feel his face redden. "Listen, Bell. Let's get something straight right now. I don't trust you." His hand began to tremble. "If you do badly, you'll sue me. If you do well, you'll forget."

Bell was silent except for his labored breathing. "I sure won't forget if you walk away," he finally said.

"No. Of course you won't. But I don't care anymore. I can live without you, this hospital, this state, or even, if I have to, without this profession."

He had people who needed him. Daniel and Megan. They deserved his time and attention.

Bell opened his mouth and gobbled air like a fish on land. Flat immobility made breathing hard for a fat man.

"You're saying you won't take care of me?"

"I'm saying you should tell me what happened, I'll take a look at you and the CT and the MRI, and we could talk about it."

"So you're saying you'll—"

Peter interrupted. "I'm saying you should tell me what happened to you."

Bell blinked twice and refocused. "I had this patient, a woman with disability forms and a chronic pain problem. I think you might have seen her once."

Peter remembered the patient who was willing to "transfer benefits."

"I told her that I was . . . ah . . . discharging her from my care. Too many requests for drugs."

Peter figured there were likely other reasons. If she had used him for drugs and a disability scam, he had used her as well. She must have upped the ante, added cash to her requests, possibly.

"She said I shouldn't do that. I could get hurt."

"And?" Peter asked.

"And when I left the hospital today, her boyfriend meets me in the parking lot. I'd met him before, but this time he shoves me, tells me I should reconsider. Just a taste, he said, of what broken promises could lead to."

"So you got beat up."

"He hit me once on the chin and my head snapped back. I felt a pop in my neck, electricity in my arms and legs. I fell back and couldn't get up. Then he kicked me in the ribs and walked away."

"What time was that?"

"I don't know. About four, I guess."

Peter checked his watch. It was now after eight. His cord had been compressed for four hours. Every additional minute made recovery less likely.

He left to look at the CT and MRI images, finding that at least in self-diagnosis Bell was correct. His best chance for recovery was with an open reduction of the dislocation, removal of the disk that was compressing his spinal cord, and fusing the vertebrae together, an operation Peter had done frequently and well. Bell was also right about timing: the quicker, the better. Transport to another facility added the risk of additional injury as well as the risk of delayed treatment, and the longer an older man like Bell was immobilized, the more likely he would suffer other medical complications.

On the other hand, this was Bell, the man who had cost Peter his job and abused his position to control a drug-dependent patient, and he was now suffering the consequences of his own shady actions. To Peter, treating Bell seemed like trying to save his own executioner. It wasn't his responsibility; he wasn't on call. Alternative providers, though not convenient, were available.

Peter slipped out of the emergency room and took the elevator to the sixth floor, the last stop, then found the stairwell and climbed up. He opened the steel door that led to the roof and walked into the warm, humid Florida night. Muffled traffic noise swirled below. The lights of the city blurred the night sky, limiting the number of visible stars to those directly overhead. This wasn't the beach, nor was it a place of silence and natural beauty, but at least it was a place of solitude, a place where he could hear his own voice.

But he chose to hear another voice. He sat on the parapet and called the room in Ponte Vedra. Karen answered.

"I'm alive," he said.

"Me too," she answered.

"How's Megan?"

"Sleepy, kind of. Didn't want to, but I made her take a pain pill."

He told her about Bell. "I don't know," he said. "I don't think I can take care of him."

"Okay. Come on back here then."

His heart started beating in his throat. "He's a nasty, evil man who abuses his role as a physician to hurt anybody who stands in the way of his power and his vanity."

"Right," she said. "He can find somebody else."

His hands trembled now as he stifled his anger. "Yes, he can."

"So what's the problem?"

"If I walk away, he never walks again."

The phone went silent. Peter thought he had lost the connection. Then Karen said, "I'm here. We'll be okay."

Peter wondered if this is why he'd called. To get permission. But he said, "I don't have to do it."

"If you don't," Karen said, "you will remember for the rest of your life why you didn't, and you will feel guilty. To justify what you didn't do, you will rekindle your anger, and that anger will consume you. You will grant him the power to make you angry for the rest of your life."

What she said sounded right. But when he tried again to imagine treating Bell, rage rose inside of him. "I don't think it's possible."

"It's possible," Karen said, "but you have to give it over to your higher power."

Karen was talking AA ten steps lingo about that same *Father God* that Megan had prayed to, not a resource available to him. He didn't have a higher power.

"What are you suggesting?"

"I'm suggesting that you trust the One who saved me from alcohol and Megan from a life on the streets, the One I think you know saved you."

Peter remembered what he thought would be his last moments in a river in Costa Rica, certain he would find oblivion. He thought of the loaded Beretta and the chance circumstances that had kept him alive, given him another opportunity with his son.

"Are you trying to tell me God sent me to Bell?"

"I'm saying you have a choice between moving toward your best life in peace or drifting toward your death in anger. It's the choice between heaven and hell, right now, in this life. And if you have to ask Jesus to help, you better ask Him."

Peter stood from his perch, looking down at the cars and ambulances parked in front of the emergency room. He listened for the mockingbird's song, but heard only traffic noise.

"Peter?" Karen said. "Are you still there?"

"I'm here," he said. "Stay with Megan. I'll come by in the morning."

He put his phone away. Before he walked back to the door that led down to the hospital, the operating room, the emergency room, the world where the lessons of science intersected with the hopes of desperate men, he prayed.

Okay, he said to the Creator of the universe, the one who had sent him Luke, Karen, and mockingbirds, *if you are real and as powerful as they think, guide my words and guide my hands, because I really hate the son-of-a-bitch.*

Bell's eyes widened with fear as he made a crude attempt to sign the consent form.

"You won't regret this," he said, his gravelly voice pitched high.

Like many other things Bell had told him, Peter suspected it was untrue. But two hours later he stood over the open incision in Bell's neck, his leg already throbbing. He regretted ever coming down from the roof. The operation proceeded at a maddeningly slow pace, especially as he imagined spinal cord neurons dying with each delay. The night staff was totally inexperienced in complex spine surgery. They had to call Nancy at home to find which trays to sterilize. He had to resort to pointing at and sometimes searching the back table for instruments the tech didn't know.

And Archie Davis manned the anesthesia machines. They had not spoken for several weeks, not since Peter had written him his last prescription. Archie hadn't asked for more; maybe Peter's expression had already given the answer. But his eyes had looked uncertain.

"You need to get help, Archie," Peter had told him.

"No can do, Pete. Stigma, you know."

Archie had been at least partially right. Help would not be confidential. Every renewal of hospital privileges or his license would require him to answer whether he had been treated for mental illness, whether he had an addiction, and to provide evidence he was clean. Prove the negative. And if he slipped, his license and income would be gone, though the debts incurred by medical school would remain, immune from bankruptcy or any other relief short of death.

So Peter had let it go and hoped Archie had the strength to be clean.

Now, at midnight, he looked over the curtain and wondered why Archie wouldn't meet his eyes.

Attempting again to monitor the position of the dislocated C_5-6 vertebrae, he coaxed a sleepy X-ray technician into positioning the intraoperative X-ray unit. Bell's heavy shoulders and thick neck precluded a clear X-ray view of the dislocation, and without that ability to monitor the position, Peter's effort to realign the spine would have to be done blind. Too much traction could stretch the already injured spinal cord and cause worse damage; too little traction would leave the spine dislocated and the spinal cord compressed.

The tech fiddled with some dials on her machine and told him to try again. He hit the foot switch, looked at the screen and found he could clearly see down to the C_4 vertebra and part of C_5. But the dislocation, C_5 on C_6, was not even close to visible.

She looked at the viewing screen and tucked some stray

strands of hair back into the surgery cap that she was clearly uncomfortable wearing. She put her other hand on her hip and smacked her gum.

"Looks like that's about as good as it'll get, Doc," she said. "Maybe if you taped down his arms or something."

"I already taped his arms down," Peter snapped. "Call your supervisor."

The girl looked from her machine to the viewing screen, then to the circulating nurse, who was not Nancy, and to the scrub tech, who was not Carl—everywhere except at Peter. She smacked her gum again.

"I'm what you'd, like, call the night supervisor," she said.

"Jesus Christ," Peter said.

He peered down into the deep hole in Bell's neck. The incision was in the front of the neck, and he used the longest retractor blades he had to hold the esophagus and trachea to one side and the carotid artery and jugular vein on the other. Vertebrae were exposed, but which ones remained a mystery.

He placed a vertebral body pin in the highest vertebral body he could expose. Between gum smacks, the night X-ray supervisor took another exposure. The pin was at C_4. He could at least count down to the right level.

He looked into the wound and put his hand out for the drill guide to place a vertebral pin at C_5, but nothing happened.

If he looked up or moved his left hand, he would lose the vision of the anatomy he had fought so hard to get. So he pointedly said, "Guide, please."

The OR tech said, "Huh?"

As if he were marking the place in a book instead of an operation, he stuffed a sponge into the wound. He looked up, first at the scrub tech, who swayed on his feet with sleepiness, then at the instrument he wanted.

He pointed to it. "Guide, please! Then drill, then pin. Just like the last one."

"Yeah, yeah, I got it now. Sorry, Doc."

The night dragged on. The operation, which could have taken as little as two hours with experienced staff and a normal-sized patient, took nearly five. With each passing hour, his leg swelled, and the pain became distracting. After the pins were placed, he put only enough traction on the vertebrae to expose the damaged disk. Working through an operating microscope, he removed the disk and the fragment that compressed the spinal cord. Then he applied more traction until C_5 lined up correctly above C_6—at least he guessed it was correct, given the limited information the portable X-rays gave him—and placed a bone graft where the disk had once been. He released the traction, locking the graft into position, and a metal plate and four screws completed the surgery.

At four o'clock in the morning, he placed the last skin suture and looked over the drapes at Archie Davis. He looked as tired as Peter.

"You going to extubate him in recovery?" Peter asked.

Archie blinked, squinted, and took a breath. "The recovery room has one nurse until 8:00 a.m. I think he'd be safer if we left him sedated and intubated until morning, then wake him up in the ICU and extubate him there where he can be monitored closely."

"I agree," Peter said. "What are you going to sedate him with?"

"Sufentanil now. That should last for about two or three hours. I can leave him on a propofol drip until the ICU staff is ready to extubate."

Peter nodded. The mention of sufentanil reminded him of his promise to Megan. The drug was a highly potent narcotic, ten times as powerful as fentanyl, usually only used in surgery or intensive care. If he could get her a couple of vials, she would have the option she wanted and his debt would be paid.

He pulled off the drapes and dressed the wound, surreptitiously watching Archie open a ten-vial pack of sufentanil, then draw the contents from one vial into a syringe and inject it into an IV. The package containing the other nine vials stayed on the anesthesia cart as they prepared the patient for transport to the ICU. Archie held Bell's head and guarded the airway as they moved him from the OR table to a stretcher.

Peter slipped behind him and edged the medical record papers off the anesthesia cart. The papers fell, scattering across the OR floor. As Archie and the circulating nurse stooped to gather the papers, Peter said he was sorry, apologized for his clumsiness, blamed his bad leg, and slipped four vials of sufentanil into his pocket.

Archie and the circulating nurse guided the stretcher while Peter trailed behind. As the nurse and Archie signed the case off to a tired-looking ICU nurse, Peter dictated his notes and wrote his orders. Peter and Archie walked back to the locker room together.

"You okay?" Peter asked.

Archie didn't look over. "Don't need to worry about me."

But everything about the way he said it made Peter worry. He felt guilty about the four vials of narcotics in his pocket. "Thanks for your help, anyway."

"Yeah, sure. No problem. Keeps me out of trouble," Archie said. "You got plans for the day?"

"I've got a date."

He kept his voice so flat that Archie asked no more questions. By the time he left the hospital, the promise of dawn chased darkness from the sky and shadows from the streets. Pale blue in the west balanced pink and orange in the east, but above the sky remained gray. His mouth felt as though it were lined with his handkerchief, his eyelids drooping over eyes reddened with fatigue. His face and his feet felt swollen, and the right leg pain had become excruciating.

Yet, except for the theft, his conscience was clear. Or, more accurately, his conscience was safely parked where he wouldn't hear it. He was satisfied with his plan. Bell would recover or not, would keep his promises or not, but Peter had done his best. Regardless, Bell would never again have the power to determine his future happiness. And Megan would have her bargain fulfilled. After that, he would deal with his conscience.

He drove to his apartment, showered, shaved, and sent a text to Karen—*still alive.* Then, exhausted, he drove to Ponte Vedra. He would need sleep soon, but he could last until noon.

That was all the time he needed.

CHAPTER TWENTY-SEVEN

His phone signaled a text message halfway through his drive. As he parked in front of the hotel room he checked the screen—*Me* 2. He smiled wryly that they should celebrate their survival on this of all days.

The vials of anesthetic-grade pain medication weighed no more than an ounce, but they felt heavy in his pocket. He intended to break another rule, the ancient rule that admonished humans not to murder each other. Actually, he intended something so close to murder that only lawyers or ethicists would argue the difference. His promise to Megan went contrary to the law, to medical ethics, and to his training to preserve life. He hadn't wanted to make the promise, but he couldn't bring himself to break it.

He found Karen in the hotel room. Megan was outside in one of a pair of Adirondack chairs on the patch of lawn. Clean salt air blew through the room when he opened the door; the breeze seemed to cleanse him somehow, as if he had just stepped into a new world.

"So you did Bell's operation?" Karen asked.

He nodded.

She smiled. "Wasn't so hard, was it?"

This time he shook his head. "It was hard. Damn hard."

Karen looked over her shoulder at Megan. "She's not too good. Confused a little. Looks like she hurts."

It sounded like she was not going to be conscious for long. Karen looked a little rough, too.

"How about you?" he asked. "Are you okay?"

"Kinda."

He watched her eyes flick toward the refrigerator that contained the mini-bar.

"It's been a long night," she said.

His own troubles and focus on Megan had blinded him completely to how hard it must have been for Karen to spend the night with her dying friend. He cursed himself silently for using her as a substitute for a hospice nurse instead of doing what he'd intended—sharing with her the mission of terminal care for a mutual loved one.

He didn't want her to stay, not now. She would be a witness, an accessory, or both.

"You should go home," he said.

"No, I'll stay. You get some sleep."

"Go home," he said forcefully.

Too forcefully—the pain in her eyes could not have been greater had he slapped her. She stepped back, wedged her hands into the front pockets of her jeans, and turned to the open glass door, the expanse of beach and ocean beyond.

Peter cursed himself again and wondered, perhaps for the first time, what was missing in his soul that made him keep hurting the people he loved. He stared at the back of Karen's head. A turquoise and silver barrette tamed her glistening black hair into a loose ponytail; it hung over her faded blue work shirt, nearly down to her jeans. He didn't want to hurt her. He wanted to protect her. Because she was . . .

No, he told himself. *This is sleep deprivation speaking.* He was a married man, kind of. And he was about to commit something akin to murder.

Filled with regret, he said, "Karen, you've done more than enough already."

When she didn't answer, he reached out, held both her shoulders from behind, and brought his chest to her back. "Karen," he said again, gently this time.

She leaned back lightly and remained silent.

"You have been such a good friend." He looked over her head to Megan's chair on the grass and the ocean beyond. "If you . . ." He hesitated here. "If you trust me, say goodbye to Megan and leave."

Karen turned and examined his face carefully, her dark eyes shifting, searching for meaning in his expression.

"What are you going to do?" she asked.

"You can go to my place if you want, or go home," he said. "I'll come as soon as I can."

She looked as if she were going to say something more, but simply nodded. She took Peter's hand and led him out to Megan.

"Dr. Jenson's here," she said to her.

Megan looked up, squinting into the morning sun. She shaded her eyes with her hand and managed a distracted smile.

Karen leaned over and gave her an awkward hug. "I love you, sister," she whispered into her ear, "and I will see you again."

Megan held onto Karen's hands as she stood again, only letting go when Karen walked away, a single tear glistening as it slid down her cheek.

Karen gone, Peter returned to the room and changed into cargo shorts and a t-shirt. He put the pack of sufentanil in one pocket, along with the necessary supplies to start an IV. Then he went back outside and stood before Megan.

Her eyes were closed again, her expression peaceful. She wore a swimsuit covered with an unbuttoned white blouse, denim shorts, and a white scarf. Her sallow skin fit her loosely. Behind him, the breeze was offshore and the tide was out, so the sea was calm, the sound of small waves gentle on the distant sand. A quarter mile north, a woman walked with a dog that played in the surf; a jogger slogged away to the south. It was still too early for most of the beach crowd.

He sat in the chair beside Megan and took her hand. She opened her eyes and turned to him. Sapphire blue, he had called her eyes, and he had not been wrong.

"I'm glad you're here," she said.

"How are you feeling?"

She closed her eyes again and faced the morning sun. "I like the feel of the sun on my face and the sand between my toes."

"Would you like to go for a walk?"

"Already done, Doctor. I don't have the strength to do it again."

"I'm sorry."

"It's time," she said.

Peter remained silent, quite aware of what she meant.

"My head hurts, and I couldn't remember Karen's name this morning. I get foggy. I got lost walking back here from the shore."

Peter feared he would choke up if he tried to speak. He had known this time would be hard. He just hadn't understood how sad.

"Say something. Tell me you haven't forgotten your promise," she said.

"I haven't forgotten." He squeezed her hand and steeled himself. "I have everything we need."

"Good. Because today is a perfect day for banana fish."

"What?"

She shook her head slightly. "Nothing. Just a story I read once in a library book. J.D. Salinger."

She took a deep breath that made her wince. She exhaled quickly and grimaced.

"Are you okay?" he asked.

She turned to him so that he could not mistake her meaning, and she could not miss his reaction. "No. I'm not okay. I have excruciating pain. I'm confused. I'm dying. Today. Today is the day."

He didn't want today to be the day. But he needed to fulfill his promise.

"I'll miss you," he said.

She smiled. "You'll have other patients."

"None like you."

"No." She paused. "None like me."

He nodded. But she wasn't looking at him. Her gaze was fixed far out to sea.

"It's time, Doctor."

He removed the contents of his right cargo pocket, took her arm, and started an IV. He flushed the axis port with saline so the needle wouldn't clot and laid out four vials of the powerful narcotic. He cracked open each vial, filled four small syringes, and laid them out in a neat row on the arm of the Adirondack chair. Each vial was capable of causing loss of consciousness, followed rapidly by respiratory failure and death. He doubted she would ever get to the second vial, certainly not the third or fourth.

Megan looked at the vials next to her arm, her means to escape from a certain future of pain and confusion, possibly to paradise. He hoped so.

Then she looked up at Peter. "Thank you."

Grief and regret filled him. He hadn't expected this. His vision blurred with the mist of tears. He stood and bent over her, gently touching his lips to the scarf that covered her scars, but stood before his tears fell and gave him away.

"One more favor," Megan said. "Cover me with a blanket, then take a walk. Let the sand warm your feet. Swim, maybe. Then come back and tell me about everything you see."

He got a yellow wool blanket from the room and came back. As he leaned to drape it over the chair, her right arm hooked him around the neck and pulled his ear to her mouth.

"Forgive me," she whispered. "I forgive you."

He didn't trust himself to speak, but he wondered about forgiveness as he limped away from her, across the small lawn toward the sea. Had he earned her forgiveness, or had it been a gift? Or, somehow, both?

When he reached the sand, he turned back. Megan, her white scarf covering her scars, her smile concealing her pain, blew him a kiss.

The heaviness in his heart nearly kept his smile from camouflaging his grief. He turned to the wide swath of soft, white sand and walked. A seagull eyed him with a careless, cold stare before turning its attention elsewhere. He came to the wet sand and tidal pools and waded through them until waves broke at his feet. He hesitated, watching a flock of a dozen brown pelicans flying beak to tail feather, as if tied together by an invisible line. They skimmed the wave tops, the line rising and falling with the waves, then swooped upward thirty feet into the air and turned into the wind.

He pulled off his t-shirt and walked into the ocean, to his knees, to his waist, to his chest. He had nothing to forgive her for. She wanted what he wanted, what we all want someday: an easy death. And he was glad she had that. And he would soon not face the dual scars that testified to his guilt.

His tears now overflowed as a wave rolled over him, allowing him to float, weightless, free. Then, with his tears blending into the infinity of the ocean, he forgave himself for failing Megan, for failing Luke, for failing Ellen. For failing himself.

He rolled onto his back and floated, looking up at the blue sky and occasional white cumulus cloud, distant and high. He floated until he felt chilled. Then he swam until he warmed up, and rolled over to float again. He paid no attention to the direction he swam, trusting the waves and current to eventually bring him back to shore. Megan would wait.

Finally, cold and tired, he allowed the surf to wash him into the shallows. He let the waves lap against his torso for a minute, got to his feet, and looked around for his bearings. He had drifted a quarter-mile north from his hotel room. He started walking south, keeping to the firm, wet sand, stopping frequently to rest his leg.

He walked back up the beach to where Megan's inert form lay covered with a yellow blanket, her head lolled to the side, her scarf slightly askew. He sat down beside her and took her cooling hand.

"I saw blue sky and small white clouds," he said, closing her eyes. "I felt soft, white sand between my toes until the sand turned brown and hard. Sandpipers ran back and forth, pecking for buried shellfish . . ."

He continued until he told her everything he remembered—the tidal pools, the pelicans, the tears that flowed into the ocean. Then a cloud covered the sun, and he felt a chill.

He picked up the syringes, the IV tubing, and the drugs and put them in the room. Then he dressed and transferred the evidence to the trunk of his car for later disposal at the hospital among the large volume of biohazard waste. Only then did he return to the room and call the main desk of the resort to report that a guest had died.

He sat in the room expecting the arrival of the police first and later, the coroner. Full of regret and sorrow, tired beyond measure, he waited.

CHAPTER TWENTY-EIGHT

The police and coroner's assistants were satisfied quickly enough. They were happy to deal with a tragedy at a beach resort instead of other jobs that likely filled their days. But even though he told himself to relax, it didn't come easily. The sleep deprivation didn't help either. He covered his tremulous right hand with his left, constantly reminding himself not to jam both of them into his pockets.

After the evidence technicians took their photographs and the coroner's assistants their measurements, they put Megan in a black bag and zipped it closed. Some primitive reflex that had no doubt been driven out of him by medical school and years of practice resurfaced—he wanted to protest. Her life was too big to be zipped up and hauled off in the back of a van.

Before they left, the tech made a call. After talking for a few minutes, he handed the phone to Peter. A gravelly voice came on the line.

"Jenson? Vince Parker here, the medical examiner. This your patient?"

"Yes."

"What's the story?"

Peter considered how to frame this in the simplest terms, terms that would invite the fewest questions. "Thirty-two year-old white female with a recurrent glioblastoma. She was in terminal stages, hospice couldn't take her until Monday, so I arranged care for her here."

Parker paused before replying. "Seems a bit unusual. Don't recall any similar cases. She got some kind of family connection?"

"No."

"You see my problem here, Jenson? She dies in the hospital, you fill out the death certificate. Out of the hospital, it's my case. I've got to come up with a cause of death, but I got nothing but a body and your word."

"I'll get you the records."

"Don't bother. I can get 'em myself quick enough. I'm just wondering how it came to happen in your hotel room."

"Technically she was not in my room."

"I'll take that to mean you're not going to tell me."

Peter said, "Just doing a favor for a friend."

"Yeah, sure. Now it's up to me to figure out what kind of favor and what kind of friend. You got anything else you want to tell me?"

"You could write down *malignant brain tumor* and it would be the truth."

"But I wouldn't be doing my job. I'll let you know what I find. But you know that, don't you?"

Parker clicked off without waiting for a reply.

Peter considered the consequences. Maybe another board complaint, which would likely be the end of his license. Maybe an indictment for manslaughter or worse. He still had the syringes in his pocket. If Parker called the police and alerted them to his suspicions, he would need Jim Casey's help now instead of later.

But they all drove off, leaving him standing on a small lawn with an empty Adirondack chair before him, an empty beach and a big ocean behind him. Feeling small and alone, he could muster the strength for only one more task. He tapped Karen's number into his phone.

"She's gone," he said simply.

"So soon?"

"The coroner's van just left."

"You could have called."

"You didn't need to be here." He concentrated on breathing and hoped she would not ask him for any more explanation. He listened to dead air for several seconds before she spoke again. "Are you okay?" she asked.

A simple question. But the answer was not obvious, not to him, not today. He felt only numb.

"Tell me where you are," she said. "I'm coming to get you."

He had difficulty understanding what she had said; when he understood, he couldn't understand why. "But I've got my car."

"Don't move. I'm coming."

He imagined the moment he slipped into the cold black waters of a river in Central America, hoping for life, expecting death, and knowing only that he could not stay where he was.

"I'm okay," he said.

"Don't move. Don't you dare move. I'm on my way."

Later he remembered the afternoon only in brief flashes. He sat in the Adirondack chair, hot sun beating down. She appeared suddenly out of the light, black hair glistening. Then he was in her car, sunshine and shadows alternately falling on his face. They arrived at that old house, the one that still had the *Luke Ryan, MD* sign by the door on the front porch, and he didn't understand why. She led him to the stairway on the side of the house, up to the second floor entry, and into an apartment. Pictures of Luke and Karen, of formal men and women in stiff collars from a century before, and of stoic Native Americans in traditional clothes.

He gave up his phone and allowed himself to be led to her bedroom. She pulled off the duvet then left him alone, floating then falling onto cool clean sheets. He closed his eyes, exhaustion finally overcoming consciousness.

His sleep was deep and dreamless. He awoke hours later in the dark, disoriented and afraid. Then he remembered where he was. Safe.

He threw off the covers and stood. The syringes of narcotics remained in his pockets. He found a bathroom, emptied the syringes into the toilet, and flushed. Then he dismantled the syringes, rinsed them out, wrapped them in tissue paper, and held them over her wastebasket. He put them back into his pocket. She didn't need to know, and she didn't need evidence in her home. He slipped out of the bathroom and explored the dark rooms as quietly as he could.

Light from the street penetrated the shades and draperies, enough that he could detect Karen's form under a blanket on the couch. He watched her breathe. On other days she'd been unwilling to rescue herself, but she had driven across town to rescue him. The mutual survival pact continued. He owed her. Maybe someday he would be more willing to save her than save himself. He hoped so.

He wanted to leave, to go home, to no longer be a burden. But the practicalities were hard, and skulking out without saying *thank you* was worse. And where would he go that felt any more like home than this place? His apartment, where the Beretta awaited?

He decided to lie down again, rest his eyes for a while, and wait for morning. Then he'd express his gratitude and get out. But when he opened his eyes again a hard light penetrated the cracks around the curtains, and he knew it was at least midday. A mockingbird sang, its voice trilling up and down, mimicking a dove and a crow and a cardinal all in the space of a minute.

His waking moment of peace quickly gave way to anxiety, and he felt in his pocket for the tissue-wrapped evidence. Then he pushed himself to his feet and searched for his shoes. His face felt greasy, his mouth full of cotton. He needed to go.

The door opened widely, and Karen stood, her arms akimbo, her long hair back, her dark eyes sparkling. She gave him a wry smile, her head shaking gently, side to side. He could see why Luke had fallen for her. She was not beautiful exactly, not in the classic sense. More like handsome, the kind of beauty that comes from inner strength.

"The shower is there," she said, gesturing to the bathroom, "and some of Luke's old clothes are there." She pointed to the freshly laundered pile on a rocking chair.

"I've got to go," he said.

"You've got to take a shower and get dressed," she said. "That is all you need to think about."

"But I've got to get to the hospital. I've got to see Bell. Then I . . ."

"Bell's other partner will see him and make the rounds for your practice. I've already made the calls. It's Sunday. Rest. Save yourself."

Sunday. It was Sunday morning. He checked his watch—eleven o'clock—and anchored himself in time. He started to say something else but she cut him off with a finger pointed at the bathroom.

"Shower," she commanded. "You'll find a toothbrush, a comb, and a razor."

Twenty more minutes wouldn't make a difference. So he followed her directions. A half hour later he emerged in a gray t-shirt and jeans that were a bit big in the waist and short at the ankle. The syringes remained in the pocket of the cargo shorts, rolled up under his arm.

The smell of coffee and orange juice greeted him.

"There's bagels," Karen said, "and cream cheese. Here. Let me wash those for you."

"No." He backed away, clutching the shorts.

She looked suspiciously at him. "The bagels don't bite."

"Right. Sorry. But I don't think you need to do my laundry."

He moved to the table, and she poured him a cup of coffee.

"It's no trouble. And there's the cream and sugar." She waved faintly. "And orange juice."

Another twenty minutes wouldn't hurt. He needed the coffee anyway. She sat at the table across from him; he took a seat and a bagel. Still, he fidgeted. His hand shook as he spread cream cheese and poured orange juice.

"Am I making you nervous?"

"No," he said.

But she was. And for no other reason than that he was unaccustomed to anyone showing him kindness. Why did she care anymore? Luke was dead, now Megan, too. He must be some kind of darkness to her, bound by mutual despair and death.

She was still looking at him.

"Okay, I admit it," he said. "I'm a wreck. Just trying to get oriented. It's been a helluva couple of days."

She nodded, waiting.

He felt like he needed to go somewhere but had no destination. Maybe he just wanted to dispose of the syringes, the last evidence, before Parker started running toxicology screens. He pushed his chair back.

"Are you going to tell me what happened?" she asked.

He shrugged. "She died."

"There's more."

"You don't need to know."

"Maybe I don't want to know," she said. "Is that what you're telling me?"

He nodded.

"I'm a big girl, Jenson."

She was that, all right. He had been telling himself that the details were a secret to protect her. Now he wondered if the secret was to protect himself from what she would think of him. Would she still send her morning texts?

"Thanks for everything," he said. "I don't know what I would have done."

Her wry smile returned. "I didn't know what you would have done, either. That's what friends are for. You're always welcome here."

Peter looked down at the table, then out the window to the branches of the oak tree that screened the neighboring house. He inhaled and exhaled and thought about how few places he had ever been *welcome*. He had always found a place or claimed a place, then defended his right to be there. But in a short time, he would leave, go to his apartment, go to work in the morning, resume a life that seemed increasingly without direction. Perhaps she was serious, that he was welcome back. But what he really wanted was to never leave.

CHAPTER TWENTY-NINE

Ten days later he prepared to leave his office, now a difficult proposition during working hours. All his old patients and referral networks had returned, and in addition he had most of Bell's practice. He shot off the text, *Still alive,* and smiled, anticipating the return. The message no longer held the note of desperation for either of them. Now it was a small celebration. In a few minutes, her presence would be the only small joy at Megan's funeral.

Betsy interrupted his thoughts before he reached the door. "Dr. Parker from the medical examiner's office on line one."

He checked his watch. He had five minutes to spare, no more. He picked up the phone. "This is Peter Jenson."

"Yes," he said, dragging the s out until it sounded like a hiss. "Vince Parker, the medical examiner. It's about the Megan Kaiser case."

Peter let silence be his initial answer. A queasy sensation crept into his gut.

Parker continued. "Maybe you remember your patient with the glioblastoma that died at your beachfront hotel room?"

"How could I forget?"

"Hmm. Yes, well. Your hotel room."

"She liked the beach," Peter said.

"Lots of people like the beach. Not many get their surgeons to invite them to their hotel room."

"You have a point, Parker?"

"Cause of death, of course. Where she died is no concern of mine. But how she died is. I got to put something on this bottom line."

"Malignant brain tumor would fit."

"Yeah, well, she had that. And it would have killed her pretty quick. But it didn't."

"She was close to the end," Peter said.

"Yes, hmm, yes. But the true cause of death is narcotic overdose. She had high doses of benzyl alkaloids on her toxicology screen, pretty normal for a cancer patient taking large doses of narcotics. But still, her levels were higher than expected. And the needle mark in her left arm." He paused. "Could have been from a blood draw, hmm?"

"What are you getting at, Parker?"

"She died of a narcotic overdose," he said. "The reason I'm calling is that I'm wondering if it was self-inflicted or you-inflicted."

Peter remained silent.

"You having some kind of affair with this woman?" Parker asked.

"No affair. I just liked her," Peter said.

"Just for yuks I did an assay for the type of narcotic. I understand she had a prescription for hydrocodone, so that's what I expected to find."

"And did you?"

"Only a trace. Not enough to kill her. Know what else I found?"

Peter waited.

"That's right. Sufentanil. Enough to kill a rhino."

"I wonder where she got that," Peter said in a flat tone.

"Hmm, let me take a guess," Parker said. "Young female patient dead in her surgeon's hotel room from a massive overdose of a narcotic that's found only in operating rooms, at least legitimately. Not common as a street drug either, no." He paused again. "Maybe you should be in jail, Dr. Jenson."

"I believe this is where you tell me why I'm not."

"Because she had the goddamn brain tumor. I can't figure your angle on this." Parker's voice rose in irritation. "You trying to shut her up about an affair or something? Give me something here. Tell me she was a drug addict or something so I can write this off as just another statistic in the so-called opioid crisis."

Parker had just handed him a ticket to ride on a silver platter. All he had to do was tell a half-truth, just say she had a history of drug abuse, never mind that it was years ago and cocaine, not narcotics. Just say that and all the suspicions would go away. But he couldn't do it; it seemed too much like a lie.

"As far as I know, she was clean," he said.

"All you'd have to say is she was a user. Who'd be there to argue with you? Otherwise people have to wonder why you'd kill her."

"A woman with a malignant tumor, facing imminent death, took pain medicine and died. That's simple, and it sounds plausible."

"Only to the ignorant or the lazy." Parker gave an aggravated sigh. "I don't know if I can let this go. I'd be protecting your claim of innocence with my apparent incompetence."

"Let it go," Peter said, "and I will wish you a long life, and a quick and painless death in the far, distant future."

"Yes-s-s. Well, I know who to call, don't I? In the meantime, the hospital is auditing the inventory of sufentanil. They'll find out if any disappeared, along with the when and where. Then maybe we'll know the who. Hope it's not you, Jenson."

Peter hung up, irritated and unsettled. No doubt the hospital audit would find four vials of missing sufentanil that disappeared after Joe Bell's surgery. But he had done the right thing. At least he had done what he had promised. The consequences would have to take care of themselves, and they would be life changing. Unemployed and unlicensed would be the best-case scenario.

Jim Casey could probably recommend someone for criminal defense. Peter was going to need it, though he had no idea how he was going to pay. But the call to Jim Casey could wait until after the funeral.

The Cross Way Church called Megan's funeral a "Celebration of Life," just as they had Luke's. Somehow it didn't irritate him as much now. The church seemed far less crowded than it had then. A few men and women in the black shirts and slacks of the Waffle House uniform, plus a few more women, presumably churchgoers, filled a half-dozen pews near the front.

A table stood before the six steps up to the stage, lit by a single spotlight in the dim worship center. On the table, two modest bouquets flanked a plain urn holding the ashes. Recorded music played over the sound system—soothing music, simple guitar and piano melodies, nothing Peter recognized.

He spotted Karen and edged in beside her just as the same preacher, Pastor Nick, pressed his fingers together and greeted them. In black vestments, with his little mustache and little feet, the preacher led them in a song, the lyrics on a screen above the altar.

"She was a good, Christian woman," he said in his eulogy,

"taken from us too soon. Yes, oh too soon." He paused for effect and continued. "But we can take comfort that she now rests in the arms of Jesus. Oh yes, in the arms of Jesus." He pressed his fingers together again and rocked on his heels. "And those of us left behind can learn from her example to live in the way that leads to abiding peace."

Peter wondered if Pastor Nick knew about her past drug addiction and life as a prostitute. Or did he know only of the last chapters in her life, the ones he could preach about today? That would be for the best. She should be remembered for how she finished. Maybe we all should. Still, it was the journey that made the finish remarkable.

The preacher said other things relating to Megan's life in the church, but Peter had already tuned out, remembering her as framed by his experience of the last few months: his stupid mistake followed by her devil's bargain and, somehow, their bond. They had been like a pair in a lifeboat, expecting nothing but death and destruction, trusting only each other to mitigate the misery.

Finally, Pastor Nick said, "Now each of us must ask ourselves if we have the same confidence that Megan had, that she would live forever with the Father in heaven. If you want to have that same confidence, talk to me or one of our staff after the service. Today. Don't take a chance with your salvation."

Preachers never missed an opportunity to increase membership. What could be better motivation than a funeral, the shadow of death hovering over the sanctuary? Once, Peter had only been confident of nothingness beyond. Now, he was uncertain even of that. He hoped Megan was right. Maybe she and Luke were enjoying paradise right now. He hoped so.

Pastor Nick led them in another song, words again on the screen above the altar, and the service ended. A heavyset grizzled man in a Waffle House uniform stood and shuffled into the aisle, making his way to the table that held the urn.

"Y'all know she was one of us," he said to the church. "And y'all know the Waffle House never closes and most of us need to get back there pretty quick. But we been saving all the booths in the back and getting us a cake for folks who want to talk about her." He stood for a moment, flushing, appearing uncertain, then said, "That's all."

How apt, Peter thought. *That's all.* The chapter of reality about Megan Kaiser closed forever.

Karen went forward to retrieve the urn. Following her into the aisle, Peter sidestepped into the man from the Waffle House.

"Doc," he said, "we all want to thank you for all what you did for Megan."

Peter didn't feel worthy of thanks. The only thing he really did was hasten her death. He screwed up her operation.

"I didn't do much," he mumbled. Over the man's shoulder, he spotted Ellen in the back row, moving slowly toward the exit.

"I just know she really appreciated it," the man said.

Peter edged by him, cursing his bad leg.

The man took a step back. "And thanks for that Alvarez guy you sent over. He's covering for us right now."

So Luis had actually gotten a job. Keeping his eyes on Ellen, Peter turned to follow her.

"Y'all come by the Waffle House this afternoon," the man called. "We got a nice little spread set up."

"I'll be there," Peter said over his shoulder.

Ellen had already reached the doors to the foyer. But was it really she? The sanctuary was large, and the light was dim. What would she be doing here?

He limped his best limp, catching some help from the ends of the pews. He pushed open the sanctuary doors just as she—

Ellen?—reached the outer ones. In a moment she would be gone unless he did something.

He hesitated. If it was Ellen, she surely didn't act like she wanted to talk. He could have let her go, but instead he called out, as loudly as he could without shouting.

"Ellen!"

She stopped and turned, unsurprised, expression blank.

"I . . ." he started, but now that he had her attention he had no idea what to say. "I didn't expect to see you."

"Daniel told me I could find you here," she said in a monotone.

He watched her expression for a clue. She didn't seem to actually want to find him. He limped closer. Perhaps his face gave away his question.

She shrugged. "I'm trying to understand."

He was close enough now to smell her perfume, surprised that it was an unfamiliar scent.

"About Megan Kaiser?" he asked.

"No, about you," she said. "Twenty years I've known you, and not once did you go to a patient's funeral. Though God knows there were lots of them. So what did this waitress with the brain tumor mean to you?"

Her eyes were as intense as he had ever seen them.

"Megan taught me that I can make mistakes, mistakes that I can't fix, with consequences that don't go away."

"Everybody knows that," she said. "Everybody has regrets."

For a fleeting second he wondered if she was talking about *everybody* or herself.

She continued to stare.

"Yes," he said. "Regrets. But mostly you can make up for a mistake, pay the price." He waved his arm to indicate the place where they stood. "Atonement."

"So you made a mistake and . . . okay, *atoned* for it?"

He studied his hands, considering whether atonement was enough, whether it was ever enough. For Megan. For Luke. The momentous task of trying to explain it all.

Finally he looked at Ellen. "No, I couldn't make up for it."

She shook her head a little, enough to twinkle her dangling silver earrings. "I don't understand."

He took a chance, reaching out and taking her left hand. He gazed at her diamond sparkling between his fingers. She didn't pull away.

"I'm saying I broke something I can't fix," he told her. "That when you break something really big, the only thing you can hope for is forgiveness."

She searched his face before she withdrew her hand. "Are we talking about the waitress here?"

"We're talking about broken things."

She flushed, and her face again became a mask, her voice flat. "Some things are better left broken."

She swiveled away and walked toward the door. Peter watched the soft touch of her heels on the carpet, the familiar sway of her hips and her hair. The bright sunshine of the morning blinded him as she disappeared through the door, her scent fading.

He sighed and reached into his pocket for his phone. Anticipating a message from the office, he switched off the mute. He had a single text—*Me 2*.

CHAPTER THIRTY

Every Tuesday and Thursday night after work, he opened Luke's office and saw the patients referred by the church in a free clinic. On the Saturday mornings that he wasn't on call, he did the same. Nine hours a week, twenty-two weeks, and he would fulfill his community service requirement. His license would be clear about the time Karen's finances would no longer carry the mortgage on the office building. After that . . . he really didn't know.

Every Tuesday, every Thursday, every Saturday, he shared a meal with Karen. He learned her stories; she learned his. He looked forward to hearing her voice. It had been a long time since he had someone like this to talk to.

Once, he had reached across the table and covered her hand with his. Her eyes dropped to their hands. A moment passed, but then she pulled her hand away.

"I won't be 'the other woman.' We're not that kind of friends. If you can't handle it, don't stay."

"Sorry. It's just that I could never talk to someone like I talk to you."

She smiled her familiar wry smile. "Never?"

No. Not never. But it had been a long time.

On most Saturday afternoons and Sundays, Daniel would come over, Ellen dropping him off, Peter taking him home. On the first Saturday afternoon after Megan's funeral, Ellen came to the door. Her hair was cut to shoulder length and layered, a sharp frame to her face. She wore a designer tee with a scoop neck, pressed shorts, and heeled sandals with thin straps. She could have been on the cover of one of those women's clothing catalogs that used to come in the junk mail when he lived at home.

Home. That house no longer felt like home but like a place where he used to live. And Ellen was beginning to seem only like a woman he used to live with.

She bundled Daniel off with a pat on his butt after stooping to hug him and kiss his cheek, an affection he seemed to tolerate. (*I'm* nine, *Mom*.)

"Drop him off any time after six but before eight," she said. "If it's eight or later, I'd appreciate it if he comes in jammies after his bath."

Peter heard from behind him the plaintive cry, "Aw, Mom."

Peter nodded. "Got it."

She didn't leave. "That funeral thing," she said. "Were you trying to tell me something? Like *you* forgive *me?*"

"No," he said, "I'm trying to tell you I'm sorry." He thought for a moment, searching for the something more that he wanted to say. "And . . ."

Her eyes bored into him, waiting. She already knew he loved her. Telling her again now would just make her mad. He hoped for a smile and got nothing.

". . . and I love you. Always have." There, he said it. One more time.

"Yes, well," she said, drawing up her purse, "I'm sorry too."

She called over her shoulder as she walked away. "Between six and eight."

On Sunday night he dropped Daniel off at the house he used to call home. Dale Kelly's car, the Mercedes roadster, was parked in the driveway. Peter wondered if Ellen had been sorry she had ever been married to him, or sorry she had already moved on. It didn't look like she was sorry she threw him out.

A month later, Dr. Bell came in for his first appointment after release from the rehab hospital. Peter stood for a moment outside the exam room, took a deep breath, and blew it out. He buttoned his white coat and pulled his cuffs. Only then did he pick up the office chart and enter.

"Dr. Bell," he said without smiling or holding out his hand.

"I'm doing fine, Jenson, just fine." Bell sat on the edge of the exam table. He wore a collared polo shirt, unbuttoned at the top, and plaid-patterned slacks with a crease, a weekend look. A cane rested against the table.

"Neck pain?" asked Peter.

"Not a bit. None since I woke up from surgery. Like a damn miracle."

"How about balance? Leg strength? Any trouble with stairs?"

Bell almost shrugged, but the effort of moving such bulky shoulders required more effort. "I can walk upstairs fine. I got to hold the rail if I go down. I haven't tried running, but that I haven't done in a whole lot of years."

"How about your hands?"

Bell turned his palms up on his thighs and looked down at them. "I can button my own shirts and cut my own meat."

Peter waited.

"I can't play the piano."

"I didn't know you played."

"I don't, you idiot, never could. I'm telling you I can't operate anymore."

"I'm sorry," Peter said.

"Sure as hell, you're not."

Peter didn't argue. "It might get better with time," he lied. The type of injury that Bell had suffered nearly always led to loss of the kind of dexterity needed for surgery.

"No. I'm calling it quits."

"I'm sure you deserve some time for yourself," Peter said.

"I don't want any damn time to myself. I liked doing what I did." He hesitated for a minute. "I'm still on some boards—the Blues, the Doctor's Company. I got a little pull for a while."

"Should keep you occupied."

"Yeah, maybe. Anyway, you kept me out of a wheelchair. And I can do some office consults to pay the bills. So, thank you."

Peter allowed himself a thin smile. "You're welcome."

"Don't get smug. You remember that Kaiser case, the one you screwed up?"

Even weeks after her death, it still hurt. "How could I forget?"

"You think I messed with the OR schedule, set you up."

Yes, he thought, but kept it to himself.

"You think I put Umberto on you the day of your board hearing."

Again, Peter kept quiet.

"Yeah. I got no dog in the fight now, so I can tell you straight up and maybe you'll believe it. I didn't do any of that. You always were your own worst enemy."

Peter didn't like hearing this. Sure, he had made mistakes. But he took comfort in extenuating circumstances. If only Bell hadn't had it out for him, he wouldn't have made a mistake and maybe wouldn't make any more in the future, not big ones. But without the *if only*, he was totally responsible. And worse, fallible. If he could make those kinds of mistakes in the past, he could make them again.

"And you're telling me this, why?" Peter asked.

"I'm trying to tell you bygones are bygones. You don't like me, I don't like you. That's not about to change. But I needed you, and you showed up. Maybe someday you'll need me."

Bell slid off the exam table, took his cane in his left hand, and leaned on it. He held out his right hand.

"Sure," Peter said, but he met his eyes and shook his hand.

Then he left quickly. He had one more appointment.

In his office, he dropped his white coat on a hook behind his door and put on his gray suit jacket. He adjusted the shirt collar, the cuffs, and the tie. As requested, he went to Dale Kelly's office. The administrative assistant notified Dale that Peter was waiting through the delicate click of her well-manicured nails on an oversized telephone. She offered Peter a beverage, which he declined, and a seat, which he took, while she tried to look competent at a clean desk with nothing to do.

Dale came out, leading with his CEO smile and an open right hand as if running for office. "Pete," he said, "so glad you could make it."

Peter figured an inverse correlation between Dale's apparent happiness and the chance of an agreeable meeting. "Always happy to see you, Dale," he lied in return.

"Come in," Dale said, clapping him on the back. "Something to drink?"

"No, thanks. Your assistant," he nodded in her direction, "has been very efficient."

She smiled as if to say *of course*.

After Peter was comfortably seated before the desk, Dale said, "We've always been friends."

Peter nodded. *No, we weren't*.

"This Vince Parker fellow. The medical examiner. He called here a few weeks ago and asked us to inventory our narcotics, especially the ones in the OR. Said one of your patients had a suspicious overdose."

Here it comes.

Peter froze his expression, a polite smile. "So I've heard."

"Turns out he was right. Ten vials of sufentanil went missing the night before your patient died."

He had expected a moment like this since Parker had called. Now the bomb was about to explode. He struggled to maintain his smile while he thought about how much he would miss medicine and how much he would hate jail.

Then, just as suddenly, he felt detached, like he was watching himself on TV. The struggle to hold on to his career was over. Oddly, he felt at peace. The smile came easier.

But something didn't add up.

"*Ten* vials?" he asked. He had taken only four; he was sure of it.

"That's what I thought, too. Impossible. At our hospital. But as it turns out, it did happen, and I owe you an apology."

Peter cocked his head. "Apology?"

"I thought Parker might be right. I figured if you stole blood bank units you might steal narcotics. I thought you might be out of control. Figured I'd be glad to fire you immediately and with cause."

"And you're not?" Peter asked, his smile gone.

"Yes. I'm sorry I ever doubted you. And with Bell out, we need you here. I'm withdrawing your notice of termination."

"And the narcotics?"

"Yes, yes, didn't I say? Terrible misunderstanding. This

anesthesiologist, this Archie Davis. Who would of guessed? This wasn't the first time. He's been taking drugs for years. If it hadn't been for you, I don't know when we would have caught him. He took a leave of absence, signed into rehab." Dale shook his head. "Says we might have saved his life."

Peter blinked. He had taken four vials of sufentanil for Megan out of a ten-pack on Archie's cart. If Archie had known about Peter taking the four, he had pocketed the rest and kept his mouth shut.

"He said to thank you," Kelly said, "but I don't know what for."

A weight lifted from Peter's shoulders as he tried to reorient to a new kind of peace.

"I hope he does well in rehab."

"Yeah, sure. Then the police run the records and find this Kaiser woman had a past. A history of substance abuse. So this Parker guy got it all wrong. Sorry for the misunderstanding."

Half-truths had saved him.

Kelly continued. "Bell says he'll use his influence to mitigate the community service hours. We need to renegotiate your contract so you can get back to your life the way it was before all this started."

His life before it started. When he had all the answers. When he didn't make mistakes.

"I'll need to think about it," Peter said. "I'll be taking some time to go to Costa Rica."

"Take all the time you need," Kelly said. "A little vacation can clear out the cobwebs." He stood. "Understand that anything I might have said before wasn't personal. Just doing what I had to do for the corporation. We're still friends."

He pasted on his CEO smile and held out his hand.

Peter hesitated, but he took the hand, smiling back. "Friends?"

He kept Kelly's hand in his grip but lost the smile.

Kelly continued to smile, a bit more woodenly. "I mean to say, we can work together."

Peter freed himself. "Maybe."

He turned and marched out, taking the elevator down to the main lobby. The lobby renovation was nearly finished and looked good; Ellen had done a fine job. He walked toward the exit, feeling the weightlessness that comes from many burdens lifted. He experienced the rare luxury of having the freedom to choose his own destination. He relished the moment.

Then he saw her, standing in the lobby with her clipboard and checklist, making blue jeans look good, her tiny, dangly silver earrings sparkling. Her sharply cut hair hid her face as she concentrated on her work. But he didn't need to see her face to know her. He stood in front of the clipboard until it dropped and she lifted her head.

Any surprise on her part quickly vanished from her expression.

"It's a beautiful day," he said.

She searched his face. "You're happy."

"Yes," he said. "And it's been awhile."

"I'm done being mad." She smiled.

"I'm going for a walk on the beach."

"Alone?" She tilted her head to the side and smiled again. "Or is this an invitation?"

For the last few months—maybe even years—the beach was where he sought the freedom that solitude brings. But solitude without love, he had learned, was just loneliness.

"I was thinking of finding Daniel."

She tipped her head back to her clipboard. "I've got a few things to do . . ." she said, her voice trailing off. She looked up, green eyes sparkling. "And Daniel and I have a family therapy session scheduled for four o'clock."

Peter searched her face for clues to her heart. "I'll have him back in time."

He saw a shadow of doubt. "I promise," he added.

The shadow passed, but he couldn't read her.

"Maybe I should go too," she said, "to be sure."

He felt something warm in his chest. Not love exactly. This was what felt like hope.

"You should," he said to her. "You definitely should."

She let the clipboard drop to her side and took his hand.

They were going to the beach.

They were going home.

THE END

ACKNOWLEDGMENTS

This book would not have been possible without the wise combination of encouragement and literary criticism gifted to me by my beloved wife, Mary. I would also like to thank my children, Adam, Jay and Brieanna, who inspired and encouraged me along the way.

Several people suffered through reading early manuscripts, investing time and giving wise counsel. These include Jenn Lohse, Bob Whitmire and Steve Murray.

The River City Writers chapter of the Florida Writers Association provided necessary group therapy and instruction. Vic DiGenti and Greg Golson stand out for their unselfish leadership.

I also acknowledge the treasured professional help from editor Nancy Stone and the peerless reader review service provided by The Spun Yarn.

I am acutely aware that I am who I am and do what I do because of the people who have lovingly shaped me. There are too many to name individually, but teachers, clergymen, and doctors not only instructed me but served as models to which I can only aspire.

Lastly, I would like to remember my father who loved books, and my mother who read to me as a child, teaching me that books contain magic.

ABOUT THE AUTHOR

Dean was born and raised in Minneapolis. After receiving his BA and MD from the University of Minnesota, he did his post-doctoral training in neurological surgery at Yale University. Now, after practicing neurosurgery for three decades in Jacksonville, Florida, he builds boats, plays with grandchildren, and writes.

Made in the USA
Columbia, SC
11 September 2020